LEGENDS OF THE WEST

A DEPUTY MARSHAL BASS REEVES WESTERN

LEGENDS OF THE WEST

MICHAEL A. BLACK

WHEELER PUBLISHING
A part of Gale, a Cengage Company

LIBRARY OF CONGRESS CIP DATA ON FILE.
CATALOGUING IN PUBLICATION FOR THIS BOOK
IS AVAILABLE FROM THE LIBRARY OF CONGRESS

ISBN-13: 978-1-4328-5738-7 (softcover alk. paper)

Published in 2020 by arrangement with Michael A. Black

Printed in Mexico
Print Number: 01   Print Year: 2020

To all of us who've worn the badge

CHAPTER 1

1879: The Indian Territories

The edge of the rising sun was on the cusp of the horizon, tincturing the nascent sky with a mixture of gray and pink, and Deputy Marshal Bass Reeves knew that somebody was about to die.

He was a big man, over six feet, and powerfully built, but he moved with the smoothness of a large, feral cat. To this end, many of his Indian friends and companions referred to this grace of movement by giving him the Indian name "Creeping Panther."

Reeves found this amusing and also appropriate, given the color of his dark skin. He reined in his big, grayish-white stallion and motioned for his friend and partner, Indian Territories Lighthorse lawman David Walks As Bear, to stop as well. Reeves leaned forward, fixing his eyes on the small cabin and corral below.

A trail of smoke rolled upward from the chimney. The homestead looked reasonably well maintained, as did the nearby barn and corral, which had four horses, one of them obviously a plow horse, within its confines. Two saddles had been haphazardly slung over the uppermost rails of the fencing nearest the house.

Reeves did the figuring in his head: two riders, maybe more. But one of the animals being a plow horse, and no third saddle perched on the rail, most likely meant that those two belonged to the farmer. And, given the proclivity of the two Quint boys for taking what wasn't theirs, Reeves harbored little doubt that the other two steeds in the corral were most likely stolen.

"Looks like somebody's home," Reeves said.

"Probably cooking themselves a nice breakfast," Bear said. "Wonder if they'll mind us joining them?"

Reeves surveyed the scene, taking in all the details. From the condition of both the barn and the cabin, along with the parallel rows of crops, beans and corn, it was no doubt a working farm. This was definitely a white man's place. Or maybe some black man's who'd figured he was owed that forty acres and a mule, regardless of any territorial treaty. But they were in the Indian Territories. In any event, it was a squatter's homestead. A small, but substantial garden was on the eastern side of the cabin. A drove of slumbering hogs filled a pen to the west. Beyond that lay the barn and a vacant plow harness looking abandoned in the early morning light. Several chickens pecked at the ground, and a rooster pranced around, getting ready to crow.

Not the type of place the Quint boys would be working. Or welcomed.

Reeves scanned the scattering of tracks that had led them this far.

"You sure these are their tracks?" he asked.

Bear smirked. "You doubting your trusty Indian scout, *Gimoozabie*?"

"I'm asking you a question," Reeves said evenly. "And I thought I told you not to call me that."

"You did." Bear chuckled. "As sure as I'm part Potowatomi."

Reeves grinned. "Thought you always claiming to be Cherokee?"

Bear grinned back. "That, too." The Indian police deputy was dressed in a buckskin jacket and kept his hair wound tightly in a circular braid at the back of his head, as was the custom of the Lighthorse.

"Well," Reeves said, "if these here tracks

do belong to them Quint boys, there most likely will be some innocent people involved. The Quint boys probably rode in and took over some family's homestead."

"Serves them squatters right for breaking the treaty. This is supposed to be Indian land."

Reeves heaved a sigh. "We can take that up with them if they're still alive. Once we get the Quints."

Bear nodded. "How you want to handle it?"

"Same as we always do. Get up close and assess the situation. Then give them the chance to surrender peaceably."

Bear's mouth pulled into a slight smile. "Be a lot easier to do it the Indian way. Sneak up on 'em, set the house on fire, and shoot 'em as they run out."

Reeves knew Bear was speaking in jest, but he still felt compelled to remove all doubt in the way he wanted things handled. "We'll give them the chance to surrender. If they don't, it's on them. Besides, like I said, there just might be some other people, not involved with them, in that house."

"Well, I could climb up on that roof and cover the chimney to smoke 'em out. Maybe even send some smoke signals while I'm up there."

"Not till we're sure of who all's in the house."

Bear heaved a sigh. "All right, *Gimooza-bie.*"

Reeves looked askance. "You call me that one more time, and I'm gonna put a boot up your ass. Now, you circle around to the left. I'll go straight up the middle, through the corral."

Bear laughed as he reined his horse off to the side.

Reeves watched him go and couldn't help chuckling. Of all the Lighthorse deputies he'd worked with, he liked Bear the best. The Indian was brave and resourceful, and an excellent shot and tracker. But his sense of humor was something to be taken in small doses, like castor oil.

Reeves dismounted and secured his horse to a young oak tree. Then he surveyed the ground he had to cover and started moving. The morning sky was lightening up fast, and he trotted at a quick pace to the far edge of the corral. The four horses paced about nervously within it. Beyond the enclosure, perhaps thirty yards away, a trail of smoke continued to wind upward from the chimney. Reeves moved up through the fencing, pausing to pet one of the nervous horses on the neck, while still keeping his gaze on the house. Now that he was closer, Reeves could better judge the distance.

A privy was on the left side, about thirty feet from the front door. The barn sat about fifty feet to the right. The front doors of the barn were standing open, and Reeves could see spots of the burgeoning sunlight dappling the barn's floor through the numerous holes in the roof.

The horse relaxed under Reeves's practiced touch. He knew horses as well as he knew men, and he urged the beast forward using its bulk to obscure his movements.

Over by the barn, the rooster began emitting a series of sharp, chirping cries. The bird pranced about, stopping periodically to repeat its morning ritual, after which the pervasive silence once again settled over the scene.

As Reeves got to the end of the fencing, the front door of the cabin opened, and a man stumbled out with an uneven gait. He had one boot on and held the other in his hand. Pausing to lean against the door jamb, he pulled the second boot onto his foot. The man was clad in filthy long-johns but had his gun belt strapped over his hips, the handle of a big revolver sticking out from the holster. Straightening up, he looked around as he stretched.

Reeves stood absolutely still next to the horse. He knew it would be movement, either by him or the animal, that would betray his position.

The man in the underwear, whom Reeves assumed was Billy Quint, the younger of the two wanted brothers, spat on the ground and headed for the outhouse. Reeves followed the man's movements.

Quint pulled open the door to the privy, grabbed two of the stacked corncobs, and stepped inside. Reeves moved cautiously to the edge of the corral, still watching the house. The door remained partially open, no sign or sounds of movement inside. He glanced toward the outhouse again and saw Bear emerge from the woods. Reeves pointed to the privy and held up his index finger. Bear glanced at the outhouse, waved, and raised his rifle. With several deft steps, he covered the ground between him and the privy, stopping a few yards away from it and pointing his Winchester 1873 rifle at the wooden door. Reeves held his hand up, palm down, signaling Bear to wait.

No sense disturbing a man when he's taking care of that kind of personal business, Reeves thought with a smile.

He still had concerns that the farmer's family might be inside the dwelling with the other Quint brother. A shot from a rifle could mean complications. Besides, it was better that the potential prisoner finish his business. The trip back to Fort Smith in the wagon was long and challenging enough without having to smell a pair of soiled long-johns the whole way.

Still, both Billy and his brother, Joseph, were hardened killers. Judge Parker's warrants read dead or alive, or so Reeves had been told. He was illiterate and had to commit the names and particulars of each arrest warrant to memory. It would be easier to take Billy by surprise, shoot him while he was in the privy, and not risk a confrontation. Both brothers had killed numerous men and shown no compunction about shooting lawmen. But shooting a man without first giving him a chance to surrender wasn't what Reeves thought proper. He had been given the position as deputy marshal by Judge Parker, who had stressed that upholding the law was paramount.

"Even the white man's law?" one of Reeves's fellow Negroes had once asked him.

"The law ain't perfect," Reeves had answered back. "But it's all we got."

He'd given his word, his pledge to Judge Parker, that he would uphold it to the best of his ability.

That meant bringing them back alive to stand trial, if at all possible.

Reeves stooped and slipped through the wooden rails. The ground leading up to the house was dry and barren. Tuffs of stubborn field grass had managed to pop out in spots, but the area looked trampled upon by uncountable horse tracks.

Through the partially open door, Reeves saw a shadow move inside the house. He froze, glancing left to check on Bear. The Indian's buckskin jacket and dark pants had faded into the high shrubbery next to another oak tree.

No need to worry about him, Reeves thought. But there was no cover between him and the door, which then opened.

A large man stepped through, rolling a cigarette, obviously the older Quint brother, dressed in boots and pants, with a torn and dirty undershirt covering his upper body. Like his younger brother, he wore a gun belt, his pistol slung low, the mark of a gunfighter.

Reeves drew his own Colt .45 Peacemaker and held it down by his leg.

Quint must have caught the movement because he looked up, still holding the rolled cigarette.

"Joseph Quint," Reeves said in a loud voice. "I'm Deputy Marshal Bass Reeves. I have a warrant for your arrest."

Quint smirked and placed the cigarette between his lips. "So the hangin' judge sent a damn nigger to get me?" He shook his head and snapped a match with his thumbnail. "Guess he don't think much of me, doin' somethin' that low."

Reeves said nothing but cocked back the hammer of his Colt.

Quint raised the match with his left hand toward the cigarette, while his right hand darted for his gun. He had barely cleared leather when Reeves brought his own revolver up and extended his arm. A split second later a bullet from Quint's gun whizzed by just as Reeves squeezed the trigger of his own weapon, and saw Joseph Quint twist with the impact of the round. Quint fired another shot, which smacked the earth near the lawman's right foot. Reeves cocked back the hammer again and fired. This time Quint doubled over with a visceral grunt. Another round from his gun discharged harmlessly into the dirt. As he twisted and fell forward, the door of the outhouse burst open, and Billy Quint emerged, firing his gun wildly, the unbuttoned trapdoor of his long-johns still hanging down in back.

Reeves turned, centered his weapon on the younger Quint, and fired. The bullet caught Billy in the throat, and his head jerked back. He seemed frozen for a split second, then lurched sideways as the successive roars from Bear's Winchester rifle sounded. Billy Quint twisted as two widening, dark holes appeared on the side of the gray material. He flopped down on the ground, face first.

Reeves turned his attention back to the now prone Joseph Quint and approached the downed man carefully. Playing possum was a technique Reeves had seen before, and the lawman was always aware that a man was still a danger until you knew for sure that he wasn't. He trotted toward the older Quint at an oblique angle, affording himself a bit of an advantage should the outlaw suddenly come to life and begin firing again. But that didn't happen. As Reeves grew closer, he could discern the man's ragged breathing. Quint's hand still clutched his weapon, a long-barreled revolver, but he made no move to use it. Reeves covered the remaining distance and kicked the gun from Quint's fingers. The outlaw's other hand was empty, and Reeves flipped the man over. Twin holes, one high on Quint's chest and the other lower, on his right side, leaked crimson. The blood from the lower wound was dark, telling Reeves that the bullet had most likely hit the man's liver. It was the end of the trail for this one. Reeves glanced toward Bear, who was standing over the younger Quint brother, the barrel of the rifle pointing down at the outlaw. Bear returned the look, shaking his head.

Reeves pointed to the house and then the barn. Bear nodded and moved to the open front door.

"My brother Billy dead?" Quint said, his words laced with pain.

Reeves nodded.

Joseph Quint closed his eyes, and Reeves thought he saw a tear start to work its way down the outlaw's stubbled cheek.

"Damn," the man said. "Never thought it would turn out like this."

Reeves watched as Bear moved past them, glanced inside, and then disappeared into the semigloom.

"Anybody else in there?" Reeves asked. "Nobody else has to die."

Quint shook his head. "Nobody to speak of."

Bear exited the cabin about thirty seconds later, his face holding a sour look.

"Woman inside," he said. "Looks like they

had their way with her. She's dead now."

Reeves frowned and stared down at Quint. "One more crime you gonna answer for."

Quint's face twisted into something akin to an ironic smile. "Looks like I already have."

"I'll check the barn, *Gimoozabie,*" Bear said, moving away with a hurried pace.

Reeves frowned at the nickname but said nothing. He kept his attention on Quint, who was writhing in the dirt. "Who were these people to you?"

The tip of Quint's tongue darted over his lips. "Kin you give me a shot of whiskey?"

"I asked you a question," Reeves said. "Who were these people?"

Quint hacked out a cough that told Reeves the man's lung was collapsing. "They was just here when we rode up. We was on the run. Knowed the law was after us. They was in the way, that's all."

"Wrong place, wrong time." Reeves looked through the cabin door and saw the bare legs of a woman stretched out on the floor. These two deserved hangin', that was for sure.

"Never thought one of your kind would be able to best me," Quint said.

Reeves shrugged. "It was your choice. I gave you a chance to surrender."

"So the old hanging judge could string me up in front of all them people? No thanks."

Reeves said nothing. He figured the man didn't have much time left.

"My mama always told me to do the right thing," Quint said. "Fought with the Confederacy durin' the war. You?"

"I was in it some."

"You're a brave man, I'll give you that." More dark blood pumped from his side.

"I promise to give you and your brother both proper burials," Reeves said. "If you have any valuables you want returned to your family, tell me now."

Quint tried to lick his lips.

"We ain't got nothing," he said. "Reckon you'll take them horses. We stole 'em anyways." The outlaw coughed, sending a patch of blood dribbling down his chin. "I'd be grateful if you bury me and my brother side by side, Marshal." He coughed wetly again, then pointed to his pants pocket. "I got my father's watch here. Promise me you ain't gonna steal it. It'd give me comfort goin' to my rest and knowin' it was with me."

"I'm a lawman. I don't steal."

Quint closed his eyes, took two quick breaths, then grimaced in pain. "You can . . . take my gun . . ." He motioned with his right hand. "Presented to me by none other than Jesse James. I kilt ten men with it. Want you to have it."

Reeves looked down at the weapon. It was the kind popular with many outlaws, a long-barreled .45 Remington 1875.

"I aim to take it," Reeves said. "But not as a gift."

"You can have it, Marshal." Quint's lips twisted into something akin to a smile. "I want you to. Please. You're a good man. Better than me, even . . . I . . ."

Quint stiffened.

Reeves moved the toe of his boot against the outlaw's open eye. He didn't flinch.

"There's another dead one in the barn, *Gimoozabie,*" Bear said as he walked up. "A man. Looks like the homesteader."

"You remember what I said I was gonna do if you kept callin' me that?"

Bear smirked. "Thought I told you. Some of my people are from the north . . . Potowatomi. Maybe, Ojibwa, too. I speak their tongues. *Gimoozabie* means 'trusted friend.' "

"I know what the hell you said it means. You keep reminding me often enough."

"Trusted friend."

"I'll trust you to rustle us up a couple of

21

shovels. We got us a whole lot of burying to do."

"You ain't got to take these bodies back to show the judge?"

"No need. Judge Parker knows I tell him the truth."

Bear heaved an exaggerated sigh of relief. "Whew. And I was worrying about smelling these two all the way back."

"Just get the damn shovels."

"Okay, *Gimo*—"

Reeves jumped forward and kicked the Indian in the rump. Bear emitted something halfway between a yelp and a laugh as he walked back toward the barn.

The Indian Territories
The town of Temptation
Marion Michael Donovan stooped down and plucked one of the yellow wildflowers from the sparse patch of greenery next to the hitching post while fanning himself with his hat. He was a rather handsome man with a full head of reddish blond hair and well formed, even features. His smile looked almost boyish, and his blue eyes gleamed with what his beloved mother had called "the mischief of a leprechaun." He straightened up, brought the wildflower to his nose, and watched the five men in front of him

near the entrance to the town's lone saloon. A cluster of several more ramshackle buildings decorated the dusty street, extending perhaps five hundred feet or more. It was a blooming metropolis by western standards. Or at least it used to be. But, regardless, it was ripe for the taking for a man of shrewd intellect and extraordinary capabilities.

Harsh laughter emitted from the short, fat man standing in the middle of the five.

Donovan knew the man's name was Kenneth Cooper, the Indian agent who'd set up their little foray down Texas way with the herd of government cattle. And it hadn't been a bad drive, all things considered. Donovan had picked up some associates along the way. They now stood off to the side watching, just as he'd instructed. He didn't figure he'd need much help with this group of louts. After all, there wasn't an Irishman in the midst, and Cooper's name sounded a trifle bit English.

Cooper was squat and fat and reminded Donovan of a pig in a suit of clothes. The man's pencil-thin mustache re-enforced this image, because Donovan knew that underneath the man's sweat-soaked, brown hat was a patch of bare scalp that any swine would be proud of showing off.

Leave it to a human shoat to want to hide

it, Donovan thought as he replaced his own hat on his head.

The man on Cooper's right was Boswell, one of the soldiers who had helped them divert the herd of beef down Texas way, when it was supposed to be bound for the Indian village. Boswell's blue uniform hung loosely on his sparse frame, and his cheeks showed the stubble of several days without the benefit of a razor. He looked like Southern Missouri trash to Donovan. Probably some riffraff who'd joined the army one step ahead of the hangman. His sidearm was in the standard, hooded military holster designed for retention and protection from the elements rather than a fast draw. No, he wouldn't be much of a problem, regardless of which way this little drama played out. Cooper wouldn't be a dangerous factor, either. He most likely had a gun stuffed into the beltline of that fat belly, like any pig, but he'd be just as happy being paid off by his new boss as he was by the old one.

Hobb, the burly sheriff of the town of Temptation, and his two deputies were a different story. Most likely, they wouldn't be taking too kindly to being replaced, but there'd be room for only one rooster in this barnyard. Donovan took another sniff of the flower and then glanced to the batwing doors of the saloon. The hulking form of Finn peered over them, the derby perched upon his massive head, and next to him the swarthy, mustachioed face of Texas-Mex, as Donovan had christened him. Both of them would provide any additional support, should any be required, as would Crowe, the third and final member of Donovan's recently formed gang of four. But Crowe wouldn't be of much use in a gunfight. The scared halfwit was probably already guzzling down half a bottle of whiskey and couldn't be counted upon to shoot straight.

But none of that bothered Donovan. In fact, he actually preferred it. It was crucial that he handle this transition of power all by his lonesome. A demonstration of his skill would be an effective way of ensuring their unwavering loyalty. They were merely jackals following the lion.

Ah, the Bard, William Shakespeare himself, would be proud of that metaphor, Donovan thought as he twirled the wildflower between his fingers and smiled his leprechaun smile. Despite it being a tad too British. But, then again, there weren't really any lions in England, were there? He sniffed the flower again and mentally added, with a twinkle, that there weren't any in Ireland either.

And now it was time to dance with the devil.

"Begging your pardons, gentlemen," he said with his fine, Irish brogue. "But I believe we have a bit of unfinished business to conduct."

Hobb frowned, his thick, flat face showing more irritation than wariness. The fool was facing the sun, and the silver star shimmered on his broad chest.

A mistake he will soon be finding himself regretting, Donovan thought. He paused to let his boyish smile sink in, letting them see he was totally confident facing down the six of them alone.

"What you want, you damn mick?" Hobb asked, his voice low and gravelly.

"Just a fairly paid wage for a good bit of work," Donovan said. He winked at Cooper, whose smile had begun to fade.

"What you talkin' about?" Hobb said. "You got *yer* pay already. Now *git.*" He turned away, but Donovan stood his ground.

"I believe I'm deserving of a bit of a raise."

Hobb turned back to face him. The big sheriff's scowl grew more pronounced. "I'm tellin' you for the last time, mick. Git!"

"There's an old Irish saying." Donovan, his expression serious, made a show of looking around. "The shadow of a man at mid-day tends to rise up and meet him at day's end." He paused and let another smile curl his lips. "So tell me, would you be hearing those chimes of midnight?"

Donovan conspicuously tossed the wild-flower with his left hand while using his right thumb to lift the finely braided twine securing his gun to his holster and then lowered his hand.

Hobb's lips curled into a snarl. He was big and barrel-chested and moved fast for a big man.

But not fast enough.

Donovan's Remington .45 was in his hand in an instant and spat a burst of flame and smoke. His first shot struck Hobb's chest, the second between the big man's eyes. Donovan shifted his weight forward, pre-senting a smaller profile to the two depu-ties, who were now drawing. Donovan's next shot caught the first man just below the left eye, making a neat, round hole in his cheek and sending a spray of crimson mist out the back of his neck.

The third man hesitated and glanced toward his crumpling friend.

Bad mistake, lad, Donovan thought as he cocked back the hammer and delivered another head shot, this time in the second deputy's left temple. He stiffened, dropping his gun in the dirt, and toppled over, landing face first.

Donovan knew he only had one cartridge left, but he was gambling that he wouldn't be needing it. He pivoted ever so slightly and cocked back the hammer once more, aiming the gun in the space between the Indian agent and the trooper.

"I've got two more rounds left to fire," Donovan said, gambling that neither of these two ninnies would be willing to test his veracity. "Which one of you would prefer to go first?"

Boswell raised his hands. "Hey, you'd be a fool to shoot me. I got something good for ya. Real good." His voice had that Missouri twang to it. This one was hill trash, but perhaps he could provide a bit of usefulness.

"Do you now?"

Boswell's lips pulled back into a nervous grin, exposing a set of missing and rotting teeth. His head bobbled up and down.

Donovan swiveled the barrel toward the Indian agent. "So that leaves you."

The pant leg of Cooper's gray suit grew suddenly dark and sodden as the porcine face, now gleaming with sweat, forced itself into what he must have hoped would resemble a bit of a smile.

Cremini, Donovan thought. The fat lout's pissed his britches.

"I don't want no trouble," the agent said.

"Cooper. Now would that, perchance, be an English name?"

"I dunno." The Indian agent swallowed. "I mean, I don't think so."

Donovan kept his gun pointed at the man for a solid ten seconds more, then lowered it. "Good answer." He strode toward the two standing men, who immediately backed away. Stopping by Hobb's prone form, Donovan used the toe of his boot to flip the body over. A gold pocket watch on a chain tumbled out of Hobb's vest and fell into the dirt. Donovan reached down and retrieved it. Brushing the dust from its surface, he nodded and placed it in his pants pocket.

"To the victor belongs the spoils," he said aloud.

Then he bent down again and removed the star from Hobb's chest. Donovan blew a long breath over the silver plating and then brushed it a few times on his shirt before pinning it in place on his own shirt.

He looked over at Cooper and Boswell. "Well, let's go over yonder to the emporium and toast our new partnership. You two can buy your new boss a bit of refreshment."

He replaced his revolver in his holster and gestured toward the saloon.

Boswell and Cooper exchanged nervous glances and tried to smile. They looked like two relieved schoolboys who'd gotten a reprieve from being taken in back of the woodshed. As they began walking toward the pair of batwing doors, Donovan stooped and retrieved each of the dead men's guns.

Somewhere in southern Illinois
Lucien T. Stutley adjusted the spectacles on his nose as he stared out the window of the moving train. He wiped at his face with his crumpled handkerchief. It was insufferably hot, and the sweat inside his high, starched collar made his neck itch. The wooden bench was unpadded and uncomfortable, and the inconsiderate, bovine woman who was sitting across from him had placed her obtrusive carpet bag on the narrow expanse of floor between them. This thoughtless act necessitated that he wedge his long legs back under the seat as best he could, which was made virtually impossible because his second bag had been crammed underneath as well. As if that hadn't been ignominious enough, she'd also seated one of her two children, the smaller one, a female, next to her and then placed the larger one, a round-

faced son of a sow if there ever was one, in the vacant space on the seat next to Stutley.

The pig-faced boy, if he could be called so, continued to emit periodic bursts of foul-smelling eruptions from both ends of his corpulent little body.

Stutley would have said something, but the woman's husband, a massive man-mountain with hands the size of ham hocks, had seated himself across the way with several bundled packs.

Luckily, Stutley had been able to place his larger bag on the seat between himself and the youth, forming a rampart of sorts. It was a finely tooled, but worn, leather suitcase that had been given to him by his uncle Lewis M. Grey, who had used it in his dental practice in Zanesville, Ohio.

The suitcase provided ample room for Stutley's private papers and notebooks that would allow him to capture the picturesque images of the western towns and characters about whom he'd been commissioned to write. Of course, the stories themselves would have to be revised back in New York before publication, but that was part of the plan. Stutley's editor at Beadles had given him the assignment, and the salary advance, to travel west and find some of the lawmen and outlaws who could be immortalized in the dime novels Irwin and Erastus Beadle's company published. Stutley had brought numerous samples along to show around. They, too, resided in his leather suitcase. He dared not pull them out now, lest "Junior," as the bovine hag called her pugnacious prodigy, lean over and drool upon them.

Then another thought struck him: how many of these uneducated rubes out here would know how to read? Well, at least some of the booklets had illustrations.

The repugnant little boy turned and looked up at Stutley with a sly grin, and seconds later it become painfully obvious that the boy had silently passed another emission of malodorous flatulence.

Stutley grimaced and glanced toward the boy's mother, whose wide mouth drew back into an oblivious and totally unsympathetic smile. The kid began waving his arms to dissipate the odor, to no avail. Some of it must have wafted across to the woman, because she sniffed the air and said, "Junior, you mess your pants again?"

Junior, who had to be close to twelve, replied with a non-verbal shrug and began picking his nose. Stutley visibly recoiled as Junior rubbed some of the vile nasal contents on the side of Stutley's leather suitcase. The kid hadn't mastered proper manners any more than he had gastric restraint and, apparently, potty training.

"Junior, stop that," the woman said.

Stutley edged closer to the window and wondered if this was an accurate sampling of the creatures who populated this area. He longed to adjust the uncomfortable money belt that continued to pinch his fat belly, but it held all the funds for his trip west. To do so might alert some lurking predator. For all he knew, the hag's hulking spouse might be one of them.

"You'll be seeing things you never saw before," Uncle Lewis had told him when Stutley had stopped off at his uncle's Ohio home. While it wasn't New York City, by any stretch of the imagination, the midwestern city had been infinity more civilized than the more recent stops on his journey. He hoped St. Louis might bear the stamp of further civilization, almost wishing he could spend some time there before going further south, toward his ultimate destination, Fort Smith, Arkansas.

"The area beyond that is known as the Indian Territories," Uncle Lewis said, trying to educate him on the ever-expanding national plain. "Soldiers, Indians, and cowboys. Where disputes are settled by the point of a gun instead of with a tort in a court of law. Like I said, you'll be seeing things you never saw before, and not all of them will be remotely civilized or even pleasant."

Junior farted again, this time with an accompanying braying sound.

Uncle Lewis was right, thought Stutley. I'm already seeing, and smelling, the uncivilized and the unpleasant.

The woman ushered another admonishment to her son, then turned and smiled at Stutley. "Boys will be boys."

He'd noticed earlier that several of her front teeth were gone.

Perhaps Uncle Lewis was missing out on a whole new crop of prospective patients, he thought and returned his gaze to the flat, overgrown plains and occasional farm that decorated the sights on the other side of the window. In his head he began to fashion the beginning of one of the entries for his journal. He took out his notebook and pencil. The point was still sharp, and he began to write. Uncle Lewis had urged him to record things while traveling, lest he forget.

"Do it for little Pearl," Uncle Lewis had said, knowing his young son loved to hear stories about the West.

Stutley pushed the sliding spectacles up onto the bridge of his nose and began writing.

The land flattened out substantially as I gazed out the window. The train moved inexorably onward, speeding me toward the southern edges of the Midwest and on toward the roughness of the West itself. What would I find? What adventures lay ahead? What kind of men would I meet? What kind of women?

Stutley closed his eyes and tried to conjure up the memory of the painting he'd seen in a museum of a beautiful, nude Indian woman bathing in a stream.

Once again, Junior punctuated Stutley's musings with another foul burst of air, which had an ominous moist sound to it. The accompanying aromatic pungency hinted that this one may have been more substantial.

"That's it, Junior," the bovine yelled. She reached over and grabbed the little lout by the ear, tugging him to his feet. The boy bleated like a wounded goat. "We're going to ask the conductor for the chamber pot." As she stood, she thrust her expansive backside close to Stutley's face. The overpowering, musky smell of her body odor in this close proximity was almost as repugnant as the emissions of her offensive offspring.

She turned to Stutley and looked down at his notebook. "Mind giving me some of that paper? We got a mess to clean up, if'n I know my little darlin' like I think I do."

Stutley recoiled at the thought of the paper from his journal being used for such an ignominious purpose, but the alternative of sitting next to the unclean youth in his unsanitary state was even more painful. Perhaps there was another seat available in another car. He tore one of the blank pages free and handed it to the woman.

She frowned. "Can't you spare more than that?"

Stutley winced. Paper was a sparse commodity on this trip, but the last thing he wanted to do was antagonize these miscreants. He gave her a second sheet.

"Thank you," she said, pulling hard on Junior's ear as they moved into the aisle. The woman turned and spoke loudly to the slumbering husband. "Watch little Mary while I take him to get cleaned up."

The unsophisticated rube looked up, grunted something undistinguishable, and closed his eyes.

Yeah, Uncle Lewis, thought Stutley, *you certainly hit the nail on the head. The adventure is just beginning.*

CHAPTER 2

The Indian Territories
After burying the homesteader and his wife in front of some trees a good distance from the house, a nice spot, Reeves and Bear had transported the bodies of the two Quint boys about a hundred feet away and buried them as well. It hadn't seemed right to bury them too close, given the crimes they'd inflicted on the homesteader and his missus. Since they were technically inside the borders of the Indian Territories, they did not mark the graves, and Reeves showed particular attention in flattening out the earth so that the graves would not be noticeable. Grave desecration was common in these parts, and Reeves didn't want that to happen to the homesteaders. His concern was less for the Quints, but he assiduously flattened their gravesites as well.

Bear wiped the sweat from his forehead and spat on the closest grave.

"This is a lot better than them two coyotes deserve," he said.

Reeves reflected on this, silently agreeing with his partner's sentiments. "You know what the good book says. Judge not, lest ye be judged."

"You talkin' about the white man's good book?"

"I look white?" Reeves asked, smirking. "You best be getting your eyes checked by one of them fancy doctors once we get back to Fort Smith. If we can find one."

Reeves placed Quint's watch and the two outlaws' guns into a burlap bag for transportation back to Fort Smith. Although Reeves knew that Judge Parker would no doubt accept the account about the demise of the pair, he always brought back something to show the judge. His reports were oral recitations, since Reeves couldn't read or write, and the watch and guns would be useful augmentations. Had Joseph Quint given Reeves a location for the return of the watch to a family member, he would have done his best to see to that as well. The other recovered property, the horses, would be turned over to the judge. Reeves opened the gate of the poke, where the drove of pigs slumbered in the mud, figuring they'd eventually wander off in search of food.

"Shame to waste all that good meat," Bear said as he watched Reeves tie a line around the necks of the four horses and attach it to the wagon.

Reeves shrugged. "We got us enough supplies. No need for more, and we ain't got the time to do no curing. Besides, after being penned up all their lives, they deserve a chance to be free. Plenty of wild hogs in them woods that they can meet up with."

Bear laughed. "Some big old boss boar'll tear them apart, most likely."

"Maybe, but at least they'll die free."

Reeves knew all about freedom. He'd been born a slave and had lived his early life knowing nothing else until the war came visiting. His master, William Reeves, from whom Bass had taken his surname, had allowed him to work as a field hand alongside his mama and daddy. It was rare that slave families were allowed to remain together. Then, as Bass grew up tall and strong, his master's son, George, took a shine to him, teaching him to ride and shoot. Reeves grew proficient with both a rifle and pistol, able to shoot accurately with either hand. It was almost like he and young George were friends . . .

Almost.

Reeves had felt life was good, but only

because he'd never known anything else. And then the war came, rumbling over the Southland and sweeping both George and Bass up into the maelstrom. A true son of the Confederacy, George Reeves decided it was his duty to march off to fight, and he took Bass with him.

Reeves was a reluctant soldier, torn between loyalty to the only man he'd ever known who'd provided for him, taught things to him, and the growing realization that this same man really didn't regard him as a man at all. He was property. Other Negroes who had been similarly conscripted by the South spoke in hushed tones about the "North Country," the Underground Railroad, a man called President Lincoln and his Emancipation Proclamation. It meant freedom, if they could get there, and desertion meant death. After thinking it over, Reeves saw no disgrace in it. When he informed his master of his decision, out of respect for the man who'd befriended and taught him virtually everything, Bass suddenly found out what he was to George Reeves, who attempted to beat all "them silly Yankee ideas out of your fool head."

But the "whippin' " suddenly took an unexpected turn as Reeves fought back after feeling the sting of the whip. Young and extremely powerful, Bass left George Reeves in a bloodied heap near the rear of the Confederate encampment and then made his way through the woods. He was only twenty-three years old, dressed in rags, and on the run. Slowly he made his way to what he hoped was the North, in search of freedom and a new life. Instead, he had ventured into the Indian Territories. He stumbled upon some Indians, Cherokees, who were sympathetic to the South and became enslaved again, this time under more brutal masters. The beatings toughened Reeves, and, while pretending to be compliant, he listened and learned their ways and language.

When the opportunity to escape his new captors arose, Reeves took it. Barefoot and ragged, he began walking east. After days without food or water, existing on what wild berries and roots he could find, he came upon a wondrous sight: a seemingly endless marching column, four abreast, of bright-blue uniforms.

Union soldiers marching from Fort Gibson to Fort Smith.

Nothing had ever looked so good to him.

Reeves fell to his knees and begged the troops to let him go with them. "I want to fight for you," he said. "And I know how."

"The war's over, son," the white Union army officer told him from atop his great black steed. "Lee surrendered at Appomattox weeks ago, and you are now a free man."

A free man! The words sounded strange, almost foreign to Reeves.

Freedom!

From that moment on, he never took it for granted.

He heard the sound of Bear approaching on his horse.

Reeves tied his own mount to the opposite side of the wagon and climbed up onto the seat.

"Let's roll," he said.

Bear looked at him and nodded. "I'm ready, *Gimoozabie.*"

Reeves stared long and hard at the Indian. "How'd you like me to make up a special name to call you?"

Bear laughed. "As long as it means 'trusted friend,' I will be honored."

Reeves shook his head and snapped the reins over the flanks of the team of horses hitched to the wagon.

The Indian Territories
The town of Temptation
Marion Michael Donovan followed Kenneth Cooper, the Indian agent, and Boswell

42

through the swinging doors. Ordinarily, he would have preferred to enter first, as the newly crowned king surveying his fiefdom, but he felt it a bit more prudent to bring up the rear until he was certain that his two new partners could be trusted completely. Additionally, he wanted to reload his gun, this time taking care to put that sixth round in the cylinder. Despite running the risk of having the hammer strike it at an inopportune moment and accidentally fire, the reassurance of having six shots, instead of only five, seemed appropriate when negotiating a new business arrangement.

The saloon had a trace of unexpected elegance to it, and Donovan was pleased. A long bar of polished wood, flanked by an array of bottles and glasses and with a long mirror hanging behind it, was set on the right side of the room. The rest of the place had wooden tables for drinking and gambling. Even the walls held a bit of surprise: a rich purple colored wallpaper that extended down a long hallway toward what smelled like a kitchen. Donovan had heard that the hallway extended to a row of back rooms where the ladies of the evening — or any other time of the day — applied their trade. Hobb had bragged, when they'd first hit town after the cattle drive, that he got fifty-one percent of all the profits from the saloon and "the hog ranch," as he called it.

Donovan licked his lips, anticipating spending a little time with each of the ladies until he decided upon one for regular connubial duties. There were five of them, but, from what he knew, only two had sounded interesting: a blonde, full-figured woman named Polly, and a svelte, raven-haired Indian lass. The others had been described as "eight pounds of potatoes stuffed into five-pound bags."

Donovan looked forward to making a better assessment himself.

There were eight rooms on the second floor, forming a hotel that was generally empty, save for Hobb's room, which he had used as his primary residence. The sheriff had another room at the almost vacant boarding house across the street, as did the Indian agent, Cooper. Both had offices, too, and Donovan wondered which room would be the most logical place for them to have hidden their stashes of ill-gotten gains.

I'll have to make a point of finding that out, he thought as he gazed at the rooms on the second floor.

The sheriff's old room, the first at the top of the stairs, was now Donovan's, and he figured it was due for a bit of remodeling.

He contemplated having the royal standard of Ireland carved upon the door, if he could find someone with the skill enough to do justice to the sainted lady's profile, breasts, and wings.

But all that could be decided at another time. Donovan paused just inside the batwing doors, pulled back the left side of his leather vest, and displayed the silver star.

"I've got an announcement to make," he said, giving full weight to his fine baritone voice.

All activity in the room stopped. The faces of several cowboys and bar girls turned toward him.

He smiled, still holding the vest aside to display the shiny star. "There's a new sheriff in town."

Finn and Texas-Mex grinned from their position at the far end of the bar. Finn was a monstrously huge man with the high cheekbones of an Indian, but the lighter complexion of a white man. His eyes were a greenish blue, and his long, black hair hung to his shoulders. Perched on top of his head was a green derby. Texas-Mex wore a sombrero and had a drooping black mustache. The room was filled with more than a dozen people. Three of them were the girls from the back: a rather short, plump redhead; the tallish blonde with a half-decent shape, who must have been Polly; and the squaw, the Indian girl. Of the three, she had perhaps the best form and nicest features, but it looked like someone had sliced her nose down the middle. It had healed with a thick scar.

Donovan knew he wanted to taste all three of them, and any more of the lasses who might be sleeping or hiding, but that could wait until later. It was time to conduct business, and his sainted mother had always stressed to him the importance of putting business before pleasure.

The rest of the patrons were mostly composed of the same cowhands who'd accompanied them on the cattle drive and those who had odd jobs in the town. Rollins, the general store clerk, and Howard, the blacksmith, sat watching with rapt attention. Donovan nodded a greeting to them both. Crowe was in the back, the bottle of liquor on the table in front of him already less than half full. The afternoon sunlight streamed in the window next to him and illuminated the red, black, and purple scarring that encompassed the right half of his head. On the other half, a few wisps of brown hair resided in tufts. Donovan knew that Crowe had been partially scalped during an encounter with some not-so-friendly Indians. Although the last major battle with the red man around these parts had occurred a few years ago, the army was still tasked with keeping the overall peace, should any of the savages step out of line. But that wasn't supposed to happen, due to the treaty that had created the Indian Territories and pledged to provide beef to the various tribes through governmental supervision.

These were the same governmentally provided cattle that Donovan had helped drive down to Texas so they could be sold at a profit. Hobb and Cooper, the regional Indian agent, had been tasked with overseeing this fair and equitable distribution of the beef, and they'd had a hell of a sweet little deal going on. They'd accept the government shipment of the beef, strip off a few to give to the Indians, and run the rest down to Texas, where they were sold again, this time to ranchers who asked no questions.

Donovan gestured to the bartender to bring a bottle of his best and three glasses to the furthest, unoccupied table. Taking a seat with his back to the wall, Donovan motioned for Boswell and Cooper to take the chairs opposite. Both men exchanged

47

glances before reluctantly sitting down. The barkeep set the glasses down in front of each man, along with the bottle, and started to walk away. Donovan leaned back in his chair and said, "Hey."

The barkeep turned, lifting an eyebrow. He was a heavyset man with a bulldog's face.

"What kind of a host are you that you won't be pouring our libation?" Donovan said. "Like you know you should be doing out of sheer politeness."

The bartender's lower lip was swallowed by his upper, but he stepped back to the table, removed the cork from the bottle, and poured a finger in each glass. When he'd finished, Donovan gave an encouraging wink.

"That was a fine job. What your name, laddie?"

"Henry."

Donovan winked. "A pleasure to be making your acquaintance. I'm the new owner." He let that sink in for a few second. After Henry nodded, Donovan said, "Leave us the bottle."

The barkeep walked away, and Donovan leaned forward, his left arm on top of the table, his right underneath. "Drink up, gentlemen," he said. "To the prosperous

48

times ahead. But, first, let's put all our cards on the table, shall we?"

Boswell and Cooper exchanged glances again.

"Your guns, gentlemen," Donovan said. "Would you be so kind as to be removing them very gently from your holsters and placing them on the top of the table for my inspection?"

Boswell and Cooper exchanged yet another glance, and Boswell's lips curled back, exposing his crooked and missing teeth. "I don't reckon I like that idea much."

"All the same," Donovan said, cracking a smile, " 'tis far better than the alternative, lad, which is me holding this gun under the table that's now pointed at your privates."

Boswell's face blanched. He swallowed hard and then flipped up the flap of his holster and carefully set his gun on top of the table. It was a long barreled, single-action army .45.

Cooper laughed, shifted in his seat, and pulled out his weapon, also a single-action army, but with a smaller, four-and-three-quarter-inch barrel.

Donovan's right hand remained concealed under the table. He centered his gaze on the Indian agent.

"I do believe we're getting off to a bad

start," Donovan said.

Cooper's brow furrowed. "What you talking about? I put mine on the table."

Donovan's smile grew broader. "All of your weapons, if you please." This was accompanied by the ominous click of a revolver's hammer being cocked back.

Cooper's lips bunched up, and he shifted in the chair, reaching into the dollop of belly covering his belt and withdrawing a Sharps four-barrel Pepperbox. He set the derringer on the table.

Donovan's grin remained in place as his eyes turned back to Boswell. "What's your Christian name?"

The hill rat's nose twitched. "Daniel."

"Ah, Danny boy, would you be so kind as to remove that bit of a blade you have protruding from the inside top of your left boot?"

Boswell's tongue darted over his lips, his nose twitched, and he brought his hand up slowly, holding the knife with two fingers. He set it carefully in the middle of the table.

Donovan leaned back and carefully lowered the hammer of his gun. "Where I came from in Ireland," he said, "we have a partiality for a verse known as a limerick. Ever heard one?"

Boswell and Cooper shook their heads.

Donovan took a deep breath, conscious now that all eyes were upon him, and began to speak, the Irish brogue coloring his speech.

"There once was a sheriff named Hobb, whose mouth had the smell of a bog. He fell to the ground, after only one round . . ." He paused and tapped the silver star on his chest with his index finger. ". . . and lay in the street like a hog."

From the bar area both Finn and Texas-Mex laughed. The rest of the room was silent until Finn turned toward them and said, "How come you all ain't laughing, too?"

The crowd erupted with forced chuckles.

One man sitting at a table had remained silent, and Finn walked over to him. Bending down in front of the man's face, the giant said, "How come *you* ain't laughing?"

"Get out of my face, you lousy half-breed."

The man had a tough look about him, like he'd been in many a scrape and had no fear of anyone. His hand darted toward his holster, but the giant moved with speed that was unexpected for one of his size. Finn's big right hand gripped the cowboy's gun hand. The cowboy grimaced in pain as it became obvious that Finn was exerting

51

tremendous pressure. The cowboy lashed out with his left fist, striking Finn in the face, to no effect. It seemed to enrage the giant, who grabbed the cowboy by the neck, lifted him completely out of his chair, took several steps back to the bar, and smashed the cowboy's head against the edge several times.

The argumentative cowboy's body went limp, but Finn didn't stop. He tossed the man's gun onto the floor and then looped his left arm around the man's neck. His right hand closed over the cowboy's skull, almost obscuring the man's face completely.

A second man rose, pulling out his gun and pointing it at the half-breed's enormous back.

Texas-Mex's right hand made a blurring movement, and the second cowboy gripped his throat, from which the hilt of a thin-bladed knife now protruded.

The Mexican's grin flashed white under his bushy mustache. *"Me gusto la pistola, también."*

The second cowboy crumpled to the floor. Finn made a wrenching motion, and a sharp snapping sound was heard. The first cowboy's body convulsed and was still. The giant let the limp form drop to the floor and went back to drink at the bar.

"My deputies," Donovan said, the smile still etched on his face.

"Anybody else no wanna laugh?" Texas-Mex said, surveying the room. When no one spoke, he slapped Finn on the back. "Let's drink, *amigo.*"

Donovan smiled and said, "Ah, that has inspired another verse within me.

"There once were two fellows quite dour, who frowned when they should have endured. But like pigs in a poke, they found 'twas no joke, when they carried them out of the door."

The Mexican began clapping. Finn set his drink down and rotated his big head around the room, staring balefully at the occupants of the room.

Everyone broke into a quick round of applause.

Donovan raised his arms in acknowledgment and then pointed to two men sitting nearest the cowboy's corpse. "Would you gents be so kind as to attend to that trash?"

Both men immediately got to their feet and began dragging the bodies toward the doors.

Boswell and Cooper exchanged glances once again. The fat Indian agent's face was covered with a brocade of sweat.

"See that the poor buggers get decent,

Christian burials out back by the privy," Donovan called after them. " 'Tis the least I can do since I was educated by the Jesuits."

"Jesuits?" Boswell said.

"Priests, my boy. Priests." Donovan picked up his glass and held it to the light. "I was almost thinking of joining their ranks once, because it was the dearest wish of my sainted mother. And they provided me with a fine education, until I had my first dance with the ladies. Then I realized that wanting to be called 'father,' while taking a vow of celibacy and poverty, wasn't much to my liking." He raised his eyebrows and sighed. "Now, let's get on to bigger and better things." His eyes narrowed as he looked at each man sitting across from him. "Tell me what you're going to be doing for me."

Cooper's mouth twitched. "The next load of cattle ain't due till the beginning of the month."

"Never mind them damn cows," Boswell said, a crafty looking smile twisting his lips. "I got something better. A whole lot better."

"I'm listening," Donovan said.

Boswell glanced around nervously. "Not here. Too many ears."

Donovan stared at the man for several seconds and then said in a hushed tone,

"Let's go up to my new abode, and you can tell me all about it."

Railroad Terminal
East St. Louis, Illinois

After they'd returned from their noxious duties with the chamber pot, Junior stank worse than ever, and the hag smelled of a sweat, newly formed upon the stale, five residual rings under the arms of her dress. Miraculously, both she and Junior had fallen off to sleep as the trip progressed, and Stutley had taken the bold move of pulling a scrap of material loose from her carpetbag and using it to wipe Junior's snots from the leather suitcase.

He then tucked the scrap back from whence it came, smiling at the stealth with which he'd accomplished the task.

Tabula rasa, he thought. A clean slate.

Not that any of these miscreants would have the slightest knowledge of Latin. From the speech he'd heard thus far on his journey, they barely understood English.

The constant, unending rhythmic rocking caused Stutley to doze off as well as the train journeyed through the impending darkness. He jerked back to consciousness when he felt someone trying to remove his spectacles.

55

Junior quickly withdrew his hand as Stutley snapped awake and glared at him.

A jarring motion of the train became more pronounced, and the conductor ventured into the car and announced that they were coming to their final stop: "East St. Louis, Illinois. Last stop *fer* this train. Change in the station for all other trains heading south."

My God, Stutley thought. *Does everyone in this part of the country sound like a southerner?*

He then became cognizant of Junior's piercing gaze over a half-cocked, sly-looking smile. What was the little dullard grinning about?

Stutley thought of smacking the brat's face, since they were all disembarking, but the kid's broad-backed old man was already standing and stretching. The bovine hag had also stirred awake and began pulling at her carpet bag in the center area between the seats. She would most likely be a formidable adversary as well.

"Gowan, take this," she said to the kid. "We gotta get off here."

Junior remained immobile until his old man reached over and swatted the little reprobate and told him to "Take that bag fer yer ma."

The recalcitrant little dolt grabbed hold of the handles and began pulling the bag along the floor, still looking back at Stutley with that mocking smile.

Good riddance, Stutley thought as he watched them move toward the far door. He immediately got to his feet and, with some concerted effort, retrieved his own luggage bag from underneath the seat. The woman's bag in the space between them, and his own rather large pair of feet, had caused the luggage to become jammed.

Stutley moved to the opposite set of doors and prepared to exit. He now had to find the next train heading south toward Arkansas and the place called Fort Smith.

The train slowed and eventually came to a bumping and grinding halt. The conductor's voice could once again be heard saying, "East St. Louis, Illinois. End of the line."

Opening the door, Stutley stepped out onto the raised platform and surveyed the huge, cavern-like surroundings. Seeing the conductor a few steps away emptying a chamber pot between the railroad car and the platform, Stutley stepped over to the man, careful to avoid the splashing liquid.

"Excuse me," Stutley said. "But where do I catch the next train to Fort Smith?"

The conductor made no effort to answer

until he'd finished pouring all the yellowish-brown contents of the pot into the crevice between the train and platform planks. No wonder the pervasive odor of the place was so putrid.

Stutley took a breath and had begun to repeat the question when the conductor blurted out, "Take the ferry across the river to the Missouri side, and, from there, it's right across from us." He bent and set the pot down inside the cab.

After thanking the man, Stutley glanced around to get his bearings. A feeling of immense relief flooded him as he marched toward what he hoped would be the last leg of his journey for a while, at least for the short term. His uncle had told him that Fort Smith was "a real western town."

The terminal was a huge cavern that marked the end of the line for several sets of tracks and the beginning of several more. Despite the darkness and relatively poor lighting, he was able to discern a sign about a hundred yards away with large red letters: *FERRY TO MISSOURI SIDE.* It was punctuated with an arrow. Hurrying toward it, he hoped he wouldn't be seeing any more of the deplorables.

He continued down to the gate and purchased a ticket for the ferry. None of the cretins — father, mother, daughter, or prodigal son — was present, and Stutley heaved a sigh of relief. As the ferry continued to fill with people, he felt the urge to record some of his thoughts and impressions lest they slip away. After placing the carpet bag on the floor between his feet and the leather suitcase on top of that, he began to unfasten the small leather buckles that held the two sides of the case together. He felt his brow crease as he saw they were loose. He'd secured them with vigor, assuring they would not come undone before he'd boarded the train in Chicago. But now the bag looked like it'd been opened and re-secured, and by a sloppy hand at that.

He recalled Junior's sly smile and immediately thought: did that little thief go into the bag when I dozed off?

He tore it open, hoping against hope that none of his periodicals or pamphlets were missing or damaged. As he shuffled through the contents he began to feel a growing sense of relief but then recoiled in disgust. Nothing had been taken, but something had been added.

Stutley stared down at the crumpled, brown stained pieces of journal paper he'd given to the bovine hag upon her request.

They were smeared with foul smelling fecal matter.

No wonder that little son of a bitch had been smiling all the way to the door.

As he extricated the refuse, he wondered once more, what manner of people were these creatures, and what had he gotten himself into?

The Indian Territories Near the Arkansas Border

As the sun was rising in the east, they came to the fork in the trail. Bear pulled back on the reins and halted the forward movement of the team of horses. They'd spent one night on the trail and gotten an early start on this second day so that Reeves could get back to Fort Smith in time to report to the judge.

Bear wound the long leather strands around the perpendicular brake lever and smacked his hands together.

"Looks like this is where we part company, Bass," he said.

Reeves rode up beside him and dismounted. As Bear jumped down from the buckboard seat, Reeves secured the reins of his horse to the rear of the wagon and untied Bear's horse.

He held the reins as the Lighthorse deputy

re-tightened the saddle cinch. Then the two men shook hands.

"Thanks," Reeves said.

"Anytime, *Gimoozabie.*"

Reeves had been reaching into his vest pocket but stopped and looked at his Indian partner. "I thought I told you not to call me that?"

Bear grinned. "And I thought I told you. It means 'trusted friend.' From my people in the north, the Potowatomi."

Reeves removed a silver dollar from his vest pocket and rotated it in the sun's rays.

"And to think I was planning on giving you one of these."

Bear eyed the gleaming coin. "It ain't too late for that."

"Well, I only give these to people who helped me. Who deserve it."

Bear lifted an eyebrow. "You know, now that I think on it, I ain't so sure that I'm part Potowatomi after all."

Reeves laughed and flipped the coin. Bear's hand shot out and snared it in midair. As he held it in his palm he gazed down on it with fondness.

"That silver lady sure is pretty, ain't she?" He rotated it with his fingers. "And this must be an Indian eagle. Look, he's carrying arrows."

61

Reeves slapped Bear's shoulder, turned, and began climbing up to the wagon seat.

"Hey," Bear said. "This all I get?"

"For now," Reeves said. "I gotta make my report to Judge Parker 'fore we get paid in full. I'll bring your'n out to you."

"And how soon's that gonna be?"

Reeves settled himself in the seat and stroked his thick mustache. "Well, reckon it might be a while, seein' as how I'm gonna have to brush up on my Potowatomi."

Bear laughed and swung up onto the saddle. He steered his horse toward the opposite fork and began heading toward the reservation lodge that was reserved for the Lighthorse. "I'll be waiting, *Gimoozabie.* You know where I'll be."

Reeves swore and looked for something to throw at the Indian but then stopped and laughed. "That's bold talk for a man who's expecting to be paid down the road."

"I ain't worried." Bear's grin was wide as he turned in the saddle and waved. "That's why I call you trusted friend."

Reeves chuckled as he lightly slapped the reins and headed toward Arkansas. The sun showed the curved edge of a bright-orange globe rising through the tree line on the horizon. The trip was mostly over now. He'd be at his ranch shortly, and then at Fort

Smith. He'd been away from home the better part of a week and felt that familiar ache of absence. Did it really make the heart grow fonder, as the saying went? Reeves believed that it did. He longed for the warmth of Jennie's embrace. They had been married for a lot of years, but the fire was still there, eight kids later. Most of their children had grown up tall and straight, and, more importantly, they were all free. He and Jennie always stressed the importance of freedom to them, both of them having been born into slavery.

The clip-clop of the horses' hooves lulled Reeves into a deeper reverie. He worried about his second son, George W. The boy was essentially good but had a temper that sometimes overrode his better judgment. Impetuosity had done in many a good man, and Reeves hoped his son wouldn't succumb to any violent impulses down the road. Many times when Georgie was growing up, Reeves had taken him behind the woodshed for talking back to his mother. The boy was ten and getting close to being grown now and still had some learning to do. Reeves couldn't think of anything worse than having one of his boys caught up in some trouble down the road. He hoped that day would never come.

"Honor thy father and thy mother," Reeves had told Georgie. "It's one of the Ten Commandments."

The boy's defiant eyes seemed to hold trouble, and he never flinched even when Reeves laid on the switch. It hurt Reeves to do it, but he knew it was for the boy's own good. Still, it was hard. Reeves was glad when the boy's tears finally came. It signaled that it was time to stop.

Reeves was also glad that all of his children, especially the girls, had received enough schooling to be able to read the Bible. He'd never been afforded that chance. His mother had been literate, though, having been educated and taught by the first master Reeves on the plantation. It hadn't been something his mother had been able to teach him, though, but he possessed a sharp mind with excellent recall. When she read passages from the good book, which was nearly every night, they became instilled in his memory, and he could often recall them, as if he'd been able to read them himself. He used his good recall to his advantage as a deputy marshal, too, committing the names of the wanted men to memory before setting out on their trail.

Maybe someday Jennie can teach me, he

thought. Once all the bad men are caught, and I can devote all my time to ranching.

But deep down, Reeves knew that was only a dream. There were so many bad men out there, so little time.

Temptation City, the Indian Territories

Donovan tightened the cinch on his saddle after allowing the horse a chance to relax a bit. He knew from his own cavalry days that horses had the tendency to puff themselves up as soon as a saddle was thrown on their backs. An inexperienced rider, a greenhorn, would then have the whole saddle slide toward him as he started to mount, inevitably falling on his backside after sticking his foot in the stirrup. And Donovan was no greenhorn. Although he'd come over to this country fleeing the potato famine in 1856, he'd quickly adapted to the ways of the world in this new and wonderful country. The trip over had been sheer hell, and Donovan had actually killed his first man during that voyage.

The memory floated back to him.

A rough and tumble young Irish lad of fourteen, he'd been made painfully aware that his sainted mother — a poor widow with him and his two siblings, a younger brother and sister — had been taken advantage of by the unscrupulous captain of the vessel, and not only just a time or two. While his mother had forbade Donovan not to "do anything foolish," the boy had sworn a blood oath that this indignity, this stain on his mother's honor, would not go unpunished. As the ship docked in Boston, Donovan sneaked down to the captain's quarters and found the man imbibing from a bottle of gin. He was a big man with a coarse looking face covered with unshaved whiskers that were turning white.

"*Whatchya* want, boy?" the captain asked, bringing the bottle to his lips.

The slurring of the words gave Donovan a confidence that he could handle this big bugger. Carefully closing the door behind him, he stood there smiling his leprechaun smile. The room was small and had few amenities. A big desk made of a dark wood lay in the center, heavy so it wouldn't slide around in rough seas. Maybe it was nailed to the floor. Across the way was the captain's bed, a tangle of filthy sheets covering a reinforced cot, where, no doubt, Donovan's mother, and any other of the attractive Irish lassies, had been tasked with earning the additional cost of the long passage.

Donovan looked directly at the big pile of muscle and blubber. "I've come for the payment for our passage, sir," he said.

The captain's brow furrowed as he brought the bottle away from his mouth. His lips were still wet with the liquor. He snorted out two sonorous breaths through his large, crooked nose and fixed Donovan with a stare. "Payment? What the hell you talking about?" He squinted, lowering one side of his face as if to better assess the youth who stood before him. "Hey, ain't you one of pretty Mary's boys?"

Donovan kept the smile as disarming as possible. "You referring to my sainted mother, Mary Mildred Donovan?"

The captain blinked a few times. Obviously, her full name had eluded him. His chuckle turned into a belch, and then he shrugged. "Yeah, I guess so."

Donovan walked slowly around the big desk that separated them. The rocking motion of the ship was slowing slightly and had almost subsided. Above, the deck hands were no doubt securing the mooring lines so the passengers and cargo could be unloaded.

The captain started to lift the bottle again but hesitated and set it back down on the desk. His hand went to his lap, resting on his leg near the center drawer. "So whatchaya want? We're docking. We're here." His expression turned sour. "So git, ya little bastard."

"Bastard?" Donovan raised his eyebrows. "First, you've been treating my sainted mother like a ship's whore all these long weeks, and now you would be insulting my father as well? I assure you, they were wed very proper in a church in Dublin."

The captain's big belly rose and fell. He snorted a laugh and picked up the bottle again.

"So I'm here to collect the pay," Donovan said.

"Pay? What pay?"

Donovan took another step closer to the big man. The captain's hand lashed out and struck the boy across the face. Donovan tasted blood from his lips, but he remained on his feet. He'd learned how to slip a punch in many a schoolyard fight back in the old country.

The captain's arm cocked back to deliver another blow, but Donovan had already let the knife drop down his sleeve and into his right hand. He ducked, and the captain's second blow missed. The power of the swing pulled the man's big belly closer, and Donovan's hand shot upward. The blade sliced across the expansive gut, cutting deeply as it traversed from one side to another.

Reeling back, the big man's hands went to his gut, where already the yellow globs of fat had begun to slither out, covered with blood, followed by the purplish pink intestines that began to pop out of the wound as well. The captain collapsed back into his chair and started to pull open the center drawer, but Donovan jammed the blade into the big man's neck and twisted. A gush of blood poured down the front of his shirt.

The boy glanced around quickly, assuring they were still alone, then pulled open the desk drawers as the captain sat there moaning. The center desk drawer contained a long-barreled revolver. Sticking it into his belt, Donovan opened the other drawers and found what he was looking for: a big leather pouch that was packed full of money. All sorts of money, most of it Irish and English currency, which was probably useless here in this new place, but there were still a lot of gold and silver coins. He jammed the pouch between his pants and belly and pulled his shirt over the newly acquired items. Gripping the captain's head, Donovan looked into the man's eyes, which were starting to glaze over. He spat in the captain's face before shoving it down onto the desk top, then folded the big man's arms in front to make it look like he was sleeping off a drunk.

Donovan stepped back to admire his work. A puddle of blood was dripping to the floor, but it wouldn't be visible from in front of the desk.

Smiling, Donovan inspected his own shirt. A few bloody spots here and there, but the material was dark enough so that no one should take any notice. He looked again at his handiwork. The captain's dangling guts looked like a nest of writhing vipers sagging between his legs.

Good old St. Patrick was right, Donovan thought, bringing his attention back to Finn, Texas-Mex, and Boswell. *Looks like there are no more snakes in Ireland.*

"What you smiling about?" Finn asked, staring at Donovan.

Donovan looked at the big half-breed. The others, Texas-Mex and Boswell, were already mounted and ready to go. "Just reliving a pleasant memory." Donovan stuck his left foot in the stirrup and swung up into the saddle. Finn did likewise.

"Did I ever tell you the story of St. Patrick?" Donovan asked, the grin still on his face. "And why there are no snakes in Ireland?"

CHAPTER 3

Fort Smith, Arkansas

Bass Reeves secured the reins of his horse's bridle to the hitching post at the stable and nodded to the young boy pitching hay.

"Want me to rub him down, Marshal?" the boy asked. His ears protruded at right angles from the sides of his head, and a spray of freckles covered his nose and cheeks.

"I'd 'preciate that," Reeves said, reaching into his vest pocket and withdrawing a penny. He flipped it to the boy, who dropped the pitchfork and caught the coin with a smile.

"Make sure he don't drink no water till he cools down," Reeves said. He then patted the big stallion's flank and pulled off the saddlebags.

Reeves always marveled at how busy Fort Smith was. Originally a military fort built in 1817, a burgeoning settlement had sprung

71

up around the installation. The army left but then came back during the Indian Wars, now called the "Indian Relocation," when the army killed or ran off the Cherokee and Choctow tribes and forced then into the territories. Reeves hadn't even been born then, but he remembered his father telling him about it: "A whole lot of killing."

Fort Smith had been abandoned again and then taken over by the Confederates during the early days of the Civil War. When the Union army took it back, the place became a haven for war orphans, southern Unionists, and runaway slaves. It was the place Reeves had been trying to get to when he'd escaped the Indian Territories during the waning days of the war. The army had stayed on for a few more years and then left again, leaving a fairly good sized settlement in its wake. The town kept the name and became a bastion of civilization on a rugged frontier that was known for lawlessness and brutality. That was when Judge Isaac Parker came to Fort Smith.

As Reeves strode across the long, grassy area that led to the courthouse, he glanced to the southwest and saw the sixteen-foot, whitewashed fence that surrounded the gallows. He'd seen the gallows up close and personal early that week, when he escorted two men who'd been sentenced to death. Reeves had been appointed a deputy marshal by the judge, at the behest of Marshal John Fenton, who knew of Reeves's reputation and ability to track, speak several Indian languages, and, if he had to, shoot. Parker had taken one look at Reeves and sworn him in, admonishing him of the responsibility he now carried. The judge treated him as a man, not a freed slave, and, for that, Reeves pledged his total and unqualified loyalty to the judge and to the law.

"All a black man's got is his word and his honor," Reeves told one of his fellow Negroes who questioned why Reeves was going to risk his life for some old white man sitting up on a bench. "The law's for everybody. And it's all we got keeping us here."

The other man shook his head and seemed not to understand, but that didn't matter to Reeves. He understood just fine.

The gate leading into the gallows opened, and Reeves caught a glimpse of the powerful construction: set against a stone wall that had once housed a black powder magazine, the platform of the massive stage had a sixteen-foot floor with eight trapdoors that could accommodate the hanging nooses. The most Reeves had ever heard of being used at one time was six. Six condemned men had walked up those twelve fateful steps and had the hoods placed over their heads, the ropes tightened around their necks. Reeves still recalled the day he'd witnessed his first hanging, the smell of fear tangible in the air, the hush that drew over the crowd of witnesses, the ominous thump as the lever was pulled, dropping the trapdoor, and the jerking snap of the ropes as they pulled tight.

It was justice, all right, delivered with a finality that spread the word. Judge Isaac Parker, the hanging judge, was a man not to be trifled with.

Reeves slung the saddlebags over his shoulder and pulled open the door to the courthouse. It was early, but he knew the judge would be there, and it would be best to file the report before the day's trials got started.

The finely polished wooden floor of the hallway always impressed Reeves. The walls had been painted a pale-yellow color, and numerous paintings of important men pointed the way to the courtroom. The judge's quarters were off to the side, and Reeves paused at the door and knocked.

George Dobbs, the large deputy marshal who was the judge's personal bodyguard, opened the door and regarded Reeves. His face cracked slightly, and a smile was barely visible under the bushy mustache.

"You get 'em, Bass?" he asked.

"Yep," Reeves said. "The judge in? Like to make my report and get back to my ranch."

George motioned Reeves into the office. This section was for visitors, lawyers, witnesses, and marshals. Judge Parker's private office, his chambers, was beyond a second door, which always remained closed. Reeves removed the saddlebags and sat in one of the chairs. George knocked gently on the chambers door and opened it a crack.

"Deputy Marshal Reeves is here, sir," he said.

A harsh sounding voice sounded from the other room: "Bass?"

Seconds later the door opened fully, and George stepped out of the way. Judge Parker's form filled the doorway. He wasn't a big man, but he commanded a certain presence, even though he was dressed in a white shirt, starched collar, and overalls. Reeves could see the black robe hanging on a coat rack inside the office.

Judge Parker's dark goatee split open, showing a row of more or less evenly spaced whitish teeth. His lower lip bulged from a plug of tobacco, and he turned his head to deliver a brown stream into a spittoon on the floor next to the doorjamb.

Reeves stood and removed his hat.

The judge winked. "Good to see you're still all in one piece. Any problems?"

"Only a few, sir," Reeves said. "Had to kill both of them Quint boys."

Parker's lips bunched together, and he reached into his mouth and took out the plug, dropping it into the spittoon. "Let's resume in the courtroom. George, go fetch Mary to record things."

Reeves went into the courtroom where he'd testified many times since being sworn in. The high mahogany bench that was set on a platform so the judge looked down on the proceedings from above. Since the judge had the power of life and death, the high bench exuded power and authority.

Wearing his long, black robe, Judge Parker strode into the room. Instead of going behind the bench, he walked over to Reeves and held out his hand.

"How you doing, Bass?"

Reeves stood, removed his glove, and shook the judge's hand.

"I'm fine, sir. Thank you."

"You had a rough time?"

Reeves shrugged. "I gave them the chance to surrender. They didn't take it."

Parker nodded, his face grim. He turned and went to the steps that led to the bench. Presently, George came back and ushered in a thin, middle-aged woman whose iron-gray hair was pulled back from her face and wound into a bun. Reeves knew she had the ability to write in some kind of special way so she could put down all the words anybody spoke. He never ceased to be impressed by her quick hands and nimble fingers.

"Swear in Deputy Marshal Reeves," Judge Parker said.

After this was done, Parker asked Reeves to give his account of what had occurred on the apprehension and arrest of the Quint brothers. Reeves kept it short, offering the factual account of the incident and how the two brothers had apparently murdered the homesteaders. The judge's expression tightened as he listened, especially the part about the woman. Reeves then told how he and Bear had buried both of the brothers as well as their victims. The pencil in Mary's hand danced over the paper, leaving those strange marks that Reeves thought looked like tracks left by a herd of nervous deer over a field of snow. She stopped writing, looked up at him, and smiled.

He placed the watch and gun that Jona-

77

than Quint had given him on the bench in front of Judge Parker.

"Let the court record show that Deputy Marshal Reeves has presented the court with a gold watch and a long-barreled .45 Remington 1875 pistol." The judge picked up the watch and studied it, then looked at the gun. "Is there any other property that was recovered?"

Reeves told him about the horses.

"You wish to keep the animals?" Parker asked.

"If it's all right with you, your honor, I'd like to give two of them to the Lighthorse. Once the plow horse is fattened up and given some care, he'll make a mighty fine addition to the wagon pulling team."

"So ruled," Parker said. He handed the Remington down to Reeves. "You keep the pistol, as well. Place the watch in the property room for public auction. George, draw up the appropriate pay voucher for Deputy Marshal Reeves."

Reeves felt a slight twinge since Jonathan Quint had expressed the desire that the watch be buried with him, but the man was a cold-blooded killer and didn't deserve any consideration in that respect.

And so it goes, Reeves thought, looking at the Remington, the same gun that almost killed him. *And so it goes.*

He heard the judge call to him.

Reeves turned. The judge looked somber as he stood there, both hands gripping the folds of his robe just below the collar.

"I'd like to see you in my chambers," the judge said. "I have a matter I need to speak to you about."

The Indian Territories

Donovan watched with appreciation and a tinge of envy as big Finn dragged the log across the trail with the ease of a man gathering kindling wood. The Indian was strong, that was for certain. But while Donovan admired the half-breed's strength, he wasn't the least bit leery about him. Finn, or Standing Buffalo as he was called before Donovan had taken a liking to him and rechristened him Finnegan, possessed the power of a buffalo all right, but the intelligence of one, too. The breed was dumb. The mind of a child inside the hulking body of a man in search of direction, in search of a leader . . . And that's what Donovan was. The half-breed had the muscle, but Donovan had the brains.

Texas-Mex, Donovan's second acquisition, was less physically powerful, but he more than made up for that with his speedy

79

hands and downright meanness. Quick with a gun and with a knife, Jose Alberto Eduardo Gonzales Martinez was not a man to turn one's back upon. Not that Donovan feared him. The Mexican was smarter than the big half-breed, but he still searched for direction. He, too, was nothing more than a follower, and Donovan was more than happy to provide the leadership for these two wayward souls with whom he'd gotten acquainted on the cattle drive to Texas. Donovan told the Mexican his new name was Texas-Mex.

"Hey, I like *dat,*" the swarthy rogue had said. "*Un nuevo nombre está muy bueno suerte,* eh?"

Suerte, Donovan knew, meant "luck," and he had plenty of that. The luck of the Irish. Of course, that kind of luck was proverbially bad, but Donovan felt like he was riding the crest of a wave, and he intended to keep on riding it for as long as it lasted.

"That good?" Finn asked, breathing hard as he dropped the end of the log into the dirt.

The thud told Donovan how frightfully heavy the wood was, so he decided to toss in a bit of praise to the big man. "Perfect. And a testament to the strongest man I've ever laid my eyes on."

The big breed's mouth twisted into a half smile, showing his row of crooked teeth and misaligned occlusion. His lower jaw protruded at an odd angle, reminding Donovan of the picture of an ape he'd once seen. He motioned for Finn and Texas-Mex to position themselves. They moved off to opposite sides of the road and took cover behind some trees. Donovan turned to Boswell, who was studying the road with a long telescope.

"You see anything yet?" Donovan asked.

Boswell's upper lip curled, and he grunted. "Think that's them coming now." He squinted through the telescope some more, then said, "Yeah. It's them."

Donovan smacked the soldier on the shoulder and held his hand out for the telescope. He brought it to his eye and looked through it but saw nothing but a blur. Obviously, Boswell had a vision problem. A soldier who couldn't see well was a formula for disaster. Or for desertion. Now he understood why this hill rat boy in blue had been so malleable. He was another miscreant looking for direction. The army hadn't provided that, but Donovan had.

He twisted the end piece until the image clarified. One covered wagon, two riders on either side. Far too light a contingent to safeguard such an important piece of vital military equipment.

But that was neither here, nor there. Pretty soon it would be *his* equipment, not the bloody army's.

Arkansas, between Fort Smith and Van Buren

Reeves contemplated the judge's request on the ride back to his ranch in Van Buren. It would be a bit of a challenge and wouldn't be as lucrative as the chance to pick up a couple more bounties, but the judge had promised to compensate him well for his investigative efforts. Reeves made sure to ask if this compensation would be extended to Bear as well, and the judge nodded.

"While I have no authority to order them, I was hopeful that one of the Lighthorse would accompany you. It's the kind of assignment that needs special expertise."

"I'll go, but give me a couple of days first," Reeves told the judge. "Got to take care of a few things at the ranch."

Judge Parker slapped Reeves on the shoulder. "Thanks. I knew I could count on you. And if what I've heard tell is true, a lot of lives, both Indian and white, could depend on you."

Reeves thought about that, too, as he rode.

What about Negro lives?

Still, he'd heard tell of the bitterness, the brutality of the Indian "relocation" back in '56 — the Cherokee and Choctaw forcibly removed from their ancestral lands and forced into the Indian Territories. It was supposed to permanently end the hostilities, and the treaty was promised to last as long as the sun shone, the wind blew, and the sky was blue.

Reeves shook his head. Today, there was no breeze in this hot Arkansas, and the sun was behind a row of clouds. Storm clouds, from the look of them.

Looks like the sky might be getting ready to turn black, he thought.

Before he'd left Fort Smith, he'd gone to the bank to cash in the voucher and get a new roll of silver dollars. If what Judge Parker said was right about the reports regarding illegal whiskey and gun peddling to the Indians in Texas, it could easily spill into Arkansas as well. And, as Bear had said about the homesteaders, there were a lot of squatters, white and black, nestling into the territories. Towns had sprung up, too, due to opportunities brought about from the mining expansions, not to mention the railroad going through Indian land. While some of these towns and homesteaders asked permission and officially leased the land from the Indians, many of them did not, and lawless settlements had cropped up. It was another case of the white man doing what he pleased. Well, some Negroes had been edging west, too, but they were fewer, and, after what they'd been through, who could blame them?

We was all promised them forty acres and a mule, Reeves thought.

His smile was rueful as he continued to ride.

The Indian Territories

The military wagon and the two escorting riders came into view. Donovan leaned closer to the big tree trunk that was concealing him and used the telescope to examine each of the three men. The two on horseback were Negroes. Buffalo soldiers, they'd taken to calling them because their hair was curly, like a buffalo's. Donovan had seen and even fought with a few Negroes during the war, when he was with the 69th New York Infantry, also known as the Irish Brigade. It had been toward the end of the campaigns, when a company of blacks had joined him and his fellow transplanted Irishmen during the Battle of Appomattox. Skeptical at first, Donovan had been subsequently impressed with their fighting spirit, if not their discipline. He figured a good portion of them had been conscripted, just as he was, from the ranks of northern cities where so many of them had fled. The others were most likely runaway slaves who were looking to get a few good licks in against the Confederates just as the Young Irelanders had done when fighting against the despicable English. In any case, Donovan figured that the two on horseback were not to be taken lightly.

He switched his attention to the burly man seated on the wagon directing the horses. He was white and had a chest like a barrel and arms to match. The sleeves of his blue uniform were pulled tight over bulging muscles as he drew back on the reins to halt the advancing team of horses. The three chevrons were each ringed on top by three rockers. A master sergeant, in for the duration, and probably a fellow Irishman to boot, judging from the look of his pug nose and red mustache. Donovan heaved a sigh. A damn shame he'd be killing one of his own this early in the day.

Collapsing the telescope and slipping it into his back pocket, Donovan thought how he'd taken a shine to it. Although it technically was army property and issued to

Private Boswell, the greasy lad was in Donovan's army now, and thus the telescope had now been re-commissioned.

Donovan waited until all three of the soldiers had stopped before he stepped out of the shrubbery and walked over to the log that blocked the road. He'd picked the spot carefully so that it was virtually impassable.

It was time for a bit of dancing with the Devil once again.

"Good afternoon to you," Donovan said in a loud voice. "Looks like you could be needing a bit of a hand."

The big sergeant's head swiveled toward him. The two buffalo soldiers stayed on their mounts, each resting a hand on top of those cumbersome, military-style holsters.

"And what would ye be knowing about this situation?" the big sergeant asked.

Pure Irish brogue. Not a doubt. Donovan smiled. "Now it sounds like you've a bit of the Gaelic in you," he said. "Where were your people from?"

The sergeant's eyes narrowed, and his right hand crept down toward the stock of a rifle that was next to him. It looked to be an old muzzle-loader, an 1861 Springfield. Donovan felt a bit more confidence spread over him. "Don't be laying any blarney on me, mister," the sergeant said. "We're on

86

official army business."

Donovan raised his hands. "Now what kind of reception is this that you're showing to a man who's offering to help you clear the road?"

The two buffalo soldiers didn't take their eyes off of him. Donovan kept his arms raised, waiting to give the signal. He'd already undone the twine strap from the hammer of his gun.

"That's mighty benevolent of you," the sergeant said, picking up the rifle and cocking back the hammer. It was a Springfield 1861, all right, but this one had been converted to a trapdoor: the end of the barrel had been cut away and replaced with a locking breechblock. Fifty caliber, good at a distance, but still a breechloader.

One shot, and he'd have to eject the cartridge and reload.

Then Donovan saw the brass ammo clip hanging down. The army had been updating those outdated single-shot Springfields by equipping them with cartridge clips, making the entire reloading process a lot quicker.

But it wouldn't be quick enough.

"Oh, hell. I'll move the damn piece of wood myself," Donovan called out, letting his arms fall to his sides — the signal to the others.

The first shots rang out, one from each side. One of the buffalo soldiers twisted and fell off his horse. The other was lifting the flap of his holster as a round whipped by him. He had his gun partially out when another volley sounded, dropping him as well.

Donovan brought his gun up, aimed, and shot the big sergeant right in the center of his massive chest. The man's mouth sagged, and his eyes flicked downward at the burgeoning stain spreading past the gold colored row of buttons. He attempted to bring the rifle to his shoulder, but Donovan had already cocked back the hammer and squeezed off another round. This one caught the sergeant in the center of his forehead, and his head snapped back and wobbled a bit more as his big body slumped forward, cascading over the front of the wagon and down onto the hitching.

The horses whinnied in terror as their hooves beat against the log, but they had no place to go.

As Finn, Texas-Mex, and Boswell emerged from the tree line on either side, Donovan walked forward and checked the fallen men in blue, putting a bullet in each of their heads.

It was obvious from the positioning that Texas-Mex had taken only one shot to down the one on his side. Donovan lifted an eyebrow as he looked toward Finn and Boswell.

"Which of you took that first shot?" Donovan asked.

Finn smirked and cocked his chin toward the unkempt solider.

Donovan stared at him. "Ah, Danny boy, it seems the army could have done a bit of a better job teaching you the rudiments of marksmanship."

Boswell's mouth puckered, and he shot a mean look at the big half-breed.

"It was his fault. He got in my way, and he's so damn big I couldn't see 'round him."

A poor shot, and an abdicator as well. Donovan didn't reply but filed this for future reference. It didn't bode well for Danny boy, as the last thing Donovan wanted was to be keeping an irresponsible prevaricator around any longer than necessary. He motioned for Finn to remove the log from the road and told Texas-Mex and Boswell to pull the bodies into the field and bury them.

"Why can't we just leave them there?" Boswell asked.

Donovan wasn't opposed to that idea.

During the war it was routine to leave the bodies where they'd fallen and let someone else do the burying. But neither did he want to chance the army finding them if they happened to send out a patrol. Not before the rest of it unfolded.

"I'm sure there's a shovel or two in that wagon, among other things." Donovan ripped back the white curtaining and saw several heavy, wooden boxes.

It was there, just as Boswell had described.

The shifty soldier came up on Donovan's side. "See? Didn't I tell ya?" His lips curled back, showing his rotten teeth. "And this ain't even the half of what I know."

Donovan held up a hand to silence him. Something stirred in the distance. The sound of rapidly approaching horses.

The Reeves Ranch, Van Buren, Arkansas
They were alone in the cabin, the flames crackling in the stone fireplace that Reeves had fashioned when they'd first moved here from Texas. A pot hung suspended from a splint above the fire.

"You sure you got to be going again so soon?" Jennie Reeves said, an expression of sorrow tincturing her pretty face. Reeves never got tired of seeing that face. He dreamed of it every night when he was on

90

the trail.

"Hate to be leaving again," he said. "But Judge Parker got a wire from the lawmen down in Texas. Seems they got some white men along the border down Texas way been stirring up trouble with the Indians."

Jennie's face showed her concern. "And how does that concern you?"

"It don't." Reeves smiled and, as gently as he could, stroked the side of her face. "Least not yet. But if Indian trouble spreads, we could be in for some hard times."

"There ain't been no Indian trouble 'round here for a long time," she said.

Her dark, beautiful face was showing a fierce determination, but Reeves had already given his word to the judge. "Not unless you count the fighting back in the war," he said. "Remember how the Cherokees sided with the South. Even had some of us Negroes as slaves."

She pursed her lips. "And that's even more reason for you not to go. You don't owe them Indians nothing."

"I gave the judge my word I'd look into it."

She closed her eyes, and he could see she was fighting back tears.

"You are always out doing that white judge's bidding." Her voice broke with the

91

last words.

Reeves remained silent for a few seconds, then said, "He a good man. The best I know."

The tears emerged from her still-closed eyes. Reeves stood and moved to her, looping his powerful arms around her slight form. He drew her back to his chest, his arms around her waist with a gentle firmness.

"I know you're right," she said. "But I just hate for you to be leaving out again so soon."

Reeves said nothing, still pressing her to him. They stayed in this embrace for a long time, and finally he said, "I do, too."

The Indian Territories

Two riders came into view. Donovan recognized them: Cooper, the Indian agent, and Crowe, the drunk from the saloon who'd been with them on the drive south. As they drew closer, Donovan saw they both appeared agitated. Very agitated.

Donovan signaled the others to relax and mounted his horse. While he wasn't intent on riding anywhere as of yet, he didn't want to be at a tactical disadvantage until he knew what this was all about. Nor did he relish the thought of looking upward toward either of those two buggers. He took out his bag of tobacco and began rolling a cigarette. He'd just finished sticking it into his mouth and flicking the primer on a wooden match stick when Cooper and Crowe came to an abrupt stop across from him.

Cooper surveyed the wagon and the bodies of the dead soldiers. His mouth gaped, and Donovan could see the man was breathing hard.

"We got trouble," the Indian agent said.

"Is that a fact?" Donovan drew some of the smoke into his lungs. "Do you care to elaborate?"

"I just got a wire from an associate down in Dallas. The Texas Rangers arrested Vince Webber down there."

"Webber," Donovan said. "The fellow who bought the cattle?"

Cooper's head bobbed up and down, his gaze shifting from side to side. "Confiscated his whole herd. I don't know if he'd had a chance to re-brand them yet. He'll spill his guts."

"About your little dealings? I doubt that'll bring them all the way up here."

"It will if they're chasing the Cherokeos."

"The Cherokeos?"

Cooper's mouth worked. "We made up the name. It was a rumor we had Crowe

93

here start back when we first started doing our trading down there to cover our tracks. About some white men giving whiskey and guns to the Comanche."

"Your trading?"

Cooper jerked his thumb toward his associate. "Crowe here was pretending to be friends with 'em. Take down a wagon and some old guns — unconverted muskets mostly — and whiskey and give it to 'em."

Donovan looked at the second man, Crowe. He appeared to be inebriated. His hat had been swept back from his scarred head, and the purplish scars where his hair had been skinned off gleamed in the sun.

"Trading implies something is given in exchange," Donovan said. "What is it you're forgetting to tell me?"

Cooper looked down as he licked his lips. He spat off to the side. "They would give us stuff, trinkets mostly, but sometimes gold coins they got from the raids." He spat again. "But mostly it was just to keep them damn rangers off us."

"Giving the noble savages some whiskey and guns so they could stir up trouble to keep the authorities busy whilst you did your illicit cattle dealings? You call that trading?"

"I call it smart," Cooper said. "As long as

those red bastards were doing raids down in Texas, nobody was looking for any missing government beef along the Texas trail."

"The Cherokeos." Donovan laughed. "Very creative. A fat, corrupt Indian agent, a misanthropic, porcine sheriff, now deceased, a drunkard, and a cowardly Texas cattleman. 'Tis the stuff of legends."

Cooper's scowl deepened. "Don't forget you're part of it. Them rangers are a tough bunch."

Donovan knew they were indeed. He'd tangled with a few of them and stood by while some others effected arrests, usually dispensing justice with a six-gun. He was also aware that Finn, Texas-Mex, and Boswell had emerged from their hiding places and had most likely overheard the conversation. They would be looking to see how he would deal with this unforeseen development. If he were to ensure their loyalty, and secure his position of leadership, he had to be certain that this matter was handled expeditiously. He contemplated the situation as the others approached, then looked at Crowe. The smell of the booze was exuding from his every pore. Perhaps the hot sun would sweat it out of him before he met up with the rangers.

"You look a bit pale," Donovan said. "I do hope you're up for a bit of riding."

CHAPTER 4

Lighthorse Headquarters
The Indian Territories

The next morning Reeves halted the team of horses towing the wagon and secured the reins around the brake handle before getting down and going inside the Lighthorse headquarters barracks. The large building had been fashioned out of logs and had room for at least twenty beds. A big wooden table was just inside the door, and two Indian deputies, stirring a large pot, sat near a smoldering fire. As Reeves entered, one pointed to the pot, but Reeves shook his head. He went further into the barracks and saw Bear snoring soundly on top of his bunk.

Reeves watched the rise and fall of Bear's chest, the sonorous vibration emitting from his gaping mouth, and went to stand over him. The Indian deputy's gun belt, replete with his weapon, had been draped over the bed post. Reeves put one hand on the butt of Bear's revolver, as the memories of their previous mission danced in Reeves's memory. "*Gimoozabie* means 'trusted friend.' " Bear was the best of them, this Reeves knew for a fact, but he was also one of the most irritating.

Reeves pulled a leather strand from the pocket of his shirt. Bending over, he dangled the end of the strand so that it touched the tip of the sleeping man's nose.

Bear's nostrils twitched.

Reeves rotated the thong. More twitching, then an abrupt end to the snoring as Bear snapped awake. His dark eyes centered on the lawman with a momentary fierceness that made Reeves chuckle, even as he moved back.

Bear jerked to a sitting position and grunted, staring at Reeves for a solid ten seconds. Then he snorted. "You got great timing," he said. "I was just dreaming I was chasing some beautiful Indian gal through a stream, and she didn't have any clothes on her."

"Like that painting you always talkin' about?" Reeves slowly straightened up and took his hand off Bear's gun. "The one you saw in that book?"

"That's the one. And I almost had her

98

caught this time, too. Then you come along with your damn string."

"Think of it as a lariat of righteousness." Reeves stuck the leather strand back into his pocket. "Keepin' you out of trouble."

Bear snorted again. "That'll be the day, *you* keeping *me* out of trouble." He ran his fingers through his black hair. "So, did you come by with the rest of my pay?"

"Something better."

Bear looked askance. "Why don't I like the sound of that?"

"Maybe you got a vision in the smoke lodge?"

Bear laughed. "Not hardly."

"We got to go back into the territories. Maybe into Texas, too."

Bear kept rubbing the back of his neck. "Texas? Who we looking for there?"

Reeves took a breath and sat down on the neighboring bunk. "Cherokeos."

"Who?"

"Bunch of white men supposed to be selling whiskey and guns to the Indians. Supposed to be stirring up trouble down Texas way."

"Texas? That's a long way from the territories. And that's Comanche lands down there." He shrugged. "Well, some Apache, too."

"You ever heard of these Cherokeos?"

Bear shook his head. "Don't doubt there're a lot of white men out there up to no good, but I ain't never heard 'em called by that name. Where'd you hear it?"

"Judge Parker. He got him a wire from the Texas Rangers. Said they was tracking some fellas. Judge wants us to go out and nose around."

"Us?"

"Yeah, you and me. Once we get out there, shouldn't take us long to track 'em down."

Bear grinned. "What you mean 'we'?"

Reeves took out the envelope he'd prepared with Bear's pay for the Quint brothers. He handed it to him. "Plus, I got the judge to give you two of them horses we got from the Quints."

"Yeah?" Bear opened the envelope, counted the money, and stuffed it into his pants pocket. "One of them that old plow horse?"

Reeves chuckled and stood as Bear got up and pulled his suspenders up over his shoulders. He still wore the blue pants with the yellow stripe that he'd gotten as a cavalry scout.

"You might want to take along another pair of britches," Reeves said.

Bear raised his eyebrows and sniffed the air. "Why? These starting to stink?"

"Not any more than usual, but I figured we might be using some of our disguises again."

"Trouble is, I only got one more pair, and they're just like these, yellow stripe and all."

"You can wear a pair of my britches, then. If and when the time comes."

"When we gonna leave?"

"Soon as we finish helping them polish off that mighty fine smelling rabbit stew in the other room."

Bear grabbed his buckskin jacket and gun belt. "That sounds good to me, *Gimoozabie.*"

Reeves gave him a hard look and then motioned toward the beckoning stew pot.

"You keep callin' me that," he said, "and you gonna end up like that rabbit."

Duffy's Emporium
Fort Smith, Arkansas

Stutley felt in his pocket for another coin. He hated to be spending so much on these drinks, but luckily the liquor was pretty cheap in these parts. Fort Smith, Arkansas . . . Somehow, he'd expected more, after hearing so much about this civilized bastion of culture on the edge of civilization from

101

his fellow travelers on the train.

"Fort Smith's about the last place where you're going to find real law abiding citizens," one grizzled old cowboy had told him. "It's where Judge Parker resides. He's bringing a better way of life to the West."

Stutley had offered to buy the man a drink as they'd exited the train at the Fort Smith station. The train continued to go south, toward New Orleans, but Stutley didn't want to go there. Although he'd heard a lot about the site of the famous 1815 battle, he figured it to be more a vestige of the Old South than the New West. His editor had been specific with the assignment: "Cowboys, Indians, gunfighters, outlaws, lawmen. That's what the readers are clamoring for. Go find them. Go west, young man. Go west."

The old codger accepted Stutley's offer and added with a gap-toothed grin, "I know just the place."

Duffy's Emporium was the best of the best, the geezer said. Card games, fine food, great booze, and even some "real purdy ladies to spend time with ya." The old man had punctuated his sentence with a knowing, but phlegm-filled, laugh. As if they'd shared a private joke, just between the two of them.

Stutley was intrigued enough to accompany him to Duffy's. If nothing else, it would provide some setting for the story that was perambulating about inside his head. Pretty ladies . . . Real pretty ladies . . . After more than eleven days of travel, Stutley could do with some feminine companionship, although his Uncle Lewis had cautioned him about that.

"There'll no doubt be a lot of prostitutes willing, ready, and able to take your money, but even if they're fetching, they're also a hard lot. Catching venereal disease isn't the only thing you have to worry about if you succumb to their advances. Keep one hand on your wallet the whole time."

It was mid-afternoon as Stutley and his discrepant guide walked along the side of the broken-stone roadway where horses towed wagons. Fort Smith was more built up than Stutley had imagined, with four distinct corners that appeared to have been designed as ramparts. But the place had been a military fort at one time, after all. Since the army had abandoned it, numerous shops and businesses had filled in, making it into what might be considered a substantial city.

It was certainly no New York, though.

A raised, wooden sidewalk appeared before them, and the old geezer sprang onto it with an eager agility, half turning to motion Stutley to follow. Having to keep up while carrying his carpet bag and the leather suitcase made the trundling voyage more cumbersome. Stutley noticed his eyeglasses were fogging up from exertion. Still, this was what he'd come out here for — what he needed to see, to experience. The adventure was just beginning.

"Welcome to Duffy's Gentleman's Emporium," a squat-looking man in a brown suit proclaimed from his station next to the pair of swinging doors. "Specializing in sophisticated drinks and entertainment for the true, distinguished gentleman."

Stutley was mildly impressed by the man's diction, and then he saw the hand-painted sign that hung over the bar:

Duffys Gentleman Imporeeum
Spesilizing in soffisticated drinks and
enternerment
for the troo destingwished gentlemon.

Obviously, the literacy level in these parts was sorely lacking. And so were attractive women.

Two rather portly ladies, neither of whom Stutley found the least bit attractive, leaned against a long bar. They were trying to muster engaging smiles but not succeeding very well, until the geezer whistled and waved. The women waved back.

Disgusting, thought Stutley. *Where was that beautiful Indian maiden running through the stream?*

The toothless geezer sidled up to the bar, grabbed the portly bartender by the sleeve, and said, "Willard, gimme a bottle and a couple of glasses, will ya?"

Willard, a thin man with a lizard-like look to him, frowned. "What you gonna pay for it with, Norman?"

The geezer pulled at the barkeep's sleeve and pointed with his other hand. "He's buying."

Willard's eyes locked onto Stutley. "That so?"

"Yes." Stutley walked up beside the geezer. "Perhaps we'd better start with two whiskeys and go from there." He had no intention of wasting his money or his time if this interview was not going to be fruitful.

Willard raised both his eyebrows and crossed his arms.

It took Stutley a few seconds to realize the man was waiting for payment. Stutley took some coins out of his pocket. There was no way he would dare to take anything out of

105

his money belt in a place like this.

The bartender pocketed the coins, set two small glasses on the bar, and poured what looked to be a thimble full in each glass.

"Aw, come on, Willard," Norman said. "We deserve more than that."

"You deserve a kick in the ass, you son of a bitch. What he paid didn't even come close to what you already owe me."

"Who you callin' a son of a bitch?" Norman balled up his fists.

Willard reached under the counter and came up holding a foot-long, wooden cudgel.

Stutley grabbed the two glasses and headed for one of the tables at the far end of the room. Norman followed, reciting a litany of curse words attacking Willard's parentage.

Stutley set both glasses down and took out his notebook and pencil. He then sat on the opposite side of the table. Norman eyed both drinks with a suspicious squint.

"You can have both of them," Stutley said. "Just give me a few minutes of your time."

Norman sat and reached for the first glass, but Stutley placed his notebook over both of them. "First," he said, "a little conversation, if you please. Your name is Norman, I presume."

"Sure enough. Norman T. Pierce. What you want to know that fer?"

Stutley scribbled down the name in his notebook. "I'm keeping a journal of sorts. I'm writing a book, you see."

Norman blinked twice, then wiped his nose with his fingers. "I can't read none." Licking his lips, he reached for the closest glass.

Stutley held his hand over it. "There'll be plenty more where that came from if you give me some good information." He paused to gauge the other man's reaction.

"Information about what?"

"About the West. Cowboys, Indians, outlaws, gunslingers, lawmen."

"How 'bout lettin' me have a little sip to think on?"

Stutley pushed one of the shot glasses toward him. Norman grabbed it and downed it in one gulp, then sighed. "Ah," he said. "Mighty fine stuff." He leaned back in his chair and began rubbing his grizzled jaw with his fingers. "So you're interested in what now?"

Stutley repeated his areas of interest. Norman launched into one story after another, centering on how "peaceable and civilized" Fort Smith was. "But that's all due to Judge Parker."

"Judge Parker," Stutley repeated as he wrote down the name.

"Yep. They call him the hangin' judge. That's 'cause he hung eleven men in one day."

"Eleven men," Stutley repeated, amazed.

"All at once, too." Norman picked up the second shot glass and drained it, wiped the inside with his index finger, then stuck his finger in his mouth.

"This occurred here at Fort Smith?"

Norman nodded, picked up the other glass, and ran his tongue around the inside. His words were distorted as he spoke, and Stutley asked him to repeat himself.

"I said, the gallows are at the other end of town." Norman set the glass down and glanced at the bar. "Over on the east end. I can show you, but it'll cost you another drink."

Stutley didn't want to take the chance of delving into the hidden money belt at this time, so he displayed empty palms. "I'm all out of money, Norman."

The old geezer frowned and got up, ambling toward the bar. "Hey, Willard, how about another drink on the house?"

Ignoring Norman, the bartender looked over at Stutley. "You want anything else, mister?"

Stutley shook his head and put his notebook back in his coat pocket.

What I need, he thought, *is to meet this Judge Parker.*

Temptation City
The Indian Territories

Donovan took a sip of the rot gut whiskey and expectorated into the spittoon at his feet. It tasted like Henry'd gone a little too heavy with the wood alcohol spiking. The bar was crowded with the remnants of the town, who'd gathered at Donovan's behest this sunny afternoon.

After dispatching Crowe and Cooper the previous night to intercept the rangers on the trail, and telling Boswell to report back to the fort to keep a watchful eye, Donovan drove the wagon with its special cargo back to the relative safety of the stable. Once there, he, Big Finn, and Texas-Mex unloaded the cargo from the wagon and secured it in the only room in the place that had a padlock.

Then they went back to the bar, and Donovan selected one of the girls, the Indian one, for his bed that night. Despite the facial scar, she'd turned out to be attractive enough. Although she smelled a bit musty, her body was slim and taut, like a rawhide rope, and he'd enjoyed their encounter. Her face was a bit of a far cry from the painting of the nude Indian female bathing in the stream, but it had been a while since he'd had a woman, and he made do.

After an hour or so, he grabbed her clothes, escorted her to the door of his new room, pushed her out, then locked the door behind her. He didn't know or trust enough people in this town and decided that caution and moderation in all things was the prudent approach. At least until he could fully establish himself with certainty.

Now, the afternoon sunlight was streaming through the windows, and his audience of perhaps fifteen men was assembled. Big Finn and Texas-Mex had joined him for reinforcement, but Donovan knew it was crucial that he handle this alone. He gripped the shot glass, which was still full of the rot gut, and motioned to Henry, the fat, bald man behind the bar. Henry's big mustache twitched as he sauntered over, and Donovan waved him closer.

When their faces were about six inches apart, Donovan tossed the rot gut into the other man's face. The bartender sputtered and tried to jerk back, but Donovan grabbed the front ruffles of the man's white shirt.

"I'll tell you this once, and once only, laddie," Donovan said in a low, guttural tone. "I'm the new owner here, and if you ever give me this rotten shit again, I'll slice open your throat and pour it up your arse. Understand?"

Henry blinked, nodded, the wetness of his perspiration now mixing with the stale booze.

Donovan pulled the man's face closer to his own. "Now get the good stuff from wherever you hide it, and pour me a new drink. And ones for my friends here." He cocked his head toward Finn and the Mexican.

When he released Henry's shirt, the bartender stepped back, worked his mouth, then grabbed a towel from behind the bar and wiped off his face. He walked to the opposite end of the bar, reached underneath it.

Donovan's right hand dropped down and undid the leather thong that secured his revolver. He knew the bartender kept a shotgun underneath the bar — Texas-Mex had told him — but Donovan felt confident that he could draw and drop Henry if his hands came out with anything other than a bottle. Besides, he was good at reading people and didn't figure the barkeep possessed the internal fortitude, the guts, to try anything. And Donovan prided himself on being an expert on guts.

Henry straightened up, holding a fancy glass bottle full of a fine-looking, amber-colored liquid.

Donovan smiled. He'd been right. No guts.

Texas-Mex, who'd also been watching, emitted a gurgling laugh. "See? I tol' you. *Pequeno cajones.*"

Donovan waited for Henry to pour the three drinks, then he turned around and held his glass high. "May I have your undivided attention for a moment?" he said, using his finest speaking voice.

The group of prostitutes had gathered in the hallway leading back to the hog ranch. He saw the Indian girl staring at him with her dark, impassive eyes. Word was that she was Cooper's favorite. Next time Donovan decided he'd sample the blonde, Polly. She didn't look half bad.

The rest of the crowd had grown silent, all eyes focusing on him.

He could tell they were curious, fearful, and eager for a leader.

And here I am, he thought.

"As you may have heard," Donovan said, pulling open his vest with his left hand to display the silver star on his shirt. "There's a new sheriff in town."

A smattering of laughter circulated, then ceased.

Donovan continued. "I'm looking for a few volunteers to help me with a little problem. Good men, good shots with a rifle." He paused and surveyed the faces in the room. "Men who can follow orders, men who aren't afraid to take a few risks."

"What's in it for us?" one cowpoke asked.

Donovan had noticed him before and sized him up. The man was big, with large hands and a belly that hung over his gun belt.

"I'm glad you asked that, friend."

"I ain't your friend." The heavyset man stood up, obviously ready to mount a challenge.

"That's a damn shame," Donovan said, cocking his head back. "Because if you're not my friend, you must be my enemy."

The big man licked his lips, unfastened his gun hammer. The crowd immediately thinned out behind him, moving to either side. Texas-Mex and Big Finn stayed put, leaning against the bar, grinning, their hands hovering over their weapons.

After a few quick breaths, the heavyset man started to look less sure of himself. His mouth worked, and then he said, "I got no quarrel with you, mister."

"Perhaps," Donovan said. "Perhaps not. But as I mentioned, I prefer to be among friends."

The big man said nothing. His hand hovered a few inches from the pearl handle of his sidearm.

Donovan winked at him. "Would you like me to recite a limerick for you?"

The big man remained silent, watching.

"Let me see," Donovan said. "My poetic juices aren't flowing so well this afternoon . . . There once was a big fat lout, who raised a ruckus with a shout. He thought he was tough, but he wasn't nearly enough . . ."

The big man went for his gun, but Donovan dropped the shot glass, brought up his own weapon, and cocked back the hammer in one smooth motion.

The Remington roared.

A small, round hole appeared in the big man's forehead, and his eyes turned completely white, the irises rolling back and up into his head. His slack fingers dropped his gun on the wooden floor, and he collapsed in sections, his knees striking first, followed by his substantial belly.

And Donovan came down on him with a clout, Donovan thought, finishing the limerick.

He assessed his performance, noting that a puddle of red was draining out of his adversary's head and soaking into the hard wood floor.

"Anyone else want to challenge me?" he asked, surveying the room with a critical eye.

He could tell from their faces that there would be no more opposition. He had them right where he wanted them.

"Very well then." He slowly lowered the cocked hammer, stopping at half-cock to rotate the cylinder so the hammer would rest on the expended round. "You two, get rid of this duffer before his damn blood irreparably stains this pretty wooden floor."

The two men moved forward, and each took a leg. Donovan stooped down and retrieved the dead man's gun.

"I've got a little proposition for you," he said, standing. "But first, I need to ask you all a question." Waiting the sufficient number of seconds to bait them, he then added, "Is there a man among you here that has an aversion to becoming rich?"

Silence reigned over the crowd until Texas-Mex chuckled. *"Es mas bueno* to laugh, *hombres."*

The crowd erupted with merriment that sounded less genuine than forced.

But that'll do, Donovan thought. *That'll do.*

"As I said, I'll be needing a few good men to accompany me tonight. We've got a little matter to attend to, and then we'll start with our plan to become the richest sons of mothers north of Texas." Donovan's gaze swept over their faces. They were ready. They were all his for the taking. "But first, drinks on the house."

A cheer erupted.

"Hey," Big Finn said. "You didn't finish your poem."

Donovan re-holstered his Remington but left the thong undone for now. He slapped the big half-breed on his massive back and turned to face him.

"Finnegan, my boy," Donovan said. "To notice that, there must be more of your father, the Irishman, in you than we thought."

Finn laughed and tossed down his whiskey.

Donovan looked over and saw the dark eyes of the Indian girl still fixed on him.

Maybe he'd take her again instead of the blonde one. He appraised the other girl.

And then again, perhaps I'll take them both.

Fort Smith, Arkansas
As the mid-morning sun shone brightly on

116

the sections of greenery in the center of the town, Stutley made it a point to stroll by the gallows on the eastern side of the encampment. It was so under-developed and rustic that he couldn't bring himself to call it a city, as some of the locals did, or even a town for that matter. Finally, after breaking down and asking directions from a store clerk, he found what he'd been searching for: the gallows.

The area was enclosed by a sixteen-foot-high, whitewashed fence, but Stutley was able to find a gap in the slats wide enough to peer through. He pressed his spectacles up on the bridge of his nose and leaned forward to look through the gap.

The gallows themselves were also painted white. They were about fifty feet away, beyond a field of green grass, and anchored into the earth by massive, square-cut timbers that looked like they could support a railroad bridge. The horizontal wooden beams were equally as thick and angular, and the structure reposed against the backdrop of an artistically fashioned stone wall. The scaffold section was covered by a roof, allowing protection from the rain, but no walls descended from either side to temper the wind. The main horizontal beam, the one around which the ropes were no doubt secured, stretched twelve feet high over the trapdoors in the floor, and the scaffold itself was perhaps twelve feet above the ground, ensuring a long enough drop that no man's feet would have a chance of striking the earth.

Stutley wondered how many slots were in the scaffold. How many men could be hanged at once? The stairway on the left side had thirteen steps — he counted them — to the top. Thirteen. What an unlucky number for a man to walk on his way to meet his maker.

After studying the details for a good ten minutes, Stutley turned and removed his notebook and pencil from his coat pocket. He began to make some rough sketches of the scene.

A few passersby glanced at him, but he did his best not to pay them any attention. A few laughed out loud.

The rubes, he thought. He'd show them. He'd show them all when his book came out.

After completing the sketch, he replaced the notebook in his coat pocket and headed across the square toward the large, white building that bore the well-crafted, painted sign: Federal Courthouse. Stutley felt a tingle of excitement. This was where he'd find the famous hanging judge . . . Judge Parker. Maybe fortune would smile upon him, and there would be a trial in progress. Perhaps he'd be able to see the judge hand down a death sentence, maybe even be able to witness an execution up close. What would that be like? To see a wretched convict marched up those thirteen white steps . . . To watch the black hood being placed over the condemned man's head . . . To hear the snap of the bolt as the trapdoor opened beneath the criminal's feet . . .

Stutley wondered if the man's neck would make an audible snap, if he'd be able to hear it from his position in front of the gallows? Imagining what it might sound like, Stutley wrote the first lines in his mind:

The crowd of perhaps fifty people speckled the green grass on the hot summer day —

Would it be better set in the autumn, a symbolic time of death?

The crowd of perhaps fifty people speckled the green grass in the coolness of the bright autumn day —

A bright day? Perhaps one that was overcast. Perhaps, *dark and dreary, dappling the crowd with a light rain —*

Yes, he liked that better. Committing those phrases to memory, he paused again to take in the ambiance from across the street.

The building did not look particularly busy, or even occupied.

His dream of getting to witness an execution drifted further away, like a runaway canoe edging along with the errant current of a river.

Straightening his hat and tie with a renewed determination, Stutley began to walk across the street toward the court building.

A harsh yell jolted him, accompanied by the thunderous sound of clopping horse hooves and straining wood, as a wagon being pulled at a relatively fast clip rumbled in front of him. The driver leaned over to deliver an epithet along with a well-aimed globule of spittle.

"Git out the damn way, ya fool!"

Stutley ducked back to the relative safety of the wooden sidewalk and cast a look of disdain toward the reckless man in the wagon. Had he more time, he should like to look that ruffian up and deliver a punch to the man's nose. But the lout had appeared quite large and formidable. Probably wouldn't know the first thing about a fair fight.

No, Stutley thought. Better to sit back and observe. Place the mongrel in a story and depict him as the pathetic creature he was. That would serve Stutley's purpose better than administering a well-deserved beating.

He readjusted his clothes and then stepped back into the street, taking particular care to look both ways this time before venturing out too far.

Along the Texas Trail
The Indian Territories
Bass Reeves held up his hand as he saw the wagon approaching. It was coming from the west. Bear, who was driving their wagon, pulled back on the reins to bring the team of horses to a halt.

"Wonder who they are?" he said, then added with a grin, "How you want to handle this, *Gimoozabie?*"

Reeves cast him a quick look. "Whoever they might be," he said, "they just might be adding one beat-to-hell Indian to their wagon, if you don't stop calling me that."

Bear chuckled. "I told you, it means 'trusted friend.' "

As the wagon drew closer Reeves saw that it was filled with a family of white settlers with as many of their possessions as it could bear. The wagon slowed to a halt on the road, and the driver nudged a young boy of about ten or twelve. The youth reached behind the seat and pulled up an old, double-barreled shotgun and handed it to the man. The man cocked open the breech, inserted two shells, and slammed it shut. He kept the weapon on his lap as Reeves rode up, with Bear and the wagon creeping behind him.

"I'm telling you right now," the man said, keeping his right hand on the stock near the trigger. "We don't want no trouble, mister."

"That's good," Reeves said. "It ain't something I'm seeking neither."

The man looked confused.

Reeves slowly brought his left hand up, gripped the lapel of his long range jacket, and pulled it back, exposing his star.

"I'm Deputy Marshal Bass Reeves. This is my *trusted friend* from the Lighthorse, Walks as Bear. Where you folks heading?"

"Arkansas," the man said. He seemed to relax slightly at the sight of the star.

"You got a ways to go, then," Reeves said. "Better be careful. We heard tell there might be Indian trouble 'round these parts."

"I wouldn't doubt it." The man glared at Bear. "Damn savages. They can't keep a promise to save their lives."

Bear smirked. "Yeah, we're known for breaking our promises. Just like the one that said we could keep our lands."

The man frowned but said nothing. Reeves saw his fingers tightening around the shotgun.

"You got inclination of using that, mister," Reeves said, "I'd strongly advise against it. I showed you my badge."

The man's mouth puckered a bit, then his grip on the shotgun relaxed. "Sorry, marshal. It's just that we come through a hell of a lot of bad luck."

"How so?"

"We just come from Temptation."

"You talking about the town called Temptation?" Bear asked.

The man spat. "Hell on earth."

Reeves glanced back at his partner.

"I thought it was some kind of railroad settlement," Bear said. "Didn't you all sign a lease with the Cherokee for use of the land?"

"That was the plan originally," the man said. "We signed the lease agreement and started building. First year or two things was going along pretty well. We built up a nice little town — stores, a hotel, a stable, even got us a telegraph office. Then things began fizzling out quicker than a campfire in a drizzle." His hand left the shotgun so he could tick off points on his fingers. "We'd been paying the money, but the Indians

123

began using it to buy whiskey. Most of them that come into the town were so drunk they just fall down in the street and lay there till somebody pulled 'em off to the side." He paused and licked his lips. "Second, the damn railroad was gonna put in a special section of track coming right into the town station. Would've been a gold mine for all of us merchants, and then they stopped short. Laid a bunch of track branching off from the main line that was supposed to go into town, but they must've seen what was happening and just stopped all of a sudden."

"Why'd they do that?" Reeves asked.

"Trouble," the man said. "And nothing but. All kinds of outlaws and riffraff started drifting in. They turned the hotel and saloon into a brothel. Got so bad most decent folk couldn't even walk the streets at night. Businesses been closing, people been pulling up stakes, leaving." His face took on a sad expression. "There's still a smidgeon of decent folks left, but me, I just plum had enough."

"The railroad never came back?" Bear asked.

The man shook his head. "Keeps going right on by. Got prairie weeds growing between them rails to the town now. There ain't nothing 'cept that section of tracks that ends up going nowhere."

"People have overcome worse," Reeves said.

"But that ain't the worst of it. We was getting along, barely, with our stores and such, 'cause we got us an army fort not too far away, and lots of the blue bellies would come in now and again to spend some of their money. Couple of drovers come through, too, though they're mostly just interested in the saloon and the ladies." He stopped and took out some chaw, cut off a piece, then stuck it in his mouth. "We was trying to do good. Even elected a sheriff who promised to keep order. Except him and the Indian agent turned out to be about as worthless as teats on a boar hog. A might more crooked, too."

"Crooked?" Reeves asked. "How so?"

The man looked them over and then spat prior to speaking. "Word was that instead of transferring the government beef to the Indians, like they was supposed to, they was a selling it elsewhere and giving them whiskey and guns instead. Indian village ain't too far from town. Supposed to be nothing now but a few squaws and a bunch of old men. All them young braves left, either drunk or run off."

Reeves and Bear exchanged glances again.

"What's his name?" Reeves asked. "This Indian agent."

"Cooper. Kenneth Cooper."

"You got any proof he's crooked?" Reeves asked.

He snorted. "Ride into Temptation and see for yourselves."

Reeves studied him. "You ever heard of a group calling themselves the Cherokeos?"

The man worked the tobacco around to the front of his mouth, causing his lower lips to bulge outward. "Might have. Why?"

"We heard they might be starting some trouble down Texas way. Bringing illegal whiskey and guns."

"Might have heard something 'bout somebody doin' that, but I can't say I seen any first hand. But if it's trouble you're a lookin' for," the man said, turning his head to spit again, "I'd say there's plenty of that in Temptation. And then some."

"What's that crooked sheriff's name?" Reeves asked.

"Used to be Hobb."

"Used to be?"

The man's lips worked, and he spat off to the side again. "Yep. He was shot dead a couple days ago. New one named Donovan took over."

"Who shot Sheriff Hobb?" Bear asked.

The man smirked. "Donovan did."

On the Trail
The Indian Territories
Donovan had chosen the spot with extreme care. The topography was perfect for an ambush, especially one as carefully planned as this one. After having Big Finn lift the heavy crates out of the wagon and place them behind the fallen tree off to the side of the clearing, Donovan told them to move the army wagon about a hundred feet away. He set several of the men he recruited to establishing a camp around it, even going so far as to erect a make-shift lean-to for their horses. When they'd finished, it looked like a typical place for a stop along the prairie.

But it was anything but that.

Donovan kept Finn and the Mex with him to do the heavy lifting and assembly. After prying the tops off the five wooden crates, Donovan relished the gleaming metal objects they yielded: the ten barrels, all contained within a gleaming cylinder and held by the rotating, circular plates; the massive U-shaped carrier support, which, when mounted on the gears, fitted onto the axle to allow the muzzle to be rotated right or left. He picked up the finely crafted hand crank and the long, tube-like ammunition hopper. The Gatling guns he'd seen at the end of his Army service had angled hoppers, into which an assistant would pour the new shells from the tin ammo boxes. This hopper stood straight and true, divided into two sections, one for loading and the other for feeding the unspent rounds into the breech.

For a moment his memory drifted back to the scene of his last battle . . .

The Confederates were advancing across the field, their mouths open and emitting those fierce yells, even though many wore no shoes or boots and probably had no ammunition. Then the command came to open fire, and the advancing wave of gray was peppered with splashes of red. The Gatling guns poured out the rounds, sounding like an incredibly fast beating of a giant drum, the shell casings spitting out, bouncing on the ground, and leaving trails of cooling mist as they struck the dew-moistened grass.

The rebel yells quickly dissipated into mournful cries as section after section collapsed or were trampled upon by the oncoming wave of soon-to-be-dead men. The smoke from the rotating barrels rose upward, giving off an acrid smell of burnt gunpowder, which would later be replaced by the odor of rotting bodies.

The old models had only five barrels in those days. This one had ten. Twice the firepower, twice the speed for dealing death.

"You use this one before, no?" Texas-Mex asked. "In your war?"

"We used this one's father."

Texas-Mex laughed.

Finn hoisted the assembled barrel upward and placed it on the U-brace.

"This thing's ain't that heavy," Finn said. "Sure it's gonna work?"

Donovan used the wrench to tighten the bolts that secured the barrel in place.

"It'll work, all right," he said, patting the shiny, yellow barrel.

"So how you call this one?" Texas-Mex asked. "A Gatling?"

"A Bulldog," Donovan said. "The biggest one in the fight."

Fort Smith, Arkansas

As Stutley stepped out onto the planked sidewalk once more, the door to the courthouse slammed behind him, and he tried to figure out at exactly what point his interview with the famous, or infamous, Judge Parker had gone sour. It had started out well enough, with the judge seeming almost

129

eager to talk. But then the esteemed jurist asked what newspaper Stutley was with, and, when he'd replied, "Beadles," Parker's face registered some confusion.

"I don't believe I've heard of that one. Where's it published?"

"New York City," Stutley replied.

Parker raised his eyebrows. "That's impressive."

Things went downhill from there. All it took was the simple question, "Is it true you've sentenced seventeen men and three women to death and hanged eleven of them at once?"

Stutley was imagining the crowd gathering on the green lawn in his mind's eye: the eleven men, clad in irons, being marched up the thirteen white steps toward the gallows, seeing the corresponding number of dangling hangman's nooses waiting to be filled at the top.

"Where did you hear that?" Parker asked.

"Judge," Stutley said, "let us just say that your reputation precedes you."

He punctuated his comment with a jaunty smile that he hoped Parker would take as a compliment. Unfortunately the judge's eyes narrowed, and his mouth pulled into a tight line.

"Exactly what type of newspaper do you

work for, Mr. Stutley?"

"Well, Beadles is not a newspaper. It's a publishing company owned by Irwin and Erastus Beadle, and we specialize in, uh, dime novels." Stutley flashed his ingratiating smile again. "I have some samples, if you'd like to see them. Unfortunately, my bag's rather heavy and is still in my hotel room, but —"

"I've seen the type of trash you describe," Parker said and picked up a small, gold-colored bell on his desk. He swung the bell back and forth, causing an irritating little peal, which subsequently brought back the huge deputy who had shown Stutley into the judge's chambers.

"George," Parker said, "show this gentleman, and I use that term with hesitancy, out of the building."

"But —" Stutley started to say.

The big deputy had already grabbed him by the collar of his suit and literally lifted him out of the chair. The man was a human ape, a kissing cousin to the one Stutley'd seen in the New York City zoo. Stutley's protestations lasted all the way out the building, where the ape roughly shoved him and slammed the door shut behind him. The action nearly knocked Stutley's spectacles from his face.

"This is an outrage!" Stutley yelled at the closed door. "I'm going to make sure all my readers back East find out how you treated a respectable man of my letters." Straightening his collar and readjusting his spectacles, Stutley realized the brute had popped the collar button off with his enormous hands.

"Now you've done it!" he shouted at the door. "If you'd care to step outside, we can settle this, man to man, you big dullard. And a coward to boot."

The door swung open, and the huge deputy stood there, staring at Stutley with a rather emotionless expression.

"Get outta here," the deputy said, "before I take off this badge and step out there to give you the beatin' you deserve."

Stutley noticed that the big lout was armed. A large, menacing-looking gun hung from a holster on the deputy's right side. Figuring he'd made the point of the displeasure at the treatment he'd received, Stutley shrugged and turned away. The deputy's thrashing would have to take place on the pages of one of his forthcoming stories, along with the Satanic depiction of the hanging judge. Stutley nodded his head at the image. Yes, that would be a good one. The dark-haired judge with his gleaming, pointed teeth framed by the dark goatee.

Stutley was about forty feet away from the courthouse when he heard someone calling his name. He turned and saw the old drunk, Norman, running toward him.

"Hey, you been in to see the judge?" the boozer asked, hustling up to Stutley.

"If you could call it that."

Old Norman wiped his nose with his fingers. "That's good. Glad I could help." His mouth twitched, and his lizard-like tongue darted out over his lips. "Say, I could really use a drink."

Stutley didn't want to go to the trouble of taking out his pocket watch to check the time, but he was certain it wasn't even ten thirty yet. He didn't answer the sodden old fart and kept walking.

Old Norman began to trot alongside him, speaking in rapid sentences, expelled between pants that sent invisible plumes of his hot, fetid breath in Stutley's direction.

The malodorous emissions turned Stutley's stomach, and he felt like retching up the heavily buttered biscuits the woman at the restaurant had given him. Didn't anyone know about personal hygiene in these parts?

"I thought you wanted to know about the real West," Norman huffed, his potbelly jiggling over his rapidly moving little feet.

Stutley took pity on the poor creature and

stopped.

"Here," he said removing a coin from his pocket. "This is yours if you can tell me where I can find some real westerners, the kind we were talking about last night."

Old Norman eyed the coin. His nose twitched like a starving rabbit's. "That's easy," the old drunk said. "Place you want to go is straight west of here. You can take the train out thata' way. Take you right to it. Almost." He reached for the coin, but Stutley closed his fingers over it.

"Not so fast. What's the name of this place?"

"It's called Temptation."

CHAPTER 5

Along the Texas Trail
The Indian Territories

Donovan dribbled some water from the canteen into his palm and splashed it over his face. To his left, the eastern sky was becoming suffused with pink, and he knew that dawn would be breaking shortly. He figured it would be the perfect time for the rangers to pounce.

He glanced down the embankment at the makeshift camp where the padded bedrolls had been configured around the still smoldering campfire next to the U.S. Army wagon. The horses had been tethered several yards away, and a few empty rifles were leaning against the wagon. It was the perfect picture of a bunch of lazy, whiskey-sodden "Cherokeos" who were so lax that they were almost asking to be taken by surprise.

And surprise was the kissing cousin to success.

135

Once again, he checked the dirt and shrubbery covered blankets that they'd placed over the Bulldog. In the early morning light, it would appear to be just another uneven rise along the dusty slope to those below. Donovan looked over at Texas-Mex, who slumbered a few feet away, and then to big Finnegan, who was dozing off to the side as well. Donovan knew he could awaken them both at a moment's notice, so he let them sleep. Besides, he had the high ground.

One of us staying awake is enough, he thought. *So long as it's the best one of us.*

He went back to the Bulldog and knelt behind it, gripping the hand crank and longing to line up the front sight. It graced the end of the barrel, slightly canted to the right side, looking almost misaligned until you realized that if you tried to look directly over the end of the barrel, your line of sight was interrupted by the tall-standing ammunition hopper. He stared at the lineal collection of rounds waiting to be shot and once again recalled the red mist settling over that field of gray back in the war.

The sound of a horse's neighing broke the morning stillness.

Donovan listened with more intensity, heard nothing else, but knew it had to be them. Perhaps the horse noise had been a signal from Crowe or Cooper, both of whom were supposed to be leading the rangers into the killing arena. Donovan hoped they wouldn't try to ride in shooting. He didn't want their horses to get caught in the crossfire. There'd be need of them later. More than likely the rangers would proceed on foot, leaving one man to guard their mounts, while the others crept up on the "sleeping" Cherokeos. The rangers would want to take them alive if they could. Not for any humanitarian reasons, but for the sake of gathering information on exactly who they were, how many of them there were, and what they were doing.

It was a bit of irony that they actually had the entire gang of them, Cooper and Crowe, in their clutches already.

Something moved in the bushes down below. Donovan adjusted the swivel gear on the Gatling gun. He'd put a bit of grease from the wagon's axle on the gear to make it move without sticking, and now the gears meshed together with the silence and fluidity of a snake slithering through the grass.

The movement continued, and a man emerged from the shadows, followed by three more. Without knowing the exact number, Donovan wanted to make sure to give them enough lead time. Let them get almost to the campfire before commencing the firing cycle. He imagined no more than half a dozen, perhaps eight at the very most. The rangers, he knew, prided themselves on being both tough and austere. Kicking Texas-Mex awake, Donovan held a finger to his lips, smiled, and pointed to the advancing rangers down below. They were about fifty feet away at the bottom of a shallow ridge.

The Mexican grinned. He, too, knew it was a perfect killing arena.

Texas-Mex pointed to big Finnegan, but Donovan shook his head.

"That big bugger'll wake up soon enough," he whispered. "Once the shooting starts."

Texas-Mex's grin grew wider as he picked up his Winchester rifle and cocked back the hammer.

Below, the six rangers were only a scant ten feet or so from the supposed slumbering bodies. Donovan motioned for Texas-Mex to rip away the blankets, and he swung the end of the gun toward the last advancing man. He gripped the hand crank with his right and the swivel with his left, figuring it would be better to sweep the barrel back once he began firing, then repeat the process in the opposite direction.

"Time to dance with the Devil," Donovan said and began turning the crank.

The first rounds exploded in the stillness of the morning and continued with such rapidity that even Donovan was surprised. He was filled with wonder at how easily he took the six men down, watching their bodies jerk and twist from the unending fusillade. The six rangers were all on the ground now as he swung the gun back and forth, while Texas-Mex poured more unspent rounds into the hopper.

Finally, Donovan stopped. A wispy braid of smoke twisted upward from the last fired barrel. The smell of burned gunpowder filled the air. Big Finn had jerked awake with the opening volley and had lain at Donovan's side for the duration, his huge hands clamped over his ears. Now he stood and glanced down at the carnage.

"Looks like a damn butcher shop," he said, his face showing an awe and reverence.

"*Magnifico,*" Texas-Mex said, looking like he'd just seen the rapture. "*Cuantos* — Uh, how many shots you fire?"

"Enough to get the job done," Donovan said with a smile.

The truth be told, he had no idea, and he wasn't about to stop to count the mosaic of expelled brass casings that littered the ground at his feet. "Go check on Crowe and Cooper. Hopefully there are no more rangers hiding in the woodpile."

Big Finn pointed. The two errant Cherokeos were walking into the clearing, Cooper pulling the reins of four horses and Crowe hauling five. That meant a total of seven rangers. The Cherokeos must have left a lone Ranger to guard the horses. Shot in the back, no doubt.

"All right then," Donovan said. "Tell Crowe he's to stay behind and bury all of them."

"Bury them?" Texas-Mex said. "What for?"

"Every decent man deserves a proper, Christian burial," Donovan said, patting the Bulldog. "And whether these buggers were deserving, or not, is beside the point. I'm a bit more concerned about someone stumbling over the corpses and reporting back to the rangers before that mother lode Boswell was talking about comes in."

Texas-Mex grunted a laugh. "Crowe no gonna like it. He probably got a bottle somewhere he wanting to crawl into."

"Tell him I'll have a bottle of the good stuff waiting for him in Temptation when he's done." Donovan fingered the sheriff's star on his chest. He turned to Big Finnegan. "But first, go down and get me those Texas Ranger stars."

Trans-Pacific Railroad
Heading West into the Indian Territories
Stutley stared out the window of the train car as the mid-morning sun shone over the sea of tall, greenish-brown prairie grass. At least this time he was spared the cramped, crowded quarters of his previous train trip. This car was sparsely populated, and he had the entire seat as well as the one facing him all to himself. It was refreshing not to have to endure the unpleasant presence, and odors, of any more of these crude, countrified bumpkins. He couldn't wait to depict them in his novels, but, then again, telling it like it really was might not be totally advisable. He was, after all, in the business of amassing readership, and not of accurately reporting the facts. People didn't want reality; they wanted mythology. They craved it. And he was in the myth-building business.

The area on the other side of the window looked as flat as a board and sprinkled with an occasional stunted tree. He wondered what this place called Temptation would be like. Old, drunken Norman, and a few others, had talked extensively about it. From their descriptions, it sounded primitive and raw, although the railroad ticket agent had been able to send a wire to the town, requesting them to have a buckboard meet the train at the water stop. It was purported to be a few miles from the town itself.

"They started to build a station right there in the town," the ticket agent had said. "Would've been a regular stop."

"Why didn't they finish it?" Stutley had asked.

The ticket agent had shrugged as he readied the telegraph key. "Don't know, don't care."

As he was tapping out the message, Stutley wondered about the man's apathetic response and hoped it wouldn't be shared by the residents of the town.

Temptation. He couldn't ask for a better name for a place where gunmen and lawbreakers would be congregating. Hopefully, there'd be enough real characters there to provide a wealth of information.

The train car squealed and shifted back and forth as it went over some uneven section of track. He kept his eyes peeled for buffalo herds but saw none, which made sense. The railroads had employed legions of hunters to slaughter the animals, necessitating the government agree to provide beef to the Indian tribes, who had depended on the buffalo for their sustenance.

Perhaps there was the beginning of a story in that.

A buffalo hunter befriended by the Indians. For a moment the image of the nubile young Indian woman running naked through the stream flashed in his mind's eye. He wondered how well received those hunters might have been. Perhaps the Indians resented their intrusion. But he'd also heard that many white men had been venturing west into the territories with impunity. After all, the Indians were basically ignorant savages, weren't they? Hadn't Manhattan been "sold" for a string of beads? Why should it be any different out here?

But manifest destiny didn't sell copies of dime novels. He remembered his editor's advice: "Don't let authenticity get in the way of a good story. It's not the facts or the truth that people want to read. That's not entertainment."

So they wanted to read about outlaws and lawmen, gunslingers and Indian fighters, maybe even brave cavalry soldiers like George Armstrong Custer.

Sitting back in his seat, Stutley fished out

his notebook. It was time to start writing.

He'd already formulated a title for his book: *The Legends of the West.*

Along the Texas Trail
The Indian Territories

Reeves could smell death in the air. It was unmistakable: the faint trace of bodies rotting in the hot afternoon sun. A circling gaggle of buzzards hung in the sky perhaps two hundred yards or so to the north. He turned to Bear, who was driving the wagon.

"Looks like somebody died," the Lighthorse said.

"Looks like. But them buzzards would be feasting instead of circling unless there's somebody moving around down there."

"You can read things like an Indian."

Scanning the immediate terrain, Reeves saw a small outcropping about one hundred yards to the right and pointed to it.

"Take the wagon over there," he said, "so the horses can rest in the shade while we go have a look-see."

Bear gripped the reins, steering the team off to the side.

Reeves removed his Colt Peacemaker and inserted the sixth cartridge into the space in the cylinder he usually left empty under the hammer while traveling. A sudden jerk or blow could cause the hammer to strike the primer and fire a round, so caution was the best policy, except when you were riding toward death. Then, you needed all the rounds you could hope to have.

Bear galloped up on his paint a few moments later and grinned at the sight of the big revolver. "Expecting trouble?" he asked.

"Just making sure I'm ready for any, in case I find some."

Bear nodded. "How you want to handle this?"

Reeves was already surveying the landscape. He noticed a natural acclivity rising on the right-hand side. "I'll go in first. You follow my lead, taking that high road. If there's somebody out there, it don't make sense to let them know there's two of us."

"I'll keep watch from above, *Gimoozabie.*" Bear's grin was wide. "Just like the great spirit."

Reeves stared at him. "You keep calling me that, and whatever them buzzards is circling for might be getting some company."

Bear laughed and urged his horse up the gradual incline.

Reeves rode forward, knowing that Bear would do a good job of watching.

As he grew closer, he saw a pair of horses

145

tied to a fallen log. The animals were out in the hot sun, and Reeves felt a surge of anger. He wondered who the owners were, and what they were doing, but felt that, whatever it was, it wasn't good.

Two men sat about twenty feet away from the horses, catching a bit of shade from a tall cactus and passing a bottle back and forth, a shovel lying between them. Both were white and wearing their guns strapped down. Reeves kept the edge of his vest over the badge on his chest. There was no sense advertising his position as a lawman until the time was right. The breeze kicked up and blew the odor of death over him once again, stronger and more pervasive this time. And then he saw why. Six bodies, partially stripped of their boots and clothing, lay in a row. A pile of boots and clothing sat off to the side. Next to it, another pile of watches, holsters, and weapons was on top of a blanket. A long, shallow hole was off to one side, like the open maw of a dead animal. It was a sorry excuse for a grave.

As Reeves approached, both men exchanged glances and then stood up. One man's hat fell onto his back, and Reeves saw the deep, purplish scars that decorated his scalp where there should have been hair.

He looked like he'd been partially scalped.

"Howdy, gents," Reeves said. He turned his horse slightly so that his right hand could drop down unnoticed by the two strangers as he undid the leather thong that secured his Peacemaker in its holster.

"What you want, nigger?" the man with the purple scars said. He held a partially full whiskey bottle in this right hand, and his lips curled back, exposing a set of rotten, crooked teeth.

Reeves nodded toward the row of bodies. "What happened here?"

"T'aint none a yer business," purple scars said. "Now git outta here."

" 'Fore we gets another body we gotta bury," the other man said. He was big and fat and had a nose the size and color of a plum.

"I asked you all a question," Reeves said. "What happened?"

"Nigger, I done told you: you'd best git whilst the gittin's good." Purple scar transferred the bottle to his left hand. He wore his gun on his right side.

Reeves pulled back the edge of his vest with his own left hand. "I'm Deputy Marshal Bass Reeves."

Before he could say anything more, purple scars made his move. He dove to the side, pulling his gun out of his holster and bringing it up toward Reeves, but the marshal had anticipated this and already had his Peacemaker out. With one smooth motion, he cocked back the hammer and fired, catching purple scars in the upper chest. The man grunted and stumbled backward. Reeves turned his horse and pointed his gun at the second man, who had also armed himself. Having no more than a split second to aim, Reeves squeezed off another round and saw the man's plum-like nose explode in a blossom of crimson. Purple scars was regaining his balance and brought his gun up. Reeves fired a third time. As the bullet penetrated one of the hollow scars on the bald man's head, he sank to his knees, his gun dropping from slack fingers.

Reeves immediately whipped his horse around and surveyed the rest of the area.

Nothing moved.

No one else was visible.

After riding up and back through the campsite, Reeves noticed several groups of tracks.

A lot of horses, perhaps a dozen or so, had traveled through here. A wagon, too, carrying something.

A lot of dead men, but no shell casings. The six had probably been ambushed with

148

rifles from a distance away, or else brought here from someplace else.

He heard a low whistle and recognized Bear's signal. The Lighthorse came into view on foot at the opposite end of the camp, waving for Reeves to follow. He kicked his horse's flanks and galloped over to his Indian companion.

"Find something?" Reeves asked.

Bear was standing over another downed man. Red blood stained the back of the man's shirt, but Reeves noticed a slight variance as the material rose and fell with slight movements.

"This one's still alive, *Gimoozabie.*"

Temptation
The Indian Territories

Stutley jumped down from the open buckboard and onto the dusty street. He reached into his pocket, found a nickel, and handed it to the driver. The old man flashed a gaptoothed grin and smacked the reins on the haunches of the two horses. The buckboard jolted forward, and Stutley was barely able to grab his traveling bags.

Idiotic lout, Stutley thought. He could have at least waited until I'd removed my luggage. And one would think that the railroad would have provided more accommodating transportation for such a long ride from their rail stop location. It had to be twenty-five minutes in the wind and the dust.

The wagon wheels stirred up more clouds of particulates, and Stutley stepped back as best he could. Not that there was any sidewalk to speak of. He looked around. The town consisted of two blocks of buildings on a main street. A smattering of houses were set back from this street area, dotting the landscape. Most of the buildings appeared to be in need of some upkeep. A few were decrepit stores offering canned food and other sundries for sale. The faded sign hanging askew in front of one advertised a stable, and an adjacent one, blacksmithing. A few people, looking like families, eyed him warily from the confines of the stores and a few other buildings. They looked timid and meek. Stutley resisted the temptation to let out a ferocious snarl just to see if it would frighten them back into the shadows like scared mice. He walked by a telegraph office, but it was unoccupied. At least they'd received his wire and had the transportation ready for him when he got off the train. The conductor had shown surprise when he'd told the man he wanted to get off there.

"Temptation?" the man had said. "What you want to go there for?"

A preposition at the end of a sentence! Stutley smirked. So far he was a head and shoulders above the unintelligent populace he'd encountered thus far on his trip west.

Black letters over a white background spelled out Hotel on the top story of a big, two-storied building. Directly below it, a pair of batwing doors, over which hung a hand-painted sign advertising what appeared to be a saloon, offered entry into the lower part of the structure. It looked in dire need of a coat of paint. Across the street a large house advertising Rooms sat next to what appeared to be the only brick and mortar construction in the city of Temptation: the bank. The rooming house had several of the windows boarded up.

This place could hardly be called a city, even by a fiction writer like himself.

A town in the incipient stages of decay, he thought.

He liked that verbiage but didn't know if it would work in his fictional recreation. People back East were enamored by the Western legends rather than the harsh reality of truth. "Your job is to stoke the legend, not kill it," his editor back in New York had said. "Nurture it."

As he headed down the street he began framing the description for his next dime novel.

The town of Temptation was a bustling place located in what had become known as the Indian Territories. Home of five tribes, countless outlaws, and lawmen.

He'd have to look up what those Indian tribes were, but, overall, he liked the phrasing and longed for a chance to stop and commit it to writing before the muse deserted him.

The streets were deserted, even though it was early evening, he continued in his literary mind's eye.

"However, many decent people there are left," the wagon driver had told him on the way from the railroad stop, "but they know better than to show themselves once the sun starts going down."

Great stuff, Stutley thought. He'd have to steal that.

The sound of raucous laughter filtered out of the hotel/saloon, and Stutley headed right for it. A crudely painted sign above the pair of batwing doors read: Temptation City Salloon. No Injuns or Nigers Alowed.

Stutley was mildly amused at the poor spelling but not totally surprised at the sentiment expressed. After all, this was basically a lawless area where groups of outlaws often ruled, and the point of a gun was the only law, which was why he was here.

At the point of a gun. Another good phrase he wanted to record.

He pushed through the opening and saw a crowd of men in cowboy garb standing near a long, rather well-constructed bar. Stutley was shocked that the inside of the place looked as nice as it did. The walls were adorned with some garish purple wallpaper. Rows of dark bottles and glasses were somewhat haphazardly arranged on shelves fashioned against a long mirror that lined the wall behind the bar. The floor was made up of wooden planks, some of which showed dark stains of what Stutley thought might be blood, and this sent a thrill up his spine.

This is just what I was hoping for, he thought.

Several tables and chairs were centered in the expansive room, and three women, apparently barmaids, made the rounds, placing steins of beer and glasses of whiskey in front of the customers. He noticed with interest that one of the women wore a buckskin dress and appeared to be an Indian. The brown material clung to her lithe form like a pair of gloves, and the whimsical vision of the naked Indian girl bathing in the stream flitted though his mind's eye. Until she looked up. The vision was torn away by a garish scar running up the center of her nose.

Such a pity, he thought. Otherwise, she was very comely.

Stutley turned his attention to the men in the room, who all sat quietly listening to the proclamations of a tall, rather handsome man in a blue shirt and black, leather vest. He wore no hat, and his reddish hair was long and combed back. Stutley was struck byhow picturesque the man looked. His smile was broad as he placed some kind of ornaments, one by one, onto a straight, iron bar. As Stutley drew closer, he saw that the ornaments were, in fact, badges of some sort. Five-pointed stars encased in a crescent, circular ridge. There was some kind of inscription along the ridge, but Stutley wasn't close enough to read it.

Hot damn. This place was rich in material. Just the kind of place his editor back at Beadles had told him to find.

Stutley placed his traveling bag on the floor and set his leather case onto a chair so he could dig out his notebook and a pencil. He absolutely had to get this down now.

"And here's the final one," the red-haired man holding the badges said as he slipped the last one on the iron rod. Stutley was able to count five of them. The man held the rod up for all to view and then turned to a huge brute of a man standing to his left. Stutley could only see the back of this Goliath. He had enormous shoulders and a black, Irish derby perched atop his head.

"All right, Finn," the redheaded man said. "Show all of us how strong you are."

His voice had a distinctive Irish lilt to it.

The huge man turned back to the bar and downed a drink from a shot glass. Stutley caught a glimpse of long, jet-black hair, high cheekbones, and light-blue eyes. The man's features had an Indian cast, but his complexion was that of a white man. His lips peeled back, exposing a set of very crooked teeth. His eyes locked with Stutley's.

"Hey, wait a minute," he said. "Lookie here. We got us a dude come to visit."

Stutley felt himself flush. He flashed a weak smile and removed his own hat.

"I beg your pardon, gentlemen," he said. "I didn't mean to disturb the festivities."

"Hey, you sound like a Yankee," one of the grubby cowboys said.

"Well, I am from New York," Stutley said.

"New York?" another cowboy said. "New York City?"

Stutley kept the smile on his lips, realizing

155

that might not be the best place to be from around these parts, and added, "By way of Ohio." He was suddenly cognizant that although he was in the West, he was also south of the Mason/Dixon. "Zanesville, Ohio," he added hastily.

"What you doin' here, dude?" the cowboy asked.

"Yeah, what you want?" demanded another.

Sensing that the crowd was turning a bit hostile, Stutley set his notebook and pencil on the table and opened up his traveling bag. "Perhaps these will help explain." He took out several copies of the dime novels he'd brought with him and passed them around. "I'm a writer, and I happen to be very interested in Western culture, most specifically, men like yourselves."

He saw his words were being wasted as one grubby cowboy after another paged through the dime novels with a perplexed look. It suddenly dawned on Stutley that the literacy rate among these creatures might not be too great.

"Let me see one of those," the red-headed man said.

One of the men passed him a book and said, "Here ya go, Donovan."

The red-headed man glared at the cowboy

who'd handed him the book.

The cowboy balked and added, "I mean, *Mister* Donovan."

The way the man spoke said volumes. It exuded respect and fear, as if the omission of the title was justification for a beating, or worse. Stutley regarded this red-headed man, Donovan, with a discreetness born out of trepidation. Obviously, he was the leader of this rag-tag collection of ruffians, and certainly not a man to be trifled with.

But, he thought, if I can gain his favor . . .

Donovan stared at the cowboy a few seconds more, and Stutley saw the trepidation continuing to dance over the cowboy's face with a series of twitches and half smiles.

Was calling a man only by his surname a killing offense around these parts?

Donovan transferred his gaze to the dime novel in front of him. The cover was colored with bright yellows and reds, brandishing the title *Jesse James, King of the Outlaws.*

Stutley suddenly wondered how the "outlaw" designation would be received by this crowd, but he felt it would be better than the books featuring Wild Bill Hickok. After all, he'd been a lawman at one time, and this group did not look particularly law abiding.

Donovan paged through the book, his

eyebrows rising. The room grew silent. Stutley knew this was a make-or-break moment. His whole future in Temptation, perhaps his whole future period, would be decided in the next few moments. Would he be accepted, or run out of town on a rail, or worse?

He sincerely hoped for the former.

Donovan laughed and read aloud the first line of the book he was holding: "The three riders rode into the town as the terrified townsfolk looked on with a sense of foreboding forlornness." He stopped and chuckled. "A bit turgid, but certainly not too distant from Poe and Dickens."

Turgid?

Stutley was astounded. The man's vocabulary was amazing, his commentary, astute. He was not only literate, but he was intelligent. Where did this guy come from?

Donovan seemed to be reading a bit more. He cocked his head and looked at Stutley.

"Is this your prose?"

"Well," Stutley said, "not completely. But I did have a hand in some of the writing and editing."

The Irishman smirked as he continued reading to himself.

Stutley felt a little better, but the grin had a certain, malevolent quality to it. This matter was far from closed.

Donovan folded the book closed. "So you'd like to make me as famous as Jessie James?"

Stutley's mouth was getting tired of having the smile frozen in place. He knew he had to choose his next words carefully. Very carefully.

"I'd certainly like to try," Stutley said, quickly adding, "Mister Donovan."

That made the other man smile. He left his place at the bar and strode toward Stutley, who noticed how intimidating Donovan was up close. A large pistol was housed in a finely crafted leather holster that hung low on his right side. He exuded strength and competence, and there was no doubt he was the leader of this rag-tag band of misfits.

I may have just found the protagonist for this novel in this most unlikely place.

Donovan stopped and leaned forward, his handsome face a few inches from Stutley's. The man's breath was redolent with the smell of whiskey.

"Now why would you be wanting to write about Jesse James, who's no more than an uneducated ruffian? Why, he's the kind who gives outlaws a bad name." Donovan looked around the room, and the crowd responded with a chorus of agreements.

Stutley compressed his lips, then said, "Jesse James does have a certain notoriety, but we do books about other famous men, too."

Donovan looked amused. "Famous, or infamous?"

Stutley felt a sense of desperation clawing at him. "Let me see. I might have one in here."

He sorted through his case again, finding the one that featured Wild Bill Hickok, but he remembered that Hickok was a lawman. Before he could find another, Donovan said, "This one'll do."

He held the dime novel in front of Stutley's face, then flipped the book upward, toward the ceiling, which was rather high. The book flipped open at the apex and fell to the floor in an unoccupied portion of the room. In a flash Donovan withdrew the pistol from its holster, cocked back the hammer, and fired.

The book skittered across the wooden floorboards.

Stutley cast a furtive glance downward. He gulped. The crowd was silent, or did it only seem so due to the intense ringing in Stutley's ears? He'd never been that close to a gun going off before. It wasn't pleasant at all.

Donovan stared at him for a solid ten seconds, then laughed.

Everyone else laughed, too.

Donovan holstered his gun, which made Stutley feel slightly better.

"Do you know what they say around these parts?"

Stutley shook his head.

The Irishman's lips curled back, exposing a row of white, even teeth. "Lead us not into Temptation."

Stutley waited, and, when Donovan laughed again, so did everyone else. Stutley reached for his notebook. "May I quote you on that, Mister Donovan?"

Donovan leaned close again and whispered, "You'd damn well better."

Stutley froze, and then the tall Irishman laughed and placed his arm around Stutley's shoulders, ushering him over to the bar. The iron rod still lay on top of it, and Stutley got close enough to read the inscription on the crescent stars: Texas Ranger. Two of the badges had bloody stains on them.

Good lord, Stutley thought. What have I gotten myself into?

"Let me introduce you to some of my associates," Donovan said. He slapped a hand on the huge brute's shoulder. "This big fellow here is the strongest man in these parts. Go ahead, Finn. Show the gentleman what you can do."

Big Finn swallowed the last bit of amber fluid in the glass in front of him and took the iron rod by each end, palms up. His face began to contort slightly.

Stutley suddenly realized that Finn was bending the iron rod, and he was making it look easy. The six badges jangled together in the center. Finn paused and readjusted his grip, then went back to work. He stopped when the ends of the bar met in an almost even circle.

Donovan grinned and slapped Finn's shoulder again. He grabbed the iron circle and held it up for all to admire. A round of applause swept through the room. Stutley set his notebook down and clapped as well, afraid not to.

Donovan motioned for the bartender to take the iron circle and place it on a hooked nail on the wall next to the mirror. "Then set up another round, on the house. And a double for my boy Finn here."

The giant grinned.

As cowboys began to belly up to the bar, Stutley picked up his notebook and began to scribble down the things he had seen.

"Your name's Finn, sir?" he asked.

Before the big man could reply, Donovan interceded. "His given name's actually Standing Buffalo. He's what we call a breed. Half-Cherokee, half-Irish. The whites didn't want him and neither did the Indians. But I do." Donovan smiled and looked at the big half-breed. "Which is why I give him that hat and renamed him Finnegan."

The big half-breed doffed the derby, grabbed the shot glass, and downed the rest of the whiskey.

"And then there's Texas-Mex." Donovan pointed to a Mexican in a sombrero. "The best man with a knife or a gun that I've ever seen."

The Mexican's white teeth flashed under his bushy mustache.

"Next to me, of course," Donovan said.

Stutley nodded.

"This is all very fascinating. Just totally fascinating." He scribbled in his notebook. "The people back East are going to love it."

"They'd better," Donovan said, leaning close enough that Stutley was once again reminded that the man was a bit inebriated. "Otherwise, it's not going to get written at all, is it?"

Stutley flashed the weak smile again. "May I ask you one question, Mister Donovan?"

The red-headed man raised an eyebrow.

163

"You may, since you asked so politely."

"Please don't take this the wrong way, but aren't you the least worried about the law?"

Donovan laughed. "Not at all." He grabbed his vest and pulled it away from his shirt, displaying a large, silver badge that said Sheriff across the front.

Stutley's eyes widened, and he suddenly felt a wave of relief.

A lawman, in a place like this? But what kind of a lawman?

He thought about the possibilities and how he could use a dash of artistic license to make this man into a hero. Perhaps even . . . a legend?

This is either going to be the biggest break of my career, Stutley thought, *or the worst.*

The Indian Territories

"There," Bear said, leading Reeves to a clearing about sixty feet away. A man lay face down in the dirt. A copious amount of blood had run from a wound in the center of his back and down the side of the black vest he was wearing.

Reeves had finished checking the six others. All dead. Shot to pieces. That this one was still alive, breathing, was a miracle in itself, but it looked like he'd only had one gunshot wound. Reeves grabbed his canteen, knelt beside the prone man. The Indian looked down at him and shook his head slightly.

Reeves used his own body to shield the man from the blazing sun, gently rolled him over, and bathed his face with some water.

This one wasn't shot up as bad as the others. They'd all been hit multiple times. Reeves had never seen anything like it.

The man's eyes opened, and he looked up. "Who are ya?" His voice was a husky rasp, barely audible.

"I'm a lawman." Reeves held the canteen to the man's mouth and allowed him a small drink.

The man's lips twitched into something that might have been intended to be a smile. Reeves could tell the man was close to death "Lawman?" He swallowed hard, then coughed. "A Nigra?"

"A freeman and a lawman."

"No offense."

"None taken."

"Look, I ain't got much time left. Promise me you'll bury us all so them buzzards won't feast on us."

"We'll bury anybody that needs burying," Reeves said. "You take it easy. Who done this to you?"

The man tried to swallow again.

Reeves held his canteen to the man's lips again to give him another small sip.

The man nodded a thanks and asked, "You really a lawman?"

Reeves held his vest open, displaying his deputy marshal badge.

"Reckon you are." The man's left hand moved to the blood-stained dirt, and his fingers dug back and forth. Something silver glinted in the sun. The man coughed wetly; blood splattered the ground by his mouth.

"Let me do that," Reeves said.

He took out his knife and shoved the blade into the earth, then pried out a silver star, surrounded by a circular rim, upon which was the inscription, Texas Ranger.

"You a Ranger?" Reeves asked.

"Yep. Name's Reed. We came outta Texas, tracking a gang of white men called the Cherokeos. They've been sellin' guns and whiskey to the Injuns. Causing lots of trouble."

"What tribe?"

"Cherokees, Comanche mostly." The Ranger coughed again. "Word is they been stealing the government-issued cattle from the Injuns, too. Stirring up lots of trouble. We got some information about them being up this way, in the territories."

"Been looking for them myself."

166

"We were met by two men. An Indian agent name of Cooper and —"

A fit of coughing erupted, spraying blood from the man's mouth and nose. It took him several seconds to recover, and, when he did, both his voice and his breathing sounded significantly diminished.

He ain't got long, Reeves thought.

The Ranger swallowed hard. "Cooper and a man name of Crowe. Ugly set of scars on his head."

"Like he'd been scalped?"

The Ranger's eyes seemed to light up a little. "You seen him?"

"Killed him. Tried to draw down on me."

The Ranger grunted an approval. "Good. Them two met up with us on the trail. Said they knew where the Cherokeos was. Would lead us to their camp."

He paused and coughed again. More blood spattered his chin. Reeves wiped it off.

"Damn bastards was lying the whole time. Led us into an ambush. I was back a ways, holding our horses with the two of them. Rest of the posse moved up on foot. 'Fore I knew what happened, Crowe shot me in the back. Guess him and Cooper thought I was dead. I couldn't move, but I heard this god-awful shooting over yonder. They opened fire from up on the ridge." His eyes closed.

"Lots of shell casings up on that ridge," Bear said. "Forty-five caliber."

"Gatling gun," Reeves said.

"Shot us all to hell; stole our horses."

"Your horses?"

The Ranger nodded. "I heared the bastards picking through the bodies. Laughing about stealing our Ranger stars and our horses. Managed to push my star into the dirt here and cover it over before I passed out. Couldn't move my gun arm, or I'd have taken one or two of them with me."

"Easy, Ranger," Reeves said. "We got us a wagon. We'll get you to a doc."

The Ranger's smile was wistful. "Too late. Just bury me with the others." He coughed again, and more color drained from his face. "If you could send my star back to Ranger headquarters, I'd be obliged, Marshal."

Reeves said he would, and the Ranger recited the mailing address.

Reeves didn't mention that neither he nor Bear could read or write. Instead, Reeves committed it to memory, hoping he'd be able to remember it completely by the time he got back to Fort Smith, so Judge Parker could write it down for him.

"I'll do my best to make sure it gets there," Reeves said. "And I'll get the rest of them stars back, too. I pledge to you that I'll track down them killers and bring them in for what they've done."

"I'm obliged to you." The Ranger closed his eyes and said, "Thanks for killing that bastard Crowe. He was no damn good."

His body convulsed as he expelled his last breath.

Temptation City Saloon
The Indian Territories

Stutley adjusted his spectacles on his nose and watched as Donovan fondled the blonde bargirl's full breast through the fabric of her plaid dress as he read aloud. It was one of those low-cut fancy dresses laced up the back with black string. Her corset was so tight it caused an unseemly dollop of flesh where her skin was exposed under her bare shoulders. In his other hand, Donovan held one of Stutley's dime novels. He had a fine reading voice, and his pronunciation was perfect, despite the lilting Irish brogue. Stutley, Donovan, and the bargirl sat in a remote corner, off to the side, while the rest of the crowd remained gathered around the bar and watched the big half-breed, Finnegan, arm wrestle two men at the same time, using only one of his arms. His Mexican partner cut slices of some dried up fruit with a dangerous looking knife and slid each piece into his mouth, using the edge of the blade.

"Turn the page for me, lassie," Donovan said.

The girl giggled and flipped the page over.

"The other page, my darling," Donovan said.

The girl cackled and grabbed the book, causing a rip in the paper as she flipped the page.

"Carefully, lass, carefully," Donovan said. "These books are as good as gold."

The awful smile flashed once more as Donovan continued reading.

Her teeth, Stutley noticed, were dreadful. Other than that, she wasn't bad looking, if you could get past the musky smell. He hadn't taken a bath in over a week, and he was certain that it had been much longer in her case.

This one-horse town could use the services of a public bathhouse and a good dentist.

" 'And so goes this tale of heroic stoicism in the great American West,' " Donovan read from the text.

The girl's petite mouth remained fixed in a forced looking smile.

Donovan pinched her breast, and she

winced in pain and wiggled. The other girl, the Indian, stood off to the side. Stutley silently appraised her black hair, high cheekbones, and ruddy complexion. Her body looked pretty well formed inside that tan, buckskin colored dress, but her nose was still unsettling. He found that dreadful scar unappealing. Stutley didn't even want to try to imagine how it had happened.

He sighed. She was a far cry from the image of the maiden in the painting. But still, when he wrote about her, he could use a bit of artistic license. Eliminate the scar, make her more attractive. He was going to have to do that with the other one, too. Again he thought of the nubile Indian maiden in the painting, her delicate, naked limbs testing the coolness of the stream, perhaps to bathe.

Stutley wondered about the barmaids. Did they ever bathe?

Donovan tossed the book toward Stutley. He managed to catch it as it bounced off his chest.

"You call that good writing?" Donovan asked, his right eye squinting slightly.

"Well, it's, uh —"

"It's pure *sheit,* as they say in Ireland. I certainly hope you can do better, laddie."

Stutley felt a surge of fear grip his spine. Had this menacing brigand been offended by the dime novel? Didn't he realize that the depiction was what people wanted to read? That the object was to sell books, not tell the truth?

"I'm sorry you didn't like it, Mister Donovan," Stutley managed to say. "But I am working on a new one."

"Are you, now?"

"I'm going to call it *Legends of the West.*"

Donovan laughed again and leaned back in his chair, motioning for the Indian prostitute to come over to him. When she did he let his right hand remain on the blonde bargirl's breast while his left roamed over the Indian girl's body.

"I wouldn't be opposed to being immortalized in one of your books, laddie. What did you say your name was again?"

"Stutley. Lucien T. Stutley."

Donovan's brow creased slightly. "Stutley," he said slowly. "That wouldn't be an English name by chance, would it?"

Stutley was aware of the animosity that existed across the Atlantic. "No, Mister Donovan."

Donovan snorted as he continued to fondle the two women. "It isn't important." He slapped the Indian girl's rump and said, "Go fetch us a bottle of the good stuff and a couple of glasses. Mister Stutley and I have a proposition to talk over."

The girl twisted out of his grasp and walked toward the bar.

Perhaps she did have some redeeming features. Her breasts were high and full, and her waist slim. Not that Stutley felt tempted to sample her wares to gain more insight. The scar repulsed him, and he could *imagine* her repugnant body odor. The blonde girl wasn't much better. In fact, she was somehow less attractive. Perhaps it was the image of the Indian girl in the painting that continued to dance through his memory.

No, the painting was just an artist's illusion. These were the type of women Uncle Lewis had warned him about.

Abstinence was the best policy out here in this deplorable pocket of nowhere.

Still, the Indian's buckskin dress hugged her full hips and buttocks in a way that excited Stutley. It excited him deeply.

He was suddenly aware that he hadn't heard Mister Donovan's last question. "I beg your pardon, sir?"

The Irishman's eyes lit up. "I see you have your eye on Pocahontas there, eh?"

"Pocahontas?"

Donovan winked. "Her real name's Walking Deer, or some such nonsense. After I assumed command here, I rechristened her

173

Pocahontas, after that poem, by Long-fellow." He leaned forward, an eager expression on his handsome face. "You are familiar with poetry now, aren't you?"

Stutley was again amazed by the man's literacy. Not only could he read, but he had read a lot. He made a clucking sound and nodded. "The depth of your knowledge amazes me, Mister Donovan. How did you end up in a place like . . ." He let his question taper off, realizing he might be venturing down the wrong path.

Donovan laughed. "The Jesuits. They recruited me for their ranks at an early age and taught me well. T'was my blessed mother's idea, and I did my best to accommodate them." He squeezed the blonde's breast again as Pocahontas came back with the bottle and two glasses. "Until I discovered the ladies and realized that a man wearing a dress and wanting to be called 'father' whilst taking a vow of celibacy wasn't for me."

Stutley was a Protestant and couldn't think of anything to say.

Donovan told the blonde girl to get off him. She emitted another one of her ear-grating squeals that set Stutley's teeth on edge. What a harpy.

"This gent and I have a bit of business to

discuss," Donovan said. "But don't go too far."

The blonde joined Pocahontas, and they walked hand in hand across the floor and down a narrow hallway at the back of the saloon.

Donovan pulled a table closer, set both glasses down, then poured some of the amber fluid into each. He picked up one and gestured for Stutley to pick up the other one. He did and, at Donovan's urging, took a bit of the liquid into his mouth. Its raw taste seared the inside of his mouth, and his first impulse was to spit it all out, but there was no place to void. Instead, he managed to swallow it, feeling the searing burn travel all the way down his gullet. When he finally managed to take a breath, he expelled it with a fit of coughing.

Donovan tossed his drink down and sat back with an amused look on his face.

"It take it you're not a drinking man?" he asked.

Still unable to talk, Stutley shrugged, hoping that would suffice.

Donovan poured a bit more into his glass again but left it on the table.

"Have you ever read the novels of Walter Scott?"

Stutley nodded. He'd heard of the man

but never read anything by him.

"The way he portrayed the outlaws," Donovan said. "Charitable criminals with hearts as pure as a leprechaun's gold. Rob Roy MacGregor and Locksley in *Ivanhoe.*"

"*Ivanhoe?*"

"Ah, yes." Donovan smiled. "Locksley helps the noble knight restore the rightful king to the throne. And Rob Roy Mac-Gregor. I remember reading about him when I was a wee bit of a lad. I wanted to be him, even though he was a Scot instead of an Irishman."

Stutley was finally getting his composure back.

Donovan leaned forward. Placing his elbows on his knees, he looked wistful as he said, "I've always had a secret yen" — he picked up a pair of the dime novels from Stutley's open sample case and held them up — "to be immortalized in a book, like Rob Roy. An outlaw who became a folk hero. And, perhaps now, I'll have that chance."

Stutley noticed one of the lackeys come bustling through the batwing doors, his head bobbling like a ball on a pivot.

"Boss," the man said. "I mean, Mister Donovan."

Donovan glared at the man and said,

"Can't you see I'm busy?"

The tone stopped the man as quickly as the point of a gun.

The point of a gun . . . Stutley made a mental note again to write down that line.

"Well," Donovan said, his face a mask of irritation. "What do you want?"

"It's Boswell," the man said, cocking his thumb toward the doors. "He's come to see you and says it's real important."

Donovan's face lost its irritation, and he straightened up.

"Tell him I'll be there shortly." He turned to Stutley and raised an eyebrow. "It seems I have business to attend to, laddie. In the meantime, may I offer you the diversion of one of my fine ladies for a bit whilst I attend to it?"

Stutley closed his eyes as a vision of Polly's grotesquely coquettish smile flashed in his memory.

On the Trail
The Indian Territories

Reeves and Bear placed the seven bodies in the wagon and moved them out of the clearing to a shady spot near a cluster of trees. It looked to be an appropriate resting place, and the two men set about burying the rangers. Several hours later, both covered in sweat, Reeves and Bear stood in front of the seven covered graves. These were all God-fearing lawmen, and leaving them unmarked seemed wrong. Reeves thought about placing a cross on each one but knew that was tantamount to inviting desecration in this part of the country. Instead, he and Bear left a pile of stones marking the spot. Hopefully, it would serve as a monument but not alert wandering vandals to the gravesite. There were too many renegades in the territories who would disturb the resting dead in hopes of finding something of value: a ring, a watch, or even some gold in the corpse's teeth. Instead, Reeves then carefully transplanted a cluster of wild flowers to the recently disturbed earth, hoping that the plants would flourish and form a natural marker.

Bear stood beside him watching as Reeves removed his hat and bowed his head. "Don't know the right words to say, but my mama used to be fond of the twenty-eighth psalm. Yay, though I walk through the valley of death, I shall fear no evil, for your rod and your staff, they comfort me."

After Reeves had completed his recitation, Bear said, "May the Great Spirit watch over them."

Reeves silently reaffirmed his pledge that

he would do his best to bring the rest of the outlaws who'd done this to justice.

"What now, *Gimoozabie?*" Bear asked, wiping away the sweat that had collected under his headband.

Reeves took out his handkerchief and wiped his own face, pondering their next move. The rangers had obviously been led into a death trap by two men known as Cooper and Crowe, and Reeves assumed, from the description, that the scared man he killed was Crowe. The other man with the plum nose needed his identity verified.

A search of their bodies and the area had turned up nothing besides a collection of weapons, watches, and rings they'd obviously stripped from the rangers' bodies. Reeves placed these items in a burlap sack and stowed it in the wagon. He'd committed to memory the mailing address the Ranger had recited to him and would see to it that the Ranger's star, and the possessions, were mailed back to his family. It was a matter of honor. Doing what was right, especially for another lawman, whether they served the same jurisdiction or not, was something he saw as his duty.

If that second dead man was the crooked Indian agent, Cooper, then the trail to the rest of the ambushers would be faint. But perhaps that town called Temptation would yield a few answers. If he took the two bodies there, maybe he could learn more, at the very least find out for sure who the two men he'd killed were. But, recalling what the man in the wagon had said, Temptation might not be the most hospitable of places for a lawman seeking information.

The rangers had been after the Cherokeos, so it was a good bet that they were behind the ambush. It had occurred in the Indian Territories, and, as a deputy marshal, Reeves had jurisdiction here. Additionally, he'd given his word to the last Ranger that the men responsible would be brought to justice.

Reeves pointed to the trail. "Let's see what the tracks tell us."

He and Bear moved over to the flat area and began scouring the ground. After about thirty seconds of looking, Bear grunted.

"Got some here."

Reeves joined him and studied the impressions and the surrounding area. "I'd say at least ten riders. And a wagon carrying some kind of heavy load."

"Like a Gatling gun."

"What you make out of these tracks here?"

Bear walked over and stared downward, moving his head slowly from right to left.

"Looks like some of them horses had no riders," he said.

"Just what I was thinking. Remember, the Ranger said the gang took their stars and their horses. Question is, why?"

Bear shrugged. "To sell?"

"Maybe. We need to find out a bit more about these Cherokeos."

"We gonna bring 'em in, *Gimoozabie*?"

"If you gonna keep callin' me that, I just might make up a new name for you."

Bear held his hand over his heart. "I told you, in the tongue of my people it is a name of respect."

Reeves chuckled. He'd ridden with Bear numerous times on these long chases, and the man's sense of humor always kept things interesting. "Yeah, well, maybe my new name for you will be something like Walks in Bear Dung."

"Hey." The Indian raised an eyebrow and looked insulted. "I told you, *Gimoozabie* means trusted friend — a name of respect and honor."

Reeves slung the shovel over his massive shoulder, turned, and walked back toward the wagon and their horses. "The white men we're tracking probably have a couple of special names for the likes of both of us that we'll be hearin' soon enough. And you can bet none of 'em gonna be related to respect or honor."

"You're probably right as the rain about that, *Gimoozabie.*"

Reeves shot him a harsh look, then continued walking.

Bear held his shovel by the middle of the handle and followed. "Hey," he said. "Wait for me, Bass."

CHAPTER 6

Temptation City
The Indian Territories

Donovan adjusted his gun belt as he strode toward the door and assessed the situation. The arrival of this dime novelist, this poetaster, had perhaps been arranged by the fates. He'd never looked upon this little foray here in Temptation as anything more than a temporary diversion, and the game was about played out. He surmised that if the Texas Rangers had come all this way, the little scam that Cooper and the now deceased Hobb had been running, the fictitious gang of *Cherokeos,* was pretty much finished. All that had been accomplished by killing that pig of a sheriff and recruiting Cooper and his crowd was to end up taking over the mortgage, so to speak. But it hadn't been totally without profit. Donovan had found Hobb's ill-gotten gains in a locked metal box the sheriff had stashed underneath the bed in his room. Donovan appreciated the sheer arrogance of man. Not only had he been hoarding a substantial amount of cash, he'd been sleeping over it and had the unmitigated gall to assume that no one would dare touch it.

Donovan glanced at the corner table as he went out. Cooper sat, with a bottle to keep him company. He'd most likely have a bit of a stash, as well. Locating it would be a bit more problematic, because the Indian agent, despite his obvious faults, had a tad more shrewdness than the late Sheriff Hobb. Additionally, he had more places to hide it. An office and a room at the boarding house. It could be either place, or perhaps both. Donovan knew the man was a mean drunk and made a mental note to keep an eye on him. Another problem that had come with assuming the mantle of leadership. With the Indian cattle shell game on its last legs, and the law on the trail, it might be a good time to jump ship.

Donovan smiled at the nautical reference, recalling the satisfaction he'd felt when he'd slit open the belly of that lard-ass who'd been taking advantage of Donovan's sainted mother. He weighed the choice of just grabbing Cooper and forcing him to turn over his stash, and then leaving this little hellhole before it got too hot, against the promise of the larger prize that Boswell had dangled before him.

He sighed. Regardless of which one he chose, one thing was certain. Much more scrutiny would be coming to visit, both by the law and the army. The latter would eventually be wondering about the whereabouts of their patrol that was supposed to be bringing in the Bulldog. Perhaps this was what Boswell had come to tell him. But the shiftless brigand of a soldier kept talking about the mother lode. He'd been as coy as a virgin at the whorehouse about revealing all the details, though, saying he had one more aspect to verify. Perhaps he was just making up the tune as he went along to keep on the right end of things.

Regardless, now was definitely the time to reevaluate all of the options.

Donovan saw the cavalryman standing by the water trough pouring the contents of his canteen over his head to cool off. His horse looked lathered as well and was partaking from the trough in copious fashion.

Donovan quickened his pace and reached the fake cavalryman in several bold strides. Boswell looked at him and started to grin, but Donovan pushed him out of the way and pulled the thirsty horse's muzzle out of the water.

"Didn't they teach you anything about horses, laddie?" Donovan rubbed his palms over the animal's wet neck. "Pour some of that water over him so he'll cool down in a proper fashion. Then let him drink a bit more."

Boswell stood there with his mouth agape, not moving.

Donovan grabbed the soldier's hat, filled it with water, and rubbed some of the liquid over the base of the horse's neck and shoulders.

"Hell, I was gonna do that," Boswell said.

"Then do it." Donovan shoved the half-full hat back to him.

Boswell glared at him as the water sloshed out of the hat and onto his shirt.

Donovan met the soldier's gaze and held it until the other man looked away.

"What are you doing here?" Donovan asked.

"Lots goin' on." Boswell emptied the hat and fanned it in the air, trying to dry it. "First, I wanted to tell ya they sent me out to look for the wagon 'cause it ain't showed up yet." His eyes drifted toward the bar. "Say, I could use me some whiskey."

"What else?"

"Well," Boswell's lips curled back over his misaligned teeth. "I could do with one of them whores, too."

Donovan's left hand flipped up and slapped him, not hard, but with enough impact to jerk the reverie out of him.

"Quit wasting my time, you bloody bugger. What else?"

Boswell rubbed the redness on his cheek. He stared back at Donovan with a mixture of fear and hatred. The former emotion evidently overruled the second, and he licked his lips.

"Hell, all I was saying was —"

Donovan raised his hand again, and Boswell stopped talking. After a pause of several seconds, he cleared his throat, looked down, and said, "I just wanted to tell ya, the gold shipment's on its way. Should be coming through day after tomorrow, or thereabouts."

Donovan assessed this new bit of information. This was indeed fortuitous. Just when he was beginning to get worried about things closing in with the rangers and the Cherokeos, the timetable had shifted in his favor. It was as if he'd reached the back row of the checkerboard and had another of his pieces crowned. Everything was falling into place. The gold was on its way here, the

Bulldog was waiting and ready to go, and, miraculously, his very own biographer had appeared to record the daring deeds of Marion Michael Donovan, the Rob Roy of the West.

Yes, he thought. That does have a bit of a ring to it.

On the Trail
The Indian Territories

Reeves pulled back on the reins, slowing the team bringing the wagon to a protracted halt. He scanned the darkening sky. Storm clouds. He figured they had perhaps an hour, maybe less, before the rains came. As far as he knew, the city of Temptation was about fifteen miles or so due west. To the east, a trail of smoke rose upward indicating someone was a lot closer. He looked to Bear, who was also studying the smoldering column.

"Must be that Indian camp," Bear said. "Supposed to be over that way. Cherokee, most likely, although this area up here's kind of a mixture."

Reeves thought for a moment. He had the bodies of Crowe and his compatriot wrapped in a blanket in the back of the wagon. It hadn't seemed right to bury them with the rangers, and neither did he want to leave the two corpses for the circling buzzards. Even though these two deserved no mercy, and were most likely now toiling in hell, leaving a man uncovered wasn't the right thing to do. And Reeves had taken an oath to do the right thing, as best he could. Additionally, he wanted to verify the identities of the two outlaws. From the description the dying Ranger had given, he was certain the scarred man was Crowe, but who was the other?

Reeves assumed that man had been Crowe's partner, and the Ranger had mentioned a crooked Indian agent named Cooper, which logic would point to as the second dead man. But how to confirm this was problematic. Neither Crowe nor his companion had any type of identification, not that Reeves would have been able to decipher any if they had. And, judging from the earlier report from the fleeing settler, the law in the town of Temptation might not be helpful either.

Sheriff Donovan, self-appointed lawman after a gunfight.

Reeves didn't like the sound of that situation.

Maybe the Indian village could shed some light on things. At the very least, they should be able to verify if the second dead man was Cooper, the Indian agent. And, if it wasn't, it gave Reeves another man to track down. Besides, he felt there was a lot more involved in all of this, especially if they had a Gatling gun.

"Let's us try that Indian village," Reeves said. "At worst, we can catch up on some rest and figure out a plan for checking out Temptation before we go ridin' in."

"It sounds good to me, *Gimoozabie.*"

Reeves felt his gut tighten in mild frustration. Bear's teasing had worn a little thin of late, but he knew his friend meant no true disrespect.

"It might just give me some time to figure out a new name for you, too," Reeves said, and he pulled the reins to steer the team toward the wavering tower of smoke on the horizon.

Polly's Room
Temptation City
Stutley felt drained, even though nothing substantial had actually happened between him and the girl, or should he say the *creature?* Whatever it had been, he could hardly call it pleasurable. Luckily, it was over with merciful quickness. Even with his eyes closed, the images of her dimpled, naked, white, ghoulish flesh, the pungent

190

muskiness of her body, of the matted hair of her armpits, and the breath of a dragon all seemed to converge upon him, quelling the embers of his passion as quickly as if a bucket of cold water had been thrown upon him.

"Well, that didn't take long," Polly said, swinging her legs over the side of the featherbed. "We might as well go back to the bar and see if Marion's back yet, huh?"

"Marion?" Stutley asked.

Polly giggled. "Big red. Don't call him by his first name, though. He gets real mad if you don't call him *Mister* Donovan."

"I know." Stutley retrieved his spectacles from the bedside table and put them on.

As she stood up, he noticed the lack of firmness to her form as she began squeezing herself back into the corset-like dress. "Just tell him you had a real good time, will ya?"

"Certainly," Stutley said, wishing he'd gone with the Indian girl. At least he could have closed his eyes and imagined the painting.

He pulled on his pants from the pile of his clothes and stood, carefully glancing over his shoulder to make sure Polly didn't see the money belt that he'd taken pains to hide.

He'd insisted on making a trip to the outhouse on the way to her room, despite her protestations that she had a nice chamber pot, a fact that she subsequently proved after he'd returned from the outside potty. She'd removed most of her clothes and was squatting over the pot when he came in, the money belt unfastened from around his waist and now carefully tied inside his pants. He'd even taken a coin, the lowest denomination he'd had, to give to the girl afterward, even though Donovan had told her it was "on the house." The last thing Stutley wanted to do was to provoke the Irish gunslinger by acting like an ingrate. Thus, the obligatory roll in the hay with Polly was not a choice, but an obligation.

Stutley slipped on his shirt and then turned his back, ostensibly in an offer of providing his companion with a modicum of privacy as she continued to force her bilious body into the stretched-to-the-limit fabric.

Polly laughed and said, "What you turning around for? You already seen everything, ain't ya?"

Stutley stayed with his back to her and turned his head just enough to flash a nervous smile while he looped the money belt around his waist again and quickly pulled his shirt over it.

Donovan's voice drifted in from the hallway.

"How are the two lovebirds?"

"We're fine," Stutley yelled. "Be out in a bit, Mister Donovan."

"Don't let me rush you," Donovan called back.

Stutley's shirt was still unbuttoned and hanging open as he buckled his pants and then turned to grabbed his hat and shoes. He hadn't thought it necessary to remove his stockings.

"Hey, what's that you're wearing?" Polly asked, pointing at him.

Oh, Lord, he thought. She's seen the money belt. He folded his arms across his chest.

"What?"

"That there." Her finger extended toward him, but not at his middle. Instead, she was indicating dangling suspenders.

"These?" He held one between his fingers. "They're called suspenders. They hold up my pants so I don't have to wear a belt."

"I thought I seen you wearing a belt?" She came forward and probed his middle with her fingers, tracing the edge of the leather money belt. "Yeah. What's this?"

Stutley felt another surge of panic grip his

spine. But perhaps he could salvage this. After all, she was as dumb as a box of horseshoes.

"Well," he said, slipping the suspenders over his shoulders as he edged toward the door. "That's what you call a truss. It's medicinal."

"Huh?"

"It holds in part of my bowel that's a bit ruptured." He patted his side.

"Oh," she said. "I heard of that. Hey, I'm glad you didn't shit in my bed. I ain't got time to do no washing."

That, Stutley thought, was an obvious understatement.

Feeling in desperate need of a distraction, he reached into his pants pocket and removed the coin.

"This is for you." He flipped it toward her, and she dropped the edge of the dress and used both hands to catch it.

"Thanks," she said, looking at the coin, and then jamming it between her teeth and biting down. Apparently satisfied it was real, she dropped it into the still-full chamber pot.

"You put it in there?" Stutley asked.

"So I know where it's at. And nobody'll try to take it from there." She smiled and rolled her shoulder at him. "So don't tell nobody."

Stutley opened the door and got out of the room as quickly as he could. He stumbled down the hallway while trying to make the final adjustments to his clothes. His fingers fumbled clumsily as he buttoned his shirt before pushing aside the raggedy curtain nailed to the top of the opening between the hallway and the bar area. The image of her dropping the coin into the chamber pot flashed in his memory.

That creature's a nightmare come to life, he thought. There was no way this was going in his journal. Well, perhaps with a bit of artistic license —

"Over here, laddie," Donovan called.

He saw the Irishman sitting at a table with another man who was wearing a uniform. A bottle and three shot glasses were in the middle. Stutley walked over to the table, straightening his clothes as he went.

A broad smile creased Donovan's face.

"Did you enjoy your session with Polly?" he asked.

Stutley managed to smile and nod.

"Good," Donovan said. "I was a bit worried I might have to rechristen you Lucy, instead of Lucien." He laughed and poured some whiskey into each of the three glasses. He held his high and said, "Now, here's to all the pretty ladies, wherever they may be."

Stutley reluctantly picked up his glass and delicately sipped it as the other two chugged theirs down.

The soldier looked at him with a grin that was more of a sneer than a smile. There was something about the man that reminded Stutley of a weasel. His cheeks bore at least two days' growth of beard, and his uniform shirt had four white concentric rings of sweat under each arm.

"This is Danny Boswell," Donovan said. "He's my right-hand man at the fort."

Boswell's head jerked fractionally, and he made no effort to shake hands. That suited Stutley just fine. After Polly, the less contact he had with anyone in the dreadful place, the better. Who knew where that hand had been recently, and what Boswell had done with it.

"Danny boy here's been a good soldier for a long time," Donovan said. "But he's set to get out of the cavalry soon."

Stutley watched as Boswell smirked.

"In fact," Donovan continued, "he's almost a civilian as we speak. We just have one little matter to attend to first."

This talk confused Stutley, and the small amount of whiskey he'd been obligated to drink felt like it was burning a hole in his stomach. He wasn't sure why the Irishman had introduced them, but figured he'd at least make an effort to initiate some conversation.

"Spent a lot of time fighting Indians?" Stutley asked.

Boswell poured himself another drink and snorted. "Not hardly," he said, bringing the glass to his mouth.

"Well," Stutley said. "What's it like being a soldier?"

"Mostly it's just been sleeping on the hard ground, never being warm at night, getting up at the crack of dawn to do a bunch of nothing for some worthless pieces of shit in command."

Stutley was somewhat shocked at the man's reply. It certainly didn't fit with the heroic image of the U.S. cavalrymen who rode the plains ensuring that settlers were safe and any renegade Indians were sent back to their reservations where they belonged.

"Ah, Danny boy," Donovan said. "Your testimonial's a bit harsh on this young man's idealism. He's here to write about the West."

The sneering smile remained on Boswell's face as he sipped more of the whiskey.

"Regardless," Donovan said, reaching over

to slap Boswell on the shoulder, "I promised him a bit of an interlude with Princess Polly before he got back under way for his patrol duties."

Boswell's eyes seemed to brighten at the prospect.

"That is," Donovan said, starting to pour another round of drinks, "assuming she's no longer so engaged." He hesitated with the bottle above Stutley's half-full glass. "Why, laddie, you hardly touched yours."

Stutley put a hand on his belly. "I'm feeling a little queer."

Donovan shrugged and set the bottle back down. He cocked his head toward the back rooms and told Boswell to go ahead. As the soldier started to get up, Donovan said, "And, after that, you head back to the fort tonight."

"Huh?" Boswell slumped back into his chair. "I was planning on staying here tonight."

Donovan shook his head. "I don't mind you stopping in here to wet your wick a bit, but, until the deed is done, you stay in your uniform and be a good soldier."

"Aw, Christ, Donovan." He started to get up again.

"What was that?"

Boswell muttered something else under

his breath, and, in the wink of an eye, Donovan had his gun out and was pointing it at the soldier's face.

"There's a bit of noise in here," Donovan said. "I couldn't quite hear you."

The soldier's eyes widened, and his hand gripped at his crotch, squeezing, and Stutley wondered if the man was going to piss his pants.

"Nothing," Boswell said. "I didn't say nothing."

"Aren't you forgetting something?" Donovan said.

Boswell stood frozen in place, as if he were afraid to move a muscle.

"Besides butchering the English language with your speech," Donovan continued, "you forgot to address me in the proper fashion."

Boswell swallowed, a look of bewilderment on his face.

Donovan placed his thumb on the hammer. "It's *Mister* Donovan. Get it?"

The soldier nodded.

Donovan cocked the weapon. "Then say it, you bloody bugger."

"I got it, Mister Donovan," Boswell said, his voice quavering.

"Eh? I didn't quite hear you."

Boswell repeated the sentence, still squeezing his crotch.

Donovan appraised the sentence and then slowly un-cocked the hammer of his revolver and lowered it.

"Very good," he said, holstering his weapon. "Now go ahead and dip your sorry little wick, and then get your arse back to the fort. Tell them that you found the bloody wagon, and they stopped here in Temptation to get the axle repaired."

Boswell's mouth twitched, and he nodded again, taking the glass of whiskey with him as he moved toward the back rooms.

"I wonder if she's cleaned herself yet?" Donovan said, then, with the trace of a smile, added, "But I doubt that bottom-feeder will even notice."

He chuckled and picked up his glass, but, before he could take the drink, a swarthy, heavyset man stumbled over to the table. Donovan set the glass down, and his right hand dropped out of sight.

Stutley felt a sudden surge of panic. He was certain, from the looks of the swarthy man's belt, that he was wearing a gun as well. Was this going to be a gunfight? Stutley leaned as far back as his chair would allow.

"Hey, Donovan," the swarthy man said. His words were sloppy, and he was obviously very drunk. "How does that damn blue belly get in the hog ranch, and I can't?" He cocked his thumb toward the back rooms.

Donovan leaned forward, his body shifting slightly. Stutley was sure he was drawing his gun from its holster.

"For one thing, Cooper, I run things here, and I told him he could," Donovan said. "And, for another, you're drunker than a sailor at a Portland port bar. You'd be wasting my girl's time and your money."

Cooper's face twisted with rage. He straightened up, swaying slightly, and pulled back his coat, revealing a gun in a holster.

Donovan continued to stare at him. "You go for that gun, you bloody bastard, and it'll be the last thing you ever do on God's green earth."

The words seemed to give Cooper pause, and he blinked copiously, licked his lips. "Where's Walking Deer? I want her."

"She's gone," Donovan said. "I gave her the evening off."

"Huh? Why, you can't do that."

"I can do any damn thing I please," Donovan said. "Now go crawl back into your bottle, if you know what's good for you."

Cooper swayed back and forth, apparently considering the Irishman's words. He lifted his right arm, extending his index finger as if to make a point.

The huge form of Finnegan appeared, looming over the teetering Cooper. He turned slightly and then looked up at the big half-breed.

"You'd better not ever point a finger at me again," Donovan said. "Or I'll have Finn here break it off and shove it up your bloody *arse.*"

Cooper's mouth puckered, and he lowered his hand.

Big Finn grinned, showing a row of crooked teeth.

The Indian agent belched slightly and then started to stagger away.

"And, damn, another thing . . ." Donovan said.

Cooper paused and glanced back. There was trepidation in the look.

"The next time you question my authority," Donovan said, "I'll blow a hole in your fat gut and watch you die nice and slow. Understand?"

Cooper's face showed that he did. He walked on unsteady legs back to the other part of the room.

"Want me to throw him out, Mister Donovan?" Finn asked.

Donovan watched Cooper's gait, then

shook his head.

"Just keep an eye on the bugger. Tell him he's going to buy a round for the house, and then send him on his merry way."

Finn smirked and went back into the main floor area and made the announcement. A hackneyed cheer resounded from the crowd. Texas-Mex sat at the bar and cleaned his fingernails with his thin-bladed knife while intently watching Cooper's reaction.

Stutley felt an exhilaration like none that he'd ever felt before. Being this close to life and death — two times in as many minutes. Almost seeing a man shot and killed right before his eyes, only a few feet away. This was great stuff. He pushed up his spectacles and patted his pockets for his notebook. He absolutely had to record all these experiences and the feelings that accompanied them.

"What are you doing?" Donovan's gaze had a lethal look to it.

Stutley realized the Irishman probably thought he was searching for a gun. He raised his hands in surrender. "I was just looking for my notebook. I've been keeping a journal."

Donovan's gaze softened slightly, then he laughed.

"Ah, yes, Lucien T. Stutley, the Walter

Scott of the West." He glanced back toward Cooper, who'd now settled into his chair with a dejected look on his face.

"Were you really going to shoot him?" Stutley asked, lowering his hands.

Donovan's eyes shifted to the author. "I never draw my gun without that specific intention in mind, but he hasn't quite outlived his usefulness. The son of a bitch should be thanking me."

Stutley raised his eyebrow. "Thanking you?"

Donovan leaned back in his chair and began a recitation: "There once was a surly man called Cooper, who walked 'round the hog ranch in a stupor, but an Indian maid, cut his throat with a blade, and they threw his sorry arse in the pooper."

His head lolled back in laugher, and then he lurched forward, slamming his forearms onto the table. "Ah, lad, you didn't know I was a bit of a poet, did you?"

Stutley found himself utterly fascinated by this captivating rogue.

Donovan laughed again. "A poetaster is closer to the truth."

Stutley took out his pencil and notebook. "Would you say that again so I can write it down?"

"There are more important things for you

to be writing."

Stutley waited, but Donovan didn't elaborate. Finally, Stutley asked, "So, let me get this straight. You think Pocahontas is dangerous?"

"You should never get so comfortable with a woman that you drop your guard around her." Donovan's eyes drifted over to the Indian agent, who was now slamming down one shot glass after another. "Besides, that man has a mean streak when it comes to women. It wouldn't surprise me if she does do him in one day. But, as I said, I still have a bit of use for Agent Cooper."

Stutley abandoned all hopes of writing anything in his notebook at the moment, vowing to do that later, after he'd retired to his room. He swallowed, trying to take in as much of this savage ambiance as he could. "Agent Cooper?"

"An envoy of the federal government, sent to these territories to look after the welfare of the red man." Donovan snorted a laugh. "You can see how seriously he takes his job."

"Walking Deer," Stutley asked. "That's the Indian girl? Pocahontas?"

" 'Tis. Not that I would've let him see her in his condition regardless, but the bit of irony is that I did tell her to take the evening off." He picked up the glass once again.

"The girl's in her monthly, and I didn't want anybody making a mess on those fine, white linen sheets tonight, in case I want to be visiting her in the morning." He tossed down the liquor and then refilled the glass.

Stutley was amazed that no matter how much the man seemed to drink, he never seemed to get intoxicated.

"Now that you've satisfied your curiosity about sweet Polly," Donovan said, leaning forward, "let's do a little talking about how I want you to write about Marion Michael Donovan, the Rob Roy of the West. Handle this with some artistic aplomb, and we'll both be in line for a bit of well-deserved fame."

Stutley flashed what he hoped appeared to be an eager grin, and it actually was. This was going to be one hell of a novel.

Cherokee Village
The Indian Territories
As they rode into the small village Reeves was struck by the starkness of the place. A few horses grazed nearby, tethered by a long rope to a horizontal log. One horse had a saddle, its reins lashed to a stunted pine tree. Only three houses made of woven saplings and plastered with mud under poplar-bark roofs were standing, and an old

man and two young males sat by a fire next to a blighted row of corn. The boys looked perhaps ten or eleven and were emaciated, staring up at them with hungry, empty eyes. They were hustled away by a few squaws.

Bear leaned over in his saddle and said something to one of the women, and she pointed to a house at the end of the encampment. Another old man sat in front of it, smoking a long pipe.

"That's the tribal chief," Bear said, looking around. "Or what's left of the tribe, which is not much."

"Kind of gathered that." Reeves could speak several Indian languages and had a working knowledge of Cherokee, but he wasn't totally familiar with all the words of this dialect.

Reeves halted the horses and set the wagon's brake. Bear dismounted and tied the reins of his horse to the wagon. They approached the old Indian together. He did not acknowledge their presence until Bear squatted down in front of him. Reeves glanced around the camp and saw the rest of it was in pitiful condition. He also squatted down so as to be on eye level with the old Indian.

Bear and the old man were already engaged in conversation. Reeves could understand a few words here and there and knew that Bear was describing him as a man of great integrity and honor.

Bear turned to him. "He asks if we have come about the missing beef."

"Missing beef?"

Bear nodded. "As that guy in the wagon said, it was part of the treaty. After they killed off all the buffalo, the government promised to provide beef to keep the tribes from venturing out of the territories and rustling from settlers." He smirked. "And we both know how good the government is at keeping its promises."

"Forty acres and a mule," Reeves said.

Despite having been enslaved by the Cherokees, Reeves still felt a twinge of compassion for the Indians. Both the black and the red races had been trampled on and lied to by the white man and his government, which bred a shared mistrust. He couldn't quite call it kinship between them, however, knowing they'd sided with the Confederacy during the war. But he didn't hate them for it. After all, to both the red and the black, the government was made up of white men intent on taking whatever they wanted, whenever they wanted. The Cherokee had already lost just about everything anyway. The only mistake they'd made during the war was picking the wrong horse in that particular race.

"Where are all the young braves?" Reeves asked.

Bear translated the question, and the old Indian's mouth twisted downward. When he spoke, his voice sounded brittle. After a bit of a discourse, he stopped, stared at Reeves, and then went back to smoking his pipe.

"He says many died on the Trail of Tears. The others left, a little at a time," Bear said. "Vanished. There is no hunting here, no food, except what they manage to grow. The government beef hardly ever arrives. Many of the young men were destroyed by the firewater the whites sold to them."

"Sold?" Reeves asked.

"The way it began, they traded what beef they had for the whiskey," Bear said. "When all the cows were gone, the white traders left and didn't come back. After that, many of the younglings left." He glanced at the old man, who passively stared at the fire. "Not much remains here . . . no life. He waits for death. What's left of his tribe waits with him. Soon they will be gone."

"Sad," Reeves said, thinking back on his own time as a slave: no hope, no future. Fortunately, things had changed for him.

These Indians weren't so lucky.

"Ask him if he knows anything about that Indian agent, Cooper."

Bear and the old man talked some more. From the tone of the words, it wasn't pleasant.

"He says Cooper is lower than even the snake," Bear said. "The lowest of the low. He came promising friendship to the tribe and betrayed them. He was the one who brought the whiskey, stole the beef."

The old man said something more. Reeves recognized one of the words: women.

Bear turned back to him. "He says Cooper has taken many squaws. They leave with him and are never seen again, save for one."

"One?"

Bear's eyes darted to the left, and Reeves turned to watch a young Indian woman approach. She wore a tight buckskin dress and moccasins. A thick scar ran down the tip of her nose, but she walked with alacrity and confidence. She carried two heavily laden saddlebags.

"What do you want here?" the young woman asked, her voice harsh and unforgiving. Her English was very good. She strode over to them and placed the saddlebags at the feet of the old man, who did not acknowledge her in any way.

Both Reeves and Bear stood.

"I'm Deputy Marshal Bass Reeves, ma'am. This here is Deputy Walks-As-Bear, from the Lighthorse."

Her expression showed no emotion, not curiosity, not fear.

"Lawmen?" She made a huffing sound. "I know all about your kind."

"Hey," Bear said. "I'm with the Lighthorse."

"The Lighthorse," the woman repeated with derision in her tone. "What good are you? You only make life more miserable for the Indian. You let the white man steal and destroy us. And you can't even arrest them, no matter what they do to an Indian."

Bear started to respond, then stopped.

"With all due respect, Ma'am," Reeves said. "You can't judge all of us by the misdeeds of others. We're here —"

"For what? To bring *justice* to my people?" Her expression was bitter.

"We're here to bring the law," Reeves said.

"The white man's law?" She looked him up and down and laughed. "And you're not even white."

"I'm a freeman, and a lawman," Reeves said. "The law don't know no color."

She glared at him. "You believe that?"

"That's the way I see it; that's the way I

make it."

She stood defiantly, and Reeves was suddenly cognizant that darkness had descended as the flickering of the fire danced over her features.

Finally, she relented and asked, "What do you want?" The question was the same, but the tone was less hostile.

Reeves gave her a quick account of why they'd come: the report of trouble with the Indians, white men known as Cherokeos selling whiskey and guns, the failure of the government beef program to provide adequately for the tribes.

"The *Cherokeos.*" She laughed. "There are only a handful of them. They made up that name and started telling people this gang was causing all the trouble. I heard them laughing about it. They didn't know I understood English as well as I do."

"Three men?" Reeves asked.

"Well, two now, unless the new sheriff takes the place of the man he killed."

Reeves and Bear exchanged glances.

"Who's that?" Reeves asked.

She stared at him. "I've said too much already."

"The Cherokeos," Reeves said. "Give us their names."

She shook her head.

Reeves felt his frustration growing. "Look, we found seven Texas Rangers back a ways. They'd been led into a trap."

Her eyes still flashed defiance. "So what?"

"We caught two of the men responsible," Reeves said, pointing toward the wagon.

The girl's face tightened. "Two men. Who?"

"We were hoping you could tell us," Reeves said. "I think one of them might be that Indian agent, Cooper."

The cords in the woman's neck tightened.

"They can't hurt you none," Reeves said. "They're dead."

She looked him over again. "You're not afraid to kill white men?"

"Not if they need killing."

This seemed to have a strange effect on her. Her whole body relaxed noticeably.

"It ain't so pretty," Bear said, "but we were hoping you could tell us if the one man is Cooper."

She nodded, and Reeves grabbed a burning stick from the fire to use for illumination. He kept one of his big hands cupped in front of it to protect the flame as they walked. Stopping by the rear of the wagon, Reeves told Bear to lower the back gate. Bear did so and then lifted the edge of the blanket they'd wrapped around the bodies.

The smell was horrendous, but, if it affected her she gave no sign. Reeves held the flame over the dead man's face, illuminating it.

The woman showed no emotion.

"It's not Cooper," she said. "His name was Franker. He was one of the regulars in Temptation."

"You knew him?" Reeves asked.

"Which one of you killed him?"

Bear and Reeves exchanged glances.

"That'd be me," Reeves said.

"Thank you." She spat on the dead man's face. "He was a pig. I'm glad he's dead. Show me the other one."

Bear looked at Reeves. The Lighthorse pulled the blanket back farther, exposing the scarred pate of the second dead man.

"That one's named Crowe." The woman spat on his face, too.

Bear smirked and covered the bodies.

"I take it you knew him, as well?" Reeves asked.

She turned and stared at him for several seconds. "And I'm sure you can figure out how." Her fingers touched her nose.

Reeves said nothing. He could tell the disfigurement had been intentionally inflicted. It was a common marking of an Indian woman who had been defiled by white men. Bear was silent as well. Finally,

Reeves said, "So, these dead men are part of the Cherokeos?"

"More or less," she said. "It was Crowe, the Indian agent Cooper, and a few others."

"How many others?"

She shrugged. "The sheriff, and whoever else he told to ride with them."

"The sheriff," Reeves said. "Named Hobb?"

"Yes."

"He's dead now," Reeves said. "Shot by a man called Donovan?"

Her eyebrows raised. "How do you know that?"

"Ran into some people on the trail."

"Yes," she said. "Donovan's the new boss in town. The new sheriff."

Reeves motioned for them to head back to the fire. When they got there, the old man was sorting through the saddlebags, which contained some biscuits and pieces of dried meat. He still made no acknowledgment of the young woman.

After a few moments of awkward silence, Reeves asked, "What can he tell us about the town?"

Bear addressed the chief once more. Reeves could understand a few phrases, which he interpreted as terms of disgust. When the old man finished speaking, he put the pipe back in his mouth and resumed his stoic posture.

"He calls it a pit of snakes," Bear said.

"It's worse than that," the woman said.

The old Indian looked up sharply, took a deep breath, and began talking in halting English. "It is as she says. Worse than snakes. The snake only seeks to live and takes only what he needs. The men in the town, Temptation, they live to kill for the sake of killing."

Reeves and Bear exchanged glances.

The old man laughed. "Yes, I speak your tongue. The missionaries came many years ago. I learned from them."

"Tell me more," Reeves said.

"First all the tribes were forced out here, away from their own lands, with the white man's promises," the old Indian said. "And, at first, these promises were kept. The tribes lived as best they could, for we were a beaten people. Then came the fighting — the white man's war, the blue and the gray. We were foolish and believed the gray would help us. They told us they would give us many things. In the end, they only took, as they had before."

"What about the town?" Reeves asked again.

"When the white man's iron horse came,

it pushed through Indian lands like the serpent goes through the grass, mostly unnoticed. The white men said it would bring good things to the Indian. The white men again promised that all would be good and built the town, paying the chiefs their money to stay on Indian land." He paused and placed a piece of dried meat from the saddlebag into his mouth. As he chewed, he continued his story. "Then they killed all the buffalo and promised us beef. The Indian agent lied to us. The beef stopped. The town was to be a village for the railroad, but that died as well. The serpent tracks went past it to the fort where the white soldiers live. Only the bad white men remain." He turned his face toward the woman, who looked at the ground. "And those who have shamed themselves."

"So the town became a gathering place for outlaws," Reeves said. He'd surmised as much. It was an all-too-common pattern in the territories. "Do you know anything more about the men who live there now?"

The old man said nothing.

Bear repeated the question in Cherokee.

The old Indian removed the pipe from his mouth. His face remained stoic as he spoke again. "You might ask an Indian squaw called Walking Deer. She was once my granddaughter but no more. She now lives there."

"Where can we find her?" Reeves asked.

"You already have," the woman said, her voice a shallow whisper.

In the flickering firelight, Reeves saw something akin to shame in those dark eyes. He took a deep breath, unsure of what to say next. The situation was all too familiar.

"They're all pigs there," she said. "Killers and thieves. There used to be a few decent people there, but they've mostly gone. I had a job there, cleaning rooms. The ones left cower in fear in their houses and stores and wait."

"Wait for what?"

Her lips twisted into a mirthless smile. "For the next group to come take what they want."

A few scant drops of rain touched their faces. Reeves looked up. The storm was almost here. He turned to Bear.

"Guess we got to ask him all polite like if we can bury Crowe and that other fella over yonder."

The old Indian's face twitched at the name. He muttered words in his native dialect that Reeves understood without the translation. Then he asked in English, "Crowe is dead?"

The woman, Walking Deer, nodded.

The old man's face retreated to its stern resolve once more. "Crowe was a coward. He hated the Indian because he was once scalped by the Creeks for trying to take a child. May the Great Spirit find him and make his spirit wander with no end."

"He was a bastard," Walking Deer said. Tears ran down over her high cheekbones. She got up and walked away. They all watched her disappear into the shadows. After a few moments the galloping of a horse's hooves was audible.

Reeves considered their options and decided a trip into Temptation was definitely in order, but they needed a base of operations. This was the logical spot. "Ask him for permission to camp here tonight and to leave our horses and wagon here for a day or two more. Tell him we'll pay."

Bear spoke to the old man in Cherokee. He replied in assent, then smiled at Reeves, showing the many gaps in his teeth. "Any man who killed Crowe is welcome in my camp."

Reeves reached into his pocket and felt for his supply of silver dollars. He carried them as a reward to give to people who helped him. Removing one, he handed it to Bear and motioned for him to give the coin to the old Indian.

The chief glanced at the glittering silver coin. "I do not want the white man's money," he said.

Reeves chuckled and extended his hands, pinching the flesh on the back of his left between his right thumb and forefinger. "I ain't no white man."

The old Indian chuckled and picked up the coin, looked at it, and began speaking. "It has great beauty. On one side, there is the eagle, and on the other, the face of a woman. I wonder . . . will this bring me luck in finding a new squaw?"

Reeves laughed. "Can't help you with that."

"How about two of your horses instead?" the old Indian said.

"I need mine and the ones for the wagon. As far as the others, they ain't mine to give. Got to turn 'em over to Judge Parker. But you're welcome to our extra food. Just don't take it all. We might be bringing back a few prisoners when we leave."

The old Indian looked at Reeves and then spoke in dialect to Bear.

"He says he senses you are a great warrior," Bear said. "He thanks you for the food and the coin. He will ask the Great Spirit to watch over you and me in our quest."

The rain was beginning to come down more noticeably, and a flash of lightning lit up the sky.

That storm was slow to get here, Reeves thought. But it's here now.

"Tell him thanks," Reeves said, standing up and placing four more silver dollars in front of the old Indian. "I've a feeling we're gonna need all the help we can get."

Temptation

The cacophony of the drunken men in the bar had settled into a dull hum. Stutley had finally been able to open his notebook and scribble a few lines as Donovan went to the piano, stood beside it, and announced he was going to sing an old Irish folksong.

Those in the bar hesitated, then, after an intimidating stare from the big half-breed, a smattering of applause broke out. The bartender whistled and gestured to a short guy dressed in a white shirt and rose-colored vest, who had been going around lighting the oil lamps. The short guy went to the piano seat and sat down, tapping a few of the keys.

"In Dublin's fair city," Donovan sang, waiting for the pianist to find the appropriate key. "Where the girls are so pretty . . ."

Stutley poured a bit more of the amber

liquid from the special bottle into his glass. He had to admit, the stuff had a distinctive taste and was even growing on him a bit. It still burned all the way down to his stomach, though. And he was suddenly cognizant that he'd fastened the money belt a bit too snugly. Perhaps a trip to the outhouse to adjust things would be in order.

" 'Twas there I first saw my sweet Molly Malone," Donovan sang.

The piano player was plunking on the keys with a rote skill now.

After recording a few more lines detailing the ambiance, Stutley stood on unsteady legs and began to make his way toward the hallway that led to the back rooms and the hog ranch.

The hog ranch. He'd have to think of a more delicate way to describe the series of rooms where the ladies of the evening plied their trade.

I'll have to use a bit of artistic license to describe them as well, he thought.

The pressing desire to urinate burned in his groin. He barely made it out the back door and across the twenty foot expanse to the odious privy, only to find it occupied by one of Donovan's ruffians when he tried to open the door. A light rain pelted his face as he stood there in the darkness.

"Be done in a bit," the occupant of the outhouse said, punctuating his statement with a low grunt. "Hand me another of them corncobs, will ya?"

It was so dark Stutley couldn't make out the man's features, but he appeared big and burly.

The crapper grunted again. "Gimme them damn corncobs."

"Corncobs?" Stutley glanced at a stack of cylindrical cones sitting on the shelf outside the structure and recoiled. "You want those? Two of them?"

"Yep. Dark one's for wiping and the light one's for testing," the man said, and farted mellifluously and sighed in relief. "Now gimme 'em."

The burning in Stutley's groin was getting overwhelming. He let the door swing shut and stepped to the side as the crapper inside said, "Hey, damn you!"

Stutley barely finished unbuttoning his fly before the release took place. He aimed the stream at the side of the privy, unconcerned that there were numerous gaps in the wooden slats. Hopefully, it would be put off by the crapper as rain.

The man inside swore again. "What the hell you doing? You pissin' on me?"

The harsh tone, and the concern that the

crapper might have a gun inside there, caused Stutley's stream of urine to diminish quicker than he would have liked. Any type of slight, real or imaginary, seemed to be a shooting offense around here. Tucking himself back into his trousers, he ran toward the building, not even bothering to button up.

Inside, he almost bumped into someone coming out of Polly's room. It was Boswell. The soldier was tucking his blue uniform shirt into his pants.

Stutley excused himself and hurried by him, pushing through the filthy curtain and getting into the main room of the bar just as Donovan was nearing the end of his song.

"She died of a fever," the Irishman sang.

Some bustling was occurring behind him, in the hallway. Stutley turned and saw a man in a struggle with Boswell in the hallway.

The crapper, Stutley thought. He must think that it was Boswell who'd pissed on him.

The voices of the two men escalated, causing Donovan to stop singing and motion to Finn and Texas-Mex to break things up. Stutley continued ambling toward the table in the secluded little cove where he and Donovan had been ensconced.

The big half-breed grabbed the two struggling men, pulling them apart and holding one in each of his massive hands.

"That son of a bitch pissed on me," the crapper was saying. His hand began fumbling with his holster.

"And you ruined my fine rendition of 'Sweet Molly Malone,'" Donovan said, raising his voice. He cast a glance at Texas-Mex.

The Mexican's right hand dipped toward his belt and then straightened out in a blurred motion. Seconds later, the hilt of a knife protruded from the crapper's belly, and the man howled in pain.

"Toss out the trash," Donovan said. "And send Danny boy on his way back to the fort."

Finn grunted and dragged both men toward the batwing doors, stopping near the bar to let the Mexican retrieve his knife. The crapper was still alive, groaning in pain, the front of his dirty, gray shirt awash with crimson as the blood began to drip on the floor.

Stutley couldn't believe it. He'd come so close. Despite his revulsion at the scene, a strange thrill danced up his spine. This must be what it felt like to face death and walk away.

"Well, it appears that our little boy in blue

took even less time than you," Donovan said, walking over to him. He sat down at the table.

"Is that man dead?" Stutley asked.

The Irishman shrugged. "If he isn't, I suspect he soon will be." He poured himself another drink and seemed to be contemplating something. Finally, after a few more seconds, he said, "I've got something I want to tell you, laddie. In the way of setting the grand stage for the book you're going to be writing about the Rob Roy of the West."

CHAPTER 7

Temptation City

It was mid-morning when Reeves rode into Temptation on one of the wagon-team horses with just a blanket and no saddle. The animal was functional enough and gave him the look he wanted. His own gray stallion was much too regal for this scouting mission, so he'd picked a mount to match his current incarnation: a rather bedraggled looking cowboy who had the look of being one step ahead of the law. Reeves had chosen a soiled, ripped shirt he kept in a burlap bag in his wagon. His pants were equally filthy, and the leather of the boots he wore was barely attached to the soles. He had many different disguises in his repertoire, ranging from a preacher to an itinerate cowpoke but figured this one, a down-on-his-luck fugitive, would work the best in the lawless town he saw stretching out before him.

The fleeing settler he and Bear had encountered had been right. The town had obviously been built with the best of intentions but had seen better days. Several houses and cabins lay on the outskirts, leading into a central street of well-crafted buildings that lined each side. One section by a big, two-storied structure even had a planked sidewalk. The bottom of the structure housed a pair of batwing doors at the front opening. A hand-painted sign, which Reeves couldn't read, hung above the doors, but he surmised the building was a bar of some sort. He heard raucous yelling coming from inside. What appeared to be a two-story boarding house was across from the saloon, but planks had been nailed over many of the windows now, and the paint had long since begun to fade and peel. A brick building next to it looked equally depleted. No children or families could be seen, and the burnt-out shell of one building that appeared to once have been a church, judging from the sagging wooden cross on the peak of the roof, stood dilapidated and abandoned. One house had a picket fence that now showed so many gaps in its line that it resembled a near-toothless beggar. A few stores still had open doors and intact windows, and Reeves figured them for the "smidgeon of decent folks" the man in the wagon had mentioned.

He rode past a livery stable that still looked operational and saw a boy rubbing down a horse while another, older male pounded a red-hot horseshoe on an anvil.

Reeves and Bear had taken the long way around, scouting the area as they approached. They'd found the set of dead-end railroad tracks the fleeing settler had mentioned. Foot-high weeds now sprouted up between the stone gravel and railroad ties. Reeves and Bear had split up there and decided to enter Temptation from opposite directions, figuring this would create less suspicion than two riders coming in together. And, at Reeves's behest, Bear had adopted an effective disguise as well.

Reeves rode past a few more dilapidated wooden buildings and stopped at the saloon. The second story that rested above it had the look of a hotel. Reeves assumed the brick and mortar building across the street had once been a bank. It looked deserted, which didn't surprise him, recalling what the old Indian had told them: virtually all the decent people had been driven out of town a long time ago.

Deliver us not into Temptation, Reeves thought as he rode up to the saloon and stopped.

He glanced around, scanning the area some more. Bear was coming in from the opposite side, the one closest to the Indian camp, but there was no sign of him yet. The plan was for the Lighthorse to find a suitable hiding place for his mount and then meander into Temptation on foot, disguised as a drunken Indian. Bear had reacted to the plan with his customary, wry comment: "After what the old chief told us, around these parts there most likely ain't no other kind."

Reeves dismounted and wrapped the reins around the hitching post as he stared through the opening above the batwing doors. The inside was about what he expected, given the description the fleeing settler had given him. Bright purple walls and a long bar that appeared to have a smooth wooden top. A long mirror behind it reflected a crowd of bodies between the shelves of bottles and glasses. The big room was crowded, and it was not even noon.

These fellers wouldn't know an honest day's work if it rode up and bit them on the ass, Reeves thought.

He placed his arms on top of the doors and peered inside. The odor of the whiskey was mixed with something else: a scent of cooked beans. There were a few plates scattered about on empty tables. There apparently was a kitchen of some sort in an adjacent room. At least fifteen or so men sat in a cluster in the center. One man stood with his back against the bar, delivering some kind of speech. Reeves regretted that he'd left his Colt .45 Peacemaker in the lockbox back in the wagon, but he figured that, for a man on the run, a well-maintained gun in a proper holster might look too out of place. He did have the gun Joseph Quint had given him tucked butt-forward in the left side of his belt, and the one he'd taken from Crowe, an 1873 Open Top Army Colt .45, tucked in the other side. But even with two guns, he was vastly outnumbered.

A tall man with red hair leaned with his back at the bar while a bunch of other seedy looking cowboys sat around him with expressions of adulation or fear, Reeves wasn't sure which. Something told him it was a mixture, with the latter being the dominant ingredient. The red-haired man wore a Remington .45 in a fancy holster slung low on his leg, and the partial edge of a sheriff's star on his blue shirt was visible under the edge of his black leather vest. The looping gold braid of a watch chain dangled from one of the vest's pockets.

Looks like the king's holding court, Reeves thought.

Most likely it was Donovan, and, if it was him, he had a lot of cohorts.

A bespectacled dude in a fancy suit sat at the closest table scribbling with a pencil on a piece of paper, and a giant stood at the other end of the bar. A fancy, round hat sat almost comically on the very top of his large head. He had the facial bones of an Indian, but his skin and eyes were light.

Half-breed, Reeves thought.

Something else caught his eye: a metal ring with six lawman stars hung above the bar. And not just any stars — Texas Ranger stars, like the one he'd accepted from the dying Ranger. Reeves was sure of it: this was most likely the right place.

"So all you'll be doing," the man Reeves assumed was Donovan was saying, "is watching and waiting until the time comes to start the lifting and loading."

Reeves pushed through the doors, and the red-haired man stopped talking. All the eyes in the place turned to stare.

"Hey, nigger," a fat man behind the bar said. "We don't serve your kind here. You see the sign?"

Reeves didn't let the word bother him.

He'd been called worse, and, besides, coming from a lard-ass cracker like that, it didn't mean anything anyway. And he also knew he had to remain faithful to the role he was playing: a black man down on his luck and on the run.

"Sign?" Reeves shook his head. "Never could do no readin' or writin', sir."

It grated on him to maintain the ruse of a shuffling, docile Negro, but it was what he had to do. He consoled himself that maybe, down the road a ways, there'd be a reckoning.

The bartender reached down behind the bar and came up with a Parker shotgun. Reeves pulled the Remington out of his belt and held it down by his leg, cocking back the hammer. Playing a role was one thing, but Reeves wasn't about to get shot by some Negro-hating, race-baiting son of a bitch.

Still, with the odds stacked against him, Reeves figured he'd at least be able to put a round into lard-ass and maybe fire another two as he made a rush for the doors. After that, he would probably not even make it to his horse before being cut down.

But if that was the way it was going to be, so be it. He felt the reassurance of the Remington's smooth handle in his hand.

"Why, Henry," the red-haired man said,

stepping forward and gesturing for the bartender to lower the Parker. Reeves caught another glimpse of a star on the man's shirt, partially hidden behind his leather vest. "There's no need to be so inhospitable. After all, he's what is known as a freeman now." He looked Reeves up and down, then grinned. "And he has the look of a man who's one step ahead of the Devil. Is that right?"

Reeves watched as the cracker bartender put the shotgun back under the bar. He made a mental note to remember it was there, in the likely event that he'd be making a return visit. He eased down the hammer and stuck the Remington back into his belt.

"I ain't looking for no trouble, sheriff." He tipped his hat and half turned toward the batwing doors.

"Sheriff?" The red-haired man's eyebrows rose, and he emitted a harsh laugh. Then he glanced down at his chest and laughed again. "We're on a bit of the informal side of the law here, my dark, freeman friend." He motioned for the bartender to pour Reeves a drink.

The lard-ass frowned, reached behind him, and got the bottle off the shelf. He poured the whiskey into a shot glass and shoved it down over the smooth wooden surface. It skidded over the surface, hit the end, and tipped over, spilling its contents.

Reeves stepped to the end of the bar but made no move to pick up the glass. He made sure he was still within leaping distance of the doors, should he need to take cover. The red-haired man seemed to take notice of this.

"The Lord watches over a cautious man," he said, seemingly impressed with Reeves's positioning. His voice tightened as he added, "Henry, you know better than to waste whiskey. Now go down and pour him another drink."

All eyes were upon him now, and Reeves suddenly noticed a pair of women entering the room. One was white and blonde, wearing a fancy plaid dress that was all puffy around her legs. Her face had a puffy look to it, as well. The other woman was tall and slender, with hair as black as a raven's wing, and a scar down the center of her nose. She was wearing the same buckskin dress that Reeves had seen her in the night before. Her dark eyes widened as she looked at him, and a silent recognition passed between the two of them.

He felt his gut tighten. She knew he was a lawman. One word from her, and he'd likely be gunned down before he could even draw.

For several seconds the room was draped with an eerie silence. The well-dressed dude sitting at one of the front tables leered at Reeves with a strange fascination, as if he were hoping for the gunplay to start.

The Indian girl kept staring at him.

Reeves waited, inching back from the bar, his right hand hovering over the handle of the Remington. He would use his left hand to draw the Colt Open Top from the other side.

"Well," the red-haired man said, "didn't you hear me?"

The lard-ass, Henry, picked up the bottle and said, "Yes, sir, Mister Donovan."

So the redhead was Donovan, just as Reeves had surmised.

Henry frowned as he waddled toward Reeves, righted the glass, and poured a finger into it. The bartender's beady eyes stared at Reeves with a look of pure hatred. Reeves made no motion to pick up the glass. He knew if he did, the temptation to throw it into the bigot's face would probably override his sense of discretion. Besides, if the Indian girl betrayed him, he'd need both hands free.

"Now don't tell me you aren't going to dignify my gracious hospitality by not imbibing," Donovan said.

"Sir," Reeves said, his eyes still on those of the bartender. "I 'preciates your kindness, but I can't handle no hard liquor whilst I be riding."

"Not a drinking man, eh?" A half smile crept over Donovan's face. "That leads me to surmise that there's no Irishmen hiding in your woodpile."

Reeves shook his head. "If'n you says so, sir."

Keep playing the role, he thought. *If she hasn't said nothing yet, maybe she won't.*

"Well," Donovan said, "what does bring you into my humblest of abodes, then?"

"With all due respect to you, sir," Reeves said, still feigning deference, "I been riding hard for a spell. I sure could use me a plate of beans, if'n' you got some to spare, sir."

Donovan smirked. "Beans over whiskey? You are a rare one."

Reeves kept the placid smile on his face. "I be glad to trade you a gun for a good meal, sir."

"A gun?" Donovan's left eyebrow arched upward. "What kind of gun?"

Reeves licked his lips, still playing his role of a nervous, down-on-his-luck cowpoke on the run. He gingerly withdrew the revolver that he'd taken from Crowe, held it up for

237

display, and set it on the bar.

Donovan motioned for the gun to be pushed toward him.

"What kind is it?" he asked.

"It's a seventy-two Open Top Army Colt forty-five, sir," Reeves said, giving the gun a shove.

"Is that a good one, Mister Donovan?" the dude sitting at the table asked.

Donovan glanced down at him, like he was deciding whether or not to slap him. He picked up the Open Top and immediately checked the cylinder.

"It's a bit of a relic," he said. "Shoots rim-fires."

"Yes, sir," Reeves said. "But I do have me some extra cartridges, sir."

Reeves figured the extra politeness would make him seem less of a threat. It was in keeping with his disguise.

Donovan hefted the gun in his hand, cocking back the hammer and checking the weapon's action. He lowered the hammer, then cocked it back again, repeating this several times.

The man knows how to handle a gun, Reeves thought.

He waited, his eyes drifting to the Indian woman. The old Indian had called her Walking Deer. Thus far, she had said nothing.

Reeves had a feeling that she wouldn't.

"Hell," one of the other cowpokes said. "I'll be durned if'n that don't look like Crowe's gun." He was a reed-thin man wearing a filthy, tan shirt. His face had a scruffy look to it.

Donovan's eyes narrowed, and he raised the Open Top and pointed it at Reeves.

"So tell me, darkie, where did you get this one?"

Reeves felt his gut tighten. He hadn't counted on any of the outlaws recognizing the dead man's gun. His mind raced back, trying to formulate a story that would keep him from getting shot.

"Crowe must have lost it," Walking Deer said. "He was always getting drunk."

"Shut *yer* mouth," the cowpoke said. "What you know 'bout him anyways, bitch?"

Donovan made a *tsk*ing sound as he cast a harsh glance at the cowpoke. "Now is that any way to speak to a lady?"

The cowpoke's mouth drew into a tight line.

Donovan turned back to Reeves. "Well, I asked you a question."

"I got it when I was on the trail," Reeves said slowly, picking up on the information that Walking Deer had provided. "Met up with a man and traded him some whiskey for it. He had him a bunch of new guns, and offered me that one."

Donovan considered this, then said, "Is that a fact?"

"It is, sir."

"That's a load of horse shit," the reed-thin man said. "Crowe wouldn't go trading with no nigger." He glared at Reeves, who stared back, ready to meet the man's challenge should he draw.

Donovan raised an eyebrow, then stuck the end of the barrel under his nose and sniffed it.

"Smells like it's been fired," he said.

Reeves figured his best chance was to continue with his ruse.

"Don't know nothin' 'bout that, sir. Him and this other man, they was pretty drunk. Sittin' there sayin' they run out of whiskey and wanted to know if'n I had me some. Well, I did in my saddlebags, and they offered up that there gun in trade."

"And what did this fellow look like?"

Reeves let his eyes meander toward the ceiling, as if he were having trouble recollecting.

"He was a white man. Had him some bad scars on the top of his head. I seen 'em cause he weren't wearin' no hat. The other

240

one, he was all passed out. Looked big and fat."

Donovan opened the weapon and checked the cylinder. "Looks like one round's been fired, which is appropriate." He snapped the weapon closed, scrutinized Reeves for a few more seconds, then said, "And our friend Crowe is always a tad more interested in the contents of a bottle as opposed to the contents of a cylinder." He set the gun on the bar and turned to the bartender. "I've always been a strong believer in free commerce. Henry, give the darkie here a plate of beans and a glass of beer." He glanced toward Reeves. "You can take it outside, laddie, but don't leave without bringing me the rest of those cartridges."

Reeves nodded. He'd seen all he needed to see: Donovan was the leader of fifteen heavily armed, hardened men. Outlaws. Killers. Bushwhackers, every last one of them, except perhaps for that slicked-up dude.

As he turned, Reeves overheard Donovan addressing one of the others. "Go back out there and find out why Crowe and Franker haven't yet returned. If they're still on a drunk, tell them I said they'd better get their arses back here."

Reeves half-turned to get a look and saw

Donovan was talking to the same reed-thin man who'd recognized Crowe's gun.

The thin man worked his tongue over his teeth, his expression hard as he walked by Reeves and toward the batwing doors.

The bartender, Henry, called out to the Indian girl, using the name "Pocahontas."

"Give this nigger a plate of beans and a beer," the lard-ass said and turned back to glare at Reeves with a scowl. "Outside."

Reeves stood waiting.

Walking Deer left the room and presently came back with a plate overflowing with reddish beans in one hand and a stein of beer in the other.

"Throw them things out after he's done," Henry said. "Don't bother washin' 'em."

Reeves thought that he would enjoy knocking that fat lard-ass down a peg of two, if and when the time came, and he hoped it would. For now, though, he had to wait. He held his hands out to accept the plate and beer when the batwing doors flew open, and Bear came tumbling through, his hands gripping a rope that was around his neck. He, too, had changed into filthy, raggedy clothes and had untied his long hair so it fell to his shoulders. Some of the hair was now tangled in the rope.

"Move it," a Mexican in a large *sombrero*

said from behind Bear. The Mex held the rope, walking Bear like a dog on a leash. "Hey, *Señor* Donovan, *mira.* Look what I find. This *mierda tonto* was sneaking around outside."

The Mexican forced Bear down on his knees in the middle of the floor. Reeves stayed frozen in place, his hands still free, waiting to see how this new event would play out. He regretted giving up the Open Top. If things went south, he would need all the firepower he could get.

Pulling out a knife, the Mexican held it against Bear's neck, the tip digging into his skin, causing a thread of crimson to trickle downward.

Donovan looked at the Indian girl. "Do you know him, lass?"

She stood, still holding the plate of beans and the beer. Her dark eyes studied Bear, then she said, "He's from the tribe. Left a long time ago. He's harmless."

Donovan eyed her for several seconds, then glanced back at Bear. "Is that right, chief? Are you a once-noble savage who turned into just another drunken Indian?"

Bear gasped, seemingly unable to speak.

Reeves figured if things got any worse, he'd shoot the Mexican first, then drop Donovan second. After that, he'd go for the bartender but probably wouldn't be around to fire a fourth time.

"Answer the man, *tonto mierda,*" the Mexican said, digging the point of the knife in deeper. The blood flow increased, but the wound still looked minor.

"You got firewater?" Bear croaked. "Me lookin' for firewater. Me clean 'em horses. Shit house. Good job. Gimme firewater."

"So you like shoveling the *horsesheit,* do you?" Donovan said with a smile. Then, his face dropped all signs of mirth. "Let him go."

Reeves wondered if that meant that Donovan was going to shoot Bear. He held his hand over the Remington and got ready.

"Aw, lemme cut his throat," the Mexican said, his lips curling into an evil smile.

Donovan waved his hand dismissively. "Let the once noble savage be on his way. I'm about ready to do another rendition of 'Sweet Molly Malone,' and I don't want to stink up the air in here any more than it already is."

The Mexican's face took on a sour expression. "Aw, *heeell.*" He slipped the knife back into a sheath on his belt.

Reeves took notice of the knife's location. The Mexican looked like he knew how to use it.

Donovan turned to the big half-breed. "Finn, toss the bugger out by the side of the building and let him sleep it off. Once he sobers up a tad, we'll have him clean the stables. The odor was getting a tad pungent when I was last there." He looked at the Indian girl. "Besides, for all we know, he might be related to Pocahontas, here."

Walking Deer said nothing, still holding the plate and beer.

The Mexican's lips bunched together, but he loosened the rope. Bear pulled it from around his neck and shook his head free. For a moment Reeves worried that Bear would turn around and hit the Mexican. Reeves wouldn't blame him. If the roles had been reversed, Reeves would have knocked the bastard into the bone orchard.

But Bear caught Reeves's eye, signaling he was all right and would keep to his role as the drunken Indian.

The giant half-breed lumbered forward, but Bear began scurrying toward the doors. The Mexican kicked him hard on the ass.

"Salga, mierda," the Mex said. *"Tonto."*

"Are drunken Indians a problem around here, Mister Donovan?" the dude asked, his pencil poised over the paper.

"No more so than errant darkies." Donovan looked at Reeves again. "And you take

245

your leave as well."

As Reeves turned toward the doors, Donovan called out, "Hey, freeman."

Reeves froze.

"You forgot your beans and beer," Donovan said.

Reeves turned around and accepted the plate and the stein from the Indian girl. Her dark eyes flashed knowingly at him, then she turned to leave.

"Beggin' your pardon, ma'am," Reeves said. "But would you be having an extra spoon I could use?"

"Use *yer* damn fingers," the barkeep growled.

Donovan made the *tsk*ing sound again and told Walking Deer to fetch a spoon.

"Thank you, sir," Reeves said and followed Bear out the doors. When they were both outside and Reeves estimated that they were out of earshot he whispered to Bear, asking if he was all right. He nodded fractionally and kept rubbing his neck. His hair still falling around his shoulders gave him a wild look.

"What was that stinkin' Mex calling me?" His voice was hoarse.

"*Mierda tonto,*" Reeves said. "*Tonto* means 'stupid' in Spanish." He grinned. "I don't have to tell you what *mierda* means, do I?"

246

"Shit. I owe that bastard one," Bear whispered back. "I was trying to listen in on what was going on inside there, and he snuck up on me." He rubbed his neck some more. "When the time comes, he's mine."

Walking Deer suddenly pushed through the batwing doors, her eyes darting back inside. She held out a spoon toward Reeves as she glanced back into the bar. "You both better get out of here now," she said in a hushed tone. "He'll kill you if he finds out who you really are."

"Much obliged, ma'am," Reeves said as he accepted the spoon.

She looked at each of them a moment more and then went back inside.

"What a woman," Bear whispered. "Even with that scar, she's something, ain't she?"

They both watched as the reed-thin man in the tan shirt rode slowly by them. He spat as he passed.

"Friend of yours?" Bear asked, his face breaking into a grin.

"Not hardly. He's headed out to check on Crowe and his buddy at the ambush site." Reeves took note of the horse's now escalating gait. The thin man appeared to be in a hurry.

"We best not let him find them graves," Bear said in a whisper. "We don't want him coming back to tell that guy Donovan."

"We best not," Reeves said in an equally low voice. He smirked. "And that's *Mister* Donovan."

Bear shot Reeves a knowing wink and staggered away in the direction of the stables. Reeves figured his partner had stashed his horse somewhere in that direction. Squatting down, Reeves quickly ate the beans and drank a few swallows of beer. It was warm and flat.

A rider came galloping in from the west, his horse lathered up from the pace. He pulled the animal to a halt, jumped off, wrapped the reins around the hitching rail, and ran through the batwing doors. They continued to swing wildly after his passage.

"Mister Donovan," the rider, who was as lathered up as his horse, yelled as he entered. "I got some news. Boswell says to tell ya the train already done left a lot earlier from Denver."

Reeves remained where he was, straining his ears to hear more, but all he heard was Donovan's stern voice.

"Lower your voice, you goddamn idiot." The harsh words were followed by the sound of a meaty slap and a yelp of pain.

Reeves finished the beans and saw that Bear had disappeared from the dusty street.

It was time for him to take his leave as well. For now, anyway.

He took another sip of beer and worked the sour liquid around in his mouth before spitting it out. Glancing back through the doors, Reeves took one more look inside before setting the plate and stein down by the entrance.

There was more to be learned here, but not with this masquerade. He had a different tactic in mind.

And I got me a rider to catch, he thought as he untied the reins and swung up on his horse.

Temptation City

Donovan guided the dime novelist across the dusty street, keeping an eye out for the darkie and the drunken Indian. Both of them appearing unexpectedly in Temptation had struck him as a tad strange. A co-incidence? Still, he saw no trace of them now, and neither of the two seemed to merit any more consideration. The darkie had probably ridden on his way, worried the law or some of the inhospitable bar population would be tracking him down, and the Indian was most likely curled up in a nearby gutter somewhere.

Stutley wobbled as he walked, and Donovan grabbed the man's shoulders and steered him toward the stables.

Too much of the Devil's brew, thought Donovan.

He'd have to have one of the girls put the bugger to bed to sleep it off.

The news that the train had left Denver earlier than anticipated also ate away at his thoughts. He'd have to depend on Boswell to get him the approximate time of arrival at the water stop. Perhaps cutting off the liquor at the bar now would be prudent to ensure an alert crew in the wee hours of the morning when the train would most likely arrive. But, then again, he didn't need them too alert. The Bulldog would do most of the work eliminating the soldiers, and then it would only be a matter of loading the cargo into the wagons for transportation south. Once they were set up down there, the lackeys could be rounded up and eliminated in a proper and expedient fashion. A celebration of their success would be in order, and the Bulldog could provide the final bell.

"How much farther, Mister Donovan?" Stutley asked, his feet zigzagging with every step. "I think I might be getting sick."

"Ah, laddie, I fear that I've led you astray by giving you too much of a good thing. If you feel the need to empty your gullet, go right ahead. Just give me a bit of advance notice so I might be stepping out of the way."

Stutley turned his head to smile, and then the sudden disappearance of his simper gave Donovan all the forewarning he needed. He deftly stepped back as the dime novelist bent over and vomited.

Such a price I have to pay to become the Rob Roy of the West, he thought.

But soon he'd have enough money to set up his own kingdom in Mexico and to send for his sainted mother and his two sisters, if he could find them back East and if, the Lord be willing, they were still among the living. His younger brother had passed shortly after they'd arrived in Boston. Donovan longed for what was left of his family to be reunited in some fashion, but it remained a bit of a fancy.

Stutley finally straightened up and wiped his lips with the back of his hand.

"Sorry," he said.

Donovan slapped him on the back and urged him forward, gingerly stepping around the little puddle that was quickly being absorbed into the dust of the street.

"No harm done, laddie. Just don't be a putting any of that in the story you're going to write about me."

Stutley's idiotic simper returned as he marched forward on still unsteady legs.

They came to the stables, and Donovan glanced around once more for the Indian and the darkie. Neither one was anywhere to be seen, which satisfied him a bit more. Not that he felt they represented any real threat to his plan, but he didn't want any prying eyes either. The necessity of managing the drunken gang of outlaws was a precarious enough path to walk.

Donovan made sure that Stutley was steady enough on his feet not to keel over and then moved to pull open one of the large doors. The whiff of air sailing out was increasingly pungent with horse manure, and Donovan glanced back to be sure that the smell wouldn't make the dime novelist heave again.

The lad looked unvarying enough. Donovan motioned for the other man to follow and went inside.

Stutley brought his hand up and pinched his nose. "Gosh, the smell —"

"Keep breathing through your nose, and it'll settle down a bit," Donovan said. "It appears as though that damn drunken Indian wandered off to find another bottle before he could do an honest day's work. Perhaps I should've let Texas-Mex cut his throat after all."

Stutley lowered his hand and blinked several times.

"But," Donovan said, " 'tis of no importance. I've got something to show you that I want handled with all of your literary aplomb when you write about me."

He moved forward into the dark interior of the large stable. The windows had been boarded over, but slits of the fading afternoon sunlight filtered in through the haphazardly placed planks, illuminating the agitated dust motes and dappling the dirt floor with uneven patterns of light. A couple of the horses whinnied and began stomping about within the confines of their respective stalls.

Donovan closed the door behind them and grabbed a lantern. Lifting the glass, he pulled out a big wooden match and flicked it with his thumbnail. The nearest horses whinnied with discomfort and fear. The glass being lowered over the burning wick magnified the illumination. The stable was filled with the animals, at least twenty of them. As he and Stutley moved farther in, the stench became stronger.

Stutley coughed again and Donovan gave him a quick look. "Feeling the urge again, laddie?"

"Huh-un. Just not used to smelling so many horses."

Donovan laughed. "Take note of it for your own edification. I don't plan on us being in this place much longer."

"Why're we here?"

"Patience, laddie, patience." Donovan debated again whether or not to show his hand to this Eastern dude but decided it might make a good scene in the novel. He tapped his index finger on the side of his head. "It is the plan of all plans."

Stutley had the grin plastered on his face, but Donovan could tell the man's stomach was still roiling.

Best be ready for another case of the heaves coming back on him, Donovan thought. He lifted the lantern and pointed. "Over here."

They walked in the dark interior toward the rear stalls. It was a huge place, and Donovan saw Stutley stealing a glimpse of the three large wagons off in the corner. Each one had a dirty, tan canvas covering its bed, the yokes stretched out in front.

Donovan strode toward them and stopped, turning around with a broad smile on this face. He reached in his pocket and took out a long, crumpled cigar, placing it between his lips.

Stutley eyed the cigar with an envious yearning.

"Ah, laddie, I'll give you one of these fine cigars, courtesy of the late Sheriff Hobb, but you have to promise me not to light it. We don't want to be smoking inside the stables."

The dime novelist nodded eagerly. Donovan reached inside his vest pocket, withdrew another cigar, and handed it to Stutley, who placed it in his mouth and stood there smiling, like a proud papa.

Donovan rolled the unlighted cigar between his lips, and canted his head to one side. "Remember that soldier boy I let get friendly with Polly after you'd had your way with her?"

"I do," Stutley said.

"Well," Donovan said, "little Danny boy's not much of a soldier to speak of, but he's a wealth of information. He told me about a train that left Denver a few days ago, going to be bringing something big to points east."

"Denver?"

"Aye. There's a national mint there, my boy. That's where they fashion those gold coins that they store in another mint in the East. The railroad runs through the territories from fort to fort. They'll be stopping near here."

255

"They will?"

Donovan's eyes narrowed for a moment, then he said with a hushed reverence, "It's a king's ransom in gold coins, laddie."

Stutley blinked several times and then asked, "And you're going to steal it?"

Donovan forced a benign smile onto his face. Either this bugger was as dense as the Blarney Stone, or the rot gut had dulled his senses.

But he's the only game in town. Why couldn't I have gotten a biographer as skilled as Johnson's Boswell?

He laughed at that comparison. He already had one Boswell, and that one was certainly enough. "Aye," he told Stutley. "Newly minted gold coins from the National Mint in Denver, bound for Philadelphia. In excess of twenty thousand dollars, or so I've been told. Enough for me to start my own empire a bit south of the border."

In the lantern light Donovan could see a look of confusion on Stutley's face.

"That's a lot of gold," the dime novelist said. "How're you going to do it? I mean, if it's on a train, and all. And with the soldiers guarding it."

"Sounds a tad problematic, doesn't it?" Donovan said. "An impossible task."

Stutley blinked and nodded agreement.

"That's what the generals would have you believe." Donovan motioned for Stutley to follow him through the stables toward the rear door. "But, as they say, the devil's in the details, and I've got an ace of diamonds up my sleeve."

It was time to show the novelist why he'll be writing that Marion Michael Donovan was the Rob Roy of the West.

The putrid odor of the horse shit in the stable was making Stutley's guts twist again. He swallowed, his stomach still roiling, and wondered if the swirling inebriation was now affecting his better judgment. Otherwise, he hardly would have said, "Pardon me for playing the devil's advocate, Mister Donovan, but —"

"Hush. No more jabbering until you've seen it."

"Seen it?" Stutley felt totally confused. "But —"

"Dammit, laddie. What did I just tell you?"

"Oh." Stutley could feel the whiskey's effects. He couldn't remember getting so drunk so fast. Of course, he hadn't eaten all day. He swallowed hard, wishing he at least had a crust of bread to gobble down. The unlit cigar between his lips was making him feel worse. It tasted acrid and bitter. He blinked twice, trying to clear his head and formulate his next question so it wouldn't offend the Irishman. Stutley desperately wanted to get the plan straight for the sake of his story, and what a story it would be. He'd be famous.

"Come on, hurry your arse up, laddie," Donovan said, his voice a low growl. "We haven't got all day."

Stutley forced all the fanciful thoughts out of his head. He started to speak, but the roiling suddenly reached a critical point again, and he felt the bile surging upward. Holding his gut, he ran to the corner, bent over, and regurgitated. When he finished, he looked down and saw the cigar in the midst of the vomit.

When he straightened up and wiped his mouth, he saw Donovan chuckling. "Still not holding your liquor too well, eh, laddie?"

"It's just that, um, I haven't eaten yet today."

Donovan grunted a laugh and unbuttoned his fly. "Well, I've got to get rid of some of that Devil's brew myself. But from the other end." He turned and began urinating on the support post.

"Should you be doing that in here?" Stutley asked. A second later he realized what he'd said. There was still a sufficient amount of liquor in his system to override caution.

Donovan was finishing up. "Ah, it's not like anyone's likely to notice with all this horse *sheit* around. You've got some on your shoes, by the way."

Stutley glanced done and saw the smears from toe to spats. He tried to bend down to wipe it off, but then realized that would just get it on his fingers. He straightened up. "What were you saying about the devil?"

"The devil?" Donovan laughed. "For a man of letters, you seem a tad lacking in the finer points of the English tongue, laddie." He paused and cast a look askance at Stutley. "Perhaps I should consider writing the bloody book myself."

Stutley blinked again, his faculties slowed but not dimmed. At least he didn't think so. "Oh, no, Mister Donovan. Please. You've got to let me write it. I'll do a good job. I promise."

The Irishman stared at him for several seconds and then grinned. "I was pulling your leg like a playful leprechaun, my boy. If all goes as planned, I won't even be around these parts to write it. I have a special ending in mind that I want you to do." He stopped and took the cigar out of his mouth. "Now, what was it you wanted to ask me?"

Stutley couldn't recall. His mind raced for a suitable question. "That's a lot of gold. How will you transport it? I mean, if they're using a train . . ."

Donovan held the lantern higher and pointed with his free hand — his gun hand, Stutley noticed with relief. "See those wagons there?"

Stutley looked. He remembered seeing the three huge vessels when they'd come in. He managed a nod.

"Between the three of them," Donovan said, "I'll have enough space to haul whatever cargo they're transporting. I've got an extra supply of horses, as well. Thanks to those stanchions of liberty, the Texas Rangers." He emitted a low chuckle.

Stutley laughed reflexively, then asked, "But didn't you say there will be soldiers on the train?"

Donovan frowned. "That I did."

"Well, I mean, aren't you afraid they'll . . ." He searched for the right way to phrase it.

"I'm not finished with your edification, laddie." Donovan motioned with his head for the dime novelist to follow. They went out the rear door, toward a shed about thirty feet away. The door had been chained shut, and another wagon, a slightly smaller version, was parked next to it. Donovan worked his fingers into his pants pocket and withdrew a key, which he stuck in the lock securing the chain on the shed door.

The lock popped open, and he pulled the chain out of the hasps on the doors. The Irishman turned to face Stutley.

"This will prove more than a match for any guardian soldiers," he said and stepped back as he pulled open the doors.

Stutley saw a canvas shroud covering some large mechanical item. Donovan grabbed the canvas and pulled it away, holding the lantern over a gleaming round barrel that looked like some sort of cannon. But instead of an open-ended bore, this one had a circular plate with ten holes. The handle of a sturdy crank was at the other end. Stutley struggled once again to find the right phrasing. "Is that . . ." He blinked again, trying to formulate a sentence.

Donovan chuckled, and this time Stutley felt it had a more sinister sound to it.

"Is that what I think it is?" Stutley asked, finally finding the words. In the lantern light he saw a look of pure ecstasy on the Irishman's face. "A Gatling gun?"

"Aye. It's called the Bulldog."

CHAPTER 8

On the Trail
Indian Territories

Reeves had kept his deputy marshal's star out of sight in his pocket when he'd visited Temptation, but he now removed it and pinned it to his shirt as he and Bear rode toward the ambush site. They had almost arrived when they caught sight of the spiraling dust cloud in the distance that indicated the rapid approach of a rider.

Reeves surveyed the unevenness of the ground and pointed to the left.

"Go over there and stay out of sight," he said. "It's probably our boy coming back, and he'll be less likely to stop if he sees the two of us."

Bear, whose hair was still hanging around his shoulders, said, "Sure thing, *Gimooza-bie.*"

Reeves shot a quick look at him but smiled instead of showing irritation.

"You'd best get moving," he said. "Unless you want me to bring up what that Mex was calling you back in town."

Bear frowned and tapped his heels against his horse's flanks.

Reeves laughed out loud as his partner rode off toward a swath of trees and brush, resisting the temptation to call out after him asking how he liked being called out of his name.

He turned his attention to the approaching rider. As the man drew closer, Reeves was certain that it was the reed-thin man from the saloon. Slowing his horse, Reeves pulled on the reins and steered the animal so that his left side was now facing the approaching rider. Then he pulled the Remington out of his belt and held it out of sight, down by his right thigh.

The rider slowed his horse as he approached, first to a lope, then to a halt about twenty feet away from Reeves. It was indeed the reed-thin man that Donovan had dispatched to find Crowe.

The man's eyes narrowed. "What you doing here, nigger?"

Reeves smirked at the insult. "Find what you were looking for?"

The man's mouth twisted into a nasty snarl. "How'd you know where I was?"

"Easy enough. I passed by here before."

As his horse pawed at the dirt, apparently sensing the coming danger, Reeves kept the reins tight with his left hand but rubbed the animal's neck with his right wrist, his hand still holding the Remington out of the thin man's sight.

"You didn't find your friend Crowe, did you?" Reeves asked.

The ugly snarl deepened. "How'd you know that?"

"I know a lot. Like how your bunch has been running illegal whiskey and guns in the territories. I'll bet you were in on killing them rangers, too, wasn't you?"

The thin man's eyes widened. "Who the hell are you?"

With his left hand, Reeves slowly pulled his jacket back, displaying his star. "I'm Deputy Marshal Bass Reeves, and you are under arrest."

The thin man's hand went for his gun, but Reeves brought his up, cocking the hammer back and firing in one smooth motion.

The thin man's body jerked, but he continued to draw his gun.

Reeves steadied his horse, which had jumped at the sudden explosion of the round, and then fired his Remington again, this time striking the thin man in the neck.

The man reeled backward, his hands reaching for his throat, gurgling as he tumbled from his saddle and onto the dirt.

Reeves maneuvered his horse a bit more, moving forward and turning so he had a better view of his adversary. Cocking back the hammer once more, he pointed the gun at the crumpled form and waited.

The reed-thin man lay face down on the ground. He didn't move.

Reeves slid off the horse's back and landed on the ground, his thumb securing the hammer to keep the weapon from firing prematurely. Stepping over, he knelt on the small of the fallen man's back, pulling his gun from its holster and tossing it aside. Reeves then rotated the body to check the man's carotid but felt no pulse. The round from the Remington had gone completely through, causing a crimson tear out the back of the neck. Blood was seeping into the dirt under the thin man's face. His right eye stared sightlessly into space, and a line of crimson seeped from the lower corner of his mouth.

Bear came riding up, coming to a stop several feet away.

"Bagged another one, eh, *Gimoozabie*?" he said.

265

Reeves winced. He took no pleasure in killing but didn't hesitate when it had to be done.

"Sure did, *tonto,*" Reeves said, then added, "I already done told you that means stupid in Spanish, didn't I?"

Bear stared down at him with a grin and pointed at the dead man. "Looks like he's the stupid one. What's our next move?"

Reeves stood up and tucked the Remington back into his belt. He reached over and patted his horse's muzzle, making soft cooing noises to help calm the animal. After a few seconds he glanced up at Bear.

"First, we find a suitable resting place for this fellow." He cocked his head down at the body. "Better take him away from this spot, though, just in case Donovan sends somebody else to see what's keeping him."

"Don't you mean *Mister* Donovan?" Bear said with a grin.

"I mean to take *Mister* Donovan into custody for killing them rangers." He stooped down and grabbed the lifeless body, lifting him as easily as he would a wayward calf.

Bear dismounted and helped Reeves adjust the dead man over the saddle of the Indian's horse. "And how we gonna do that, with all them hired guns backing him up?

They outnumber us three to one."

"Three to two," Reeves said.

Bear laughed. "Don't forget, I don't have any authority to arrest no white men."

"That ain't never stopped you from putting a bullet or two in 'em."

"Just don't tell Judge Parker."

Satisfied that the thin man's body would stay in place for the moment, Reeves walked over to his horse and jumped aboard. All of the horses shuffled about uneasily as the smell of death permeated the air.

"Let's ride," Reeves said. "Got to think some on our next move."

"We going back to that town tonight?"

Reeves nodded.

Once again, he thought, *Deliver us into Temptation.*

Temptation City

Donovan watched as Polly and Pocahontas helped Stutley up the stairs to his room. The bloody bugger had vomited once again in one of the spittoons near the bar. Donovan had elected to remain at the bottom and let them do the honors, lest the poetaster get the heaves again. He swayed a bit as they crested the top, and both women strained to keep the idiot from falling backwards. He took a few staggering steps forward and began to retch again, this time catching both of his helpers with some of the spraying puke. Polly screamed in anger and slapped his face. The Indian girl remained stoic.

Donovan laughed and shouted, "Put him to bed and then clean yourselves up."

Polly shot him an angry look but knew better than to say anything.

Donovan held her gaze until she turned away.

Yes, he thought. She knows better.

Of the two of them, he preferred the Indian's lithe body to the more fleshy tones of the white girl. But it mattered little at this point. With the train fast approaching, he was ready to dump both of them and get on with the building of his empire. Turning to go back into the bar, he assessed that situation. The customary raucous behavior — card games, drinking, and flirting with some of the other, less comely women of the hog ranch — was in full swing under the flickering lights of the numerous oil lamps. Donovan reached in the pocket of his vest and removed the pocket watch, courtesy of his predecessor, Sheriff Hobb, and popped open the gold case.

It was now nearing eight thirty-five.

Donovan scanned the room and caught

sight of Cooper sitting at one of the far tables with a bottle and a partially full shot glass in front of him. The man's baleful stare locked onto him.

Smiling, Donovan strolled over to the Indian agent's table. This was yet another problem that he would have to deal with when the time was right. Still, Donovan was cognizant of one burning factor. He'd found Hobb's stash of money quite easily, and it certainly followed that Cooper had an equally substantial sum hidden away. The question remained, where exactly was it? The Indian agent had a room at the boarding house across the street, and an office next to it. Either place would afford him an adequate lair for secreting his booty. Donovan knew he could draw his gun and force the man to show him where it was, but that might spark a bit of suspicion and trepidation in the rest of the group. He needed them to think of him as a powerful but benign leader who'd show them the pathway to riches, and not a greedy bully who couldn't be trusted.

Thus, finding the stash himself, without Cooper knowing, was the best course. He had no doubt he could dispose of the man later, perhaps even before they left to intercept the train. Looking down at the timepiece again, he saw that more than a minute had passed since he began his contemplations.

He snapped the lid of the watch closed and sighed with a false benevolence as he announced that everyone should be aware that they had an early departure time.

"We ride out at dawn," he said, raising his voice so he could be heard. "Our fortune awaits."

Texas-Mex and big Finn were standing apart from the others, their backs against the bar. Donovan had confided in them the real plan: ride out and switch the tracks when the train was at the water stop, then wait for the subsequent derailing. Once that had occurred, and the juggernaut had stopped, the Bulldog would provide a more than adequate method of eliminating the army guardians. The hung-over cowpokes would then remove the gold from the boxcar and place it in the waiting wagons. The Bulldog could then be used again to tidy up as the riffraff assembled for what they thought would be their payment. The three wagons could then depart, one driven by each of them, to parts farther south. Namely, Mexico.

Donovan still debated whether he should take the dime novelist with him so as to assure the completion of his tale of fame.

Marion Michael Donovan, the Rob Roy of the West.

Of course, Stutley was a liability of sorts. If he did accompany them south, there was always the danger that the lad might lead the authorities back to him. But if they settled in Mexico, the chances that some U.S. marshals or even the Texas Rangers would come after him were slim, if any. Bounty hunters might be another problem, which was why it would be prudent to keep Texas-Mex and Finnegan close at hand, at least until he was established.

But all this was moot.

First things first, he thought as he reached Cooper's table and pulled out a chair across from the man.

Cooper's eyes looked bloodshot and filled with gale. No words passed between them for several seconds, then Donovan reached over and took the half-full bottle. He poured Cooper another drink and edged forward a bit with his ingratiating grin.

"Don't let me interfere with your drinking."

Copper remained silent a bit longer, then his lips curled back into a feral sneer. "Why did you send her up to that damn dude's room?"

Donovan knew whom he meant but feigned ignorance. He raised an eyebrow. "And to whom would you be referring?"

"You know who I mean," Cooper said, his voice low and guttural. "Why'd you do it? I wanted her tonight."

"Pocahontas?" Donovan kept his smile fixed as an idea came to him. "Well, why didn't you say so?"

Cooper's face twitched. "But she's with that damn dude."

Donovan shook his head. "The lad's a bit tipsy. I just told the ladies to usher him up to bed. You're more than welcome to have your way with either of them, should you still feel the need."

Cooper licked his lips.

"In fact," Donovan said, reaching in his pocket, removing two silver dollars, and placing them on the table next to the bottle, "I'll even treat you to an overnight."

Cooper's eyes widened. His fingers edged toward the coins.

Donovan brought his hand down on top of them so fast that Cooper's head jerked back.

"Not quite yet, my friend," Donovan said. "There was a bit of untidy business involving the dude. I told her to clean herself up. Give her a few minutes to wash, and then you can have your way with her."

He could almost see the lust growing in Cooper's eyes.

Donovan winked and stood up. "Time for me to drain myself a bit." He turned and walked toward the bar. Polly and Pocahontas were coming down the stairs now, both wrinkling their noses at the unpleasantness that had occurred with Stutley.

Donovan stood in front of them and canted his head.

"Ladies, do take your time and clean your lovely selves," he said. Turning to the Indian girl he added, "Keep Cooper busy for an hour or so. I'll check on you later."

The girl frowned. "I don't want to be with him. He's ugly and mean. He wants me to do things that —"

"You'll do whatever the bloody hell I tell you to do," Donovan said. Although he didn't raise his hand toward her, the implication of the threat was clear in his tone.

She immediately fell silent.

"Now go clean yourselves."

"What about me?" Polly asked.

Donovan eyed her up and down. "The game's wide open."

He turned, looked back at Cooper, and waved. He then ambled toward the rear entrance and the outhouse. Once outside

273

he veered off from going directly toward the privy and then went to the corner of the building. The space between the buildings was wide enough to accommodate him, and he turned and walked toward the street, pausing when he got there and glancing around. All seemed quiet. He adjusted his hat and looked at the boarding house and then Cooper's office, trying to assume the logic and thinking of the Indian agent. A few lights flickered behind the windows of the boarding house, but it seemed more in keeping with Cooper's personage that he would be less trustful of a place where others would constantly be present. It would be better to check the office first.

Donovan glanced back at the saloon as he crossed the street. The street in front was still deserted. When he got to the door, he found it secured with a hasp and a hefty padlock. He briefly considered breaking out the glass window but decided against this. The noise might not be heard over the din from across the street, but climbing through the residual shards would prove treacherous. Instead, he pulled the knife from his boot and wedged it between the metal hasp and the solid wood of the door. Working the blade back and forth until the screws holding it in place gave way, Donovan pushed open the door.

He heard something undecipherable and paused. Turning around, he saw no one on the deserted street.

Once inside, he closed the door behind him. In moonlight through the adjacent window he saw an oil lamp. Picking it up, he lighted it with a wooden match and held it up, surveying the office. The place was rather tidy, which surprised him. It contained a desk and a pair of chairs, a filing cabinet, and a bookcase filled with several leather-bound volumes of what apparently were the federal statutes governing the Indian Territories. He went to the desk first, opening the side drawers and finding them empty save for a few stacks of paper. The center drawer was locked, and Donovan used the knife to force it open, smiling as he saw a stack of paper currency and five separate piles of coinage. Setting the knife on the table, he removed the money and quickly placed it on the desk as he counted it out.

It was a disappointing twenty-seven dollars.

There has to be more than this, he thought.

Donovan slowly studied the room before him, trying to take it all in, trying to think as Cooper might have thought. Perhaps there was no more. Perhaps he'd spent the rest of it.

Donovan dismissed that idea. The man's parsimony was a particularly dominant trait. There was more; there had to be.

His gaze settled on the bookshelf. As he got up, his boot shifted against something underneath the desk. He slid back in the chair and held the lamp down toward the floor. A bag lay in the shadows. Picking it up, Donovan opened it but found nothing except wadded papers. He removed one of them and pressed it open on the top of the desk.

A finely printed page, replete with a title and number along the upper part of the page was visible in the lamplight:

Revised Federal Statutes of 1876 Indian Territories 785

The rest were columns of printed text that Donovan didn't bother to try and read. He uncurled a few more and, seeing they fitted the same format, he looked to the bookshelf again.

Hiding your treasures in plain view. Cooper possessed a bit more slyness than he appeared to have.

Donovan rose and took the lamp to the

bookcase. He held the light close to the shelves and found what he was looking for: the absence of telltale dust marks in front of three of the volumes. Taking the three thick books out, he carried them to the desk and cracked one open. Three stacks of currency had been placed into the hollowed out section of the pages, each tied with a string. The other two volumes contained identical bundles.

He started to smile, but then the door burst open behind him, and a voice in the darkness snarled, "Don't you move." It was accompanied by the cocking of a gun's hammer.

Donovan turned and saw Boswell standing in the doorway. Still holding the gun outstretched, the soldier slid inside and shoved the door closed. He scanned the room and settled briefly on the stacks of money. His lips curled back to expose his foul teeth.

"I see you found it," Boswell said.

"Aye," Donovan said, debating the chances of drawing his own gun as he tried to avoid getting shot. The desk was to his left, which would have been his preferred direction of evasive movement. To his right the space between him and the bookcase was sparse. For the moment, he decided it was prudent to make no sudden motions. "Why aren't you at the fort?"

"Train's on its way," Boswell said. "Supposed to get to the water stop by dawn, or so. They sent three of us to guard the damn thing. For once, I volunteered."

Donovan forced a grin. "I bet that was a shock to your sergeant. But what if the others notice your absence and report it?"

Boswell's smile twisted into something closer to a sneer. "Dead men don't tell nothing. I killed them both 'fore I left to come here."

"Of course," Donovan said, still considering his options. His knife was lying on the desktop, obscured by stacks of money. Boswell was perhaps eight feet away from him. "Well, let's take ourselves over to the saloon, and I'll buy you a drink and set you up with one of the ladies of your choice."

Boswell shook his head and stretched out his arm, leveling the gun.

"It set me to thinking: why do I need you? I know the plan. I can take that money, the Bulldog, and me and the others can still hit the train in a couple hours."

"You think you have what it takes to be a leader of men, Private Boswell?"

"I ain't no private no more." His lips

twisted into a sneer. "I'm done with the army."

"Desertion? Isn't that a tad premature? The train hasn't arrived yet, and we planned to —"

"Shut your mouth. And don't try to tell me that you had something good in mind for me."

Donovan could see the other man's mouth working in the dim lamplight. He was trying to work up the nerve to shoot, perhaps wondering if the shot would bring others.

"Well, here," Donovan said, extending his hand toward the stacks of currency. "Take it then. Take it all."

He brushed a stack of bills onto the floor and saw Boswell's eyes follow it. Donovan grabbed the knife with his right hand and jumped forward, bridging the distance and twisting as he used his left to grab the barrel of Boswell's gun. The weapon went off, firing its round upward, and Donovan felt the hot spurt of flame singe the skin of his fingers. At the same time, he drove his shoulder against the waspish soldier's chest, pinning him against the door and then jamming the knife into Boswell's gut, twisting as it pierced the flesh. The soldier grunted and screamed. Donovan rotated the blade, and Boswell expelled a loud breath, then collapsed, emitting shallow, intermittent gasps. Donovan pulled the gun from Boswell's now slack fingers as he let the man fall all the way to the floor.

"Once a deserter, always a deserter," Donovan said.

Reeves and Bear stood in the shadows by the outhouse. Outside, all was quiet, while the sounds of merriment emanated from the rear entrance of the saloon. They both had changed into other clothes, dark outfits that would be harder to see at night. Reeves had a large, blue bandana tied around his neck. Bear had wound his long hair into its usual tight-braided bun at the back of his head and also wore a similar bandana.

One of the drunken cowpokes pushed out the back door, leaving it ajar, and walked with an unsteady gait toward the outhouse.

Reeves and Bear melted into the shadows and watched. The cowpoke pulled open the door and started unfastening his pants. Reeves moved around and struck the cowpoke behind the ear with the barrel of his gun. The cowpoke collapsed, and Reeves caught the man and arranged him on the bench in the privy.

"I hope he don't make a mess in his drawers," Bear said with a grin.

"Judging from the smell, I don't think it'd be the first time he did." Reeves closed the outhouse door.

"What now?"

"I'm going to check things out inside," Reeves said. "Stay out here and keep your ears open. I'll whistle if I need you."

"You going in there? They already seen both of us this afternoon."

"That's why I'll be wearing this." Reeves pulled the bandana up over the lower portion of his face. With his black hat pulled low on his forehead, only his eyes were visible.

Bear made a clucking sound. "You can almost pass for a white man." He brought his finger up to touch his cheek near his eye. "Except for here."

"I'll have to stay in the shadows then." Reeves adjusted his hat. "Like I said, if I need you, I'll whistle."

Bear blended into the darkness once more.

Reeves moved to the back door and peered inside. The long hallway was deserted, but, as he started inside, he caught the sound of voices, a man and a woman. Angry sounding voices.

He flattened against the outside wall and peered around the corner. A couple came bustling into the hallway.

"Let me go, you bastard."

It was the Indian girl, Walking Deer. Reeves didn't know the man, but he looked drunk and mean.

"Come on, bitch. Get yer red ass in there. I been waitin' for you all night."

Walking Deer kept struggling, and the man slapped her across the face. Hard.

Reeves felt his anger rise. He didn't cotton to hurting women.

The pair got to the door of a room about fifteen feet away, and the man pushed her inside. She continued her protests, and he drew back his arm to hit her again.

The door closed behind them.

Reeves debated what to do.

He heard muffled screams, and then the sound of more blows being delivered.

The hallway was clear, and Reeves moved through the doorway, covering the distance with three quick steps. When he reached the room, he slipped inside. A lamp illuminated the room, but the shadows reached out from the darkened corners. The front of Walking Deer's dress had been torn off, and her breasts were exposed. She was bent over holding her stomach. The man whirled and looked at Reeves.

"Hey, get outta here," he said.

Reeves smashed his left fist into the man's

substantial gut, then delivered a chopping blow to his head with his right. The man collapsed to his knees. As he started to rise, Reeves delivered a powerful blow that knocked the man out cold.

The girl had straightened up, her eyes wide open.

"Who are you?"

Even in the dim light, Reeves could see her dark eyes narrow.

"It's you," she said. Slowly, she crossed her arms across her chest.

"Yes, ma'am." Reeves tipped his hat and pulled the bandana down from his face. He took a nickel-plated Smith & Wesson Schofield with a five-inch barrel from the man's belt and shoved it in his own gun belt. "I seen him hitting you," he said. "No way I could keep lettin' him do that."

She continued to stare at him. "What are you doing here?"

Reeves ignored her question and kept searching the unconscious man, removing a straight razor, a Sharps Pepperbox derringer, and some money from his pockets.

"Who is this guy?" he asked.

"It's Cooper," she said.

"The crooked Indian agent?"

She nodded. "He told me Donovan paid for him to do an overnight with me."

283

"I've been lookin' for him." Reeves pocketed the straight razor and the derringer and then tossed the money onto the bed. "Guess this is yours then."

Her eyes followed the money, then she looked back at him, saying nothing. Keeping one arm over her breasts, she reached out with the other hand and plucked the money from the bedspread.

Reeves removed a long, leather thong from his pants pocket and began tying the Indian agent's hands behind his back. Once he was satisfied they were secured, he grabbed the man's chin and checked his eyes. Cooper was still out. Reeves lifted him as easily as if he were picking up a sleeping child and carried him to the window. He set the Indian agent down and raised the window. Leaning out, he whistled.

A whistling reply trilled in the darkness, then Bear appeared.

"What you got, *Gimoozabie*?"

"We back to that now?" Reeves reached down and grabbed Cooper, picked the man up, and shoved him through the window. The Indian agent groaned as he hit the ground.

"Better tie a gag around his mouth," Reeves said. "I'll be out shortly. Meet you by the horses."

"I'll see if I can find an extra horse for him." Bear picked up the unconscious man and disappeared once more into the shadows.

Reeves turned back to the girl.

"You gonna be all right?"

She smirked. "It's nothing I ain't handled before. They'll probably think he wandered off drunk when he was done."

Reeves said nothing.

"But what are you doing back here?" she asked. "They catch you, they'll kill you."

"They've got to catch me first. I came back to find out what Donovan's planning. You know?"

She shook her head. "He's got some kind of plan. Keeps saying it's something big. I think it involves the army. That one soldier pig, Boswell, kept coming by, talking to him."

"Boswell? He around now?"

"Ain't seen him."

Reeves mulled his choices. He had the feeling if she knew more, she would tell him. "Anybody else that might know what Donovan's planning?"

She compressed her lips, obviously thinking. "Maybe that dude. Him and Donovan have been thicker than thieves."

"The dude? The one wearing that fancy suit?"

"Yes. Donovan wants him to write some kind of book about him."

"A book?"

"He's some kind of writer, or something, from back East. New York City."

"Where's he stayin' at?"

"He's in the room directly above this one."

"Where's he at now?"

She lifted her right hand and pointed upward. She kept the other arm across her chest, her left hand cupping her right breast. "Me and Polly put him in bed a little bit ago. He was sick from the whiskey."

Reeves tilted his head toward the ceiling, judging the distance, then looked at the window. The top of the window frame jutted out several inches, and there were several barrels stacked along the wall. It would be an easy climb, as long as the dude left the window open. It was worth a try before he and Bear left with Cooper. He reached into his pocket, removed a silver dollar, and handed it to her.

She looked at it. "What's this for?"

"I give 'em to people that help me. You could've told Donovan who I was this afternoon, but you didn't. I appreciate that."

She stared at him for a long time, then

her gaze went to the coin in her hand. "This is a lot." She looked at the bed. "Enough for . . . You want to?"

Reeves smiled. "You're mighty pretty, but I got me a wife back in Arkansas, and she's my one and only."

He glanced out the window. Bear was nowhere in sight. He pulled back into the room and said, "Besides, I got to pay a visit upstairs. You say that writer fella might know what Donovan's planning?"

She shrugged. "I suppose. They're as thick as thieves. But he might call for help."

"I'll have to make sure he don't." Reeves pulled the bandana up over the lower half of his face again and adjusted his hat low as he moved to the window. "I be appreciative if you stayed in your room for a bit and didn't go out."

"As far as anybody knows," she said, dropping her arms to her sides. "I'm in for the night with Cooper."

Reeves stole a peek at her loveliness. Her breasts were high and firm. He then tipped his hat.

"Much obliged, ma'am."

He went to the open window and climbed out.

In his dream, Stutley was chasing the

beautiful, naked Indian maiden across the stream in which she'd been bathing. She gazed back at him as her strong, brownish legs made splashes in the shallow water. A verdant forest flanked both sides of the stream, and he'd almost caught her when suddenly the maiden stopped and turned to him, her face now a mask of pure terror. Stutley tried to stop running but couldn't. Something was up ahead. He didn't know what, but somehow he knew it was dangerous. It was like watching the scene play out from afar but being in the middle of it, too. Struggling to make his legs stop, to keep his stomach contents under control, but to no avail. The bile rose in his throat, the upward burn, the convulsive constrictions — he was really feeling it now.

He snapped awake, conscious that part of the dream was indeed real — the part about the imminent vomiting. Desperate not to soil the bed linens, which were foul smelling already, Stutley rolled off the featherbed and made his way to the dresser, upon which rested a wash basin. He grabbed it and held it under his face, regurgitating the vile contents that had seared his throat and palate. The ill feeling subsided, only to start again, but this time nothing came up. His stomach contracted and expanded twice more, and then he felt a modicum of relief.

He stood in the dark room hearing only the sound of his own heavy breathing. After he was convinced that the vomiting was finished, he straightened up and set the basin back on its perch on the dresser. He wanted to pour what there was of the expiation into the chamber pot. Swallowing to try and get the awful taste out of his mouth, he suddenly realized that, although he wasn't wearing his jacket and tie, he still had on his shirt and pants.

Those damn whores didn't even bother to help me get undressed, he thought, and then a surge of panic gripped him as his fingers sought and then found the money belt, which was still secured around his middle.

"Thank God," he muttered and began silently cursing that damn Donovan, who had insisted on him downing more of the rotgut whiskey as they sat at a corner table and Donovan laid out the way he wanted to be portrayed in the novel.

"Remember," the Irishman had said, "we're building a legend here. Locksley from *Ivanhoe*. Marion Michael Donovan, the Rob Roy of the West."

Stutley had simpered and guzzled his way through the conversation, scribbling down as many notes as he could. In truth, the more he heard, the more troubled he was by the details: derailing the train, killing all those soldiers — more than twenty of them, by Donovan's estimation — was, to put it bluntly, a bit troubling.

He swallowed again, but the spittle did little to remove the pervasive acidity that lingered in his mouth.

And there was something else, if he was completely honest with himself: it was troubling, yes, but also exciting. Not that he condoned Donovan's plan for the robbery and slaughter, but the Irishman said Stutley was to come along. To view the event as it unfolded. To actually be there. To see the death and destruction first hand. The thought of it took his breath away. He'd been too young to fight in the war, but one of his uncles had. As a young boy, Stutley had asked him what it was like, but his uncle said he couldn't find the words to describe it. He'd once mentioned that he'd seen a lot of men die.

Stutley had once dreamed of writing a novel about the titanic conflict, the war between the blue and the gray, a book that would be hailed as a definitive masterpiece, but, instead, he was now writing dime novels that merged fact with fiction, made heroes of killers, and created false legends.

Entertaining legends, but still false ones.

Still, the chance to see this kind of event for himself, to see real men fighting and dying — this was the chance of a lifetime.

The whiskey had burned all the way down to his crotch, and he felt the sudden urge to urinate. Stutley hoped the maid had remembered to empty the chamber pot and then remembered there wasn't any maid.

He moved on unsteady feet toward the edge of the bed. Placing one hand on the mattress for balance, he stooped over and used his other hand to feel for the chamber pot.

Somehow, it eluded him. He needed the light of the lamp but didn't know if he could hold it in that long.

But luckily there's a window, he thought with a sly smile.

Except, if he happened to piss on someone below, he could expect a retaliation that terrified him.

Still reeling a bit, he stumbled and fell toward the bed. A hint of ambient lighting from the full moon shone in through the window, allowing him to partially make things out. But everything was out of focus. Shadows merged into soft blurring things.

My spectacles, he thought. *What did those whores do with them?*

His fingers felt around the bedside table and then the surface of the bed itself.

The pressing need to void his bladder returned with a vengeance.

Rolling off the bed, he got on his hands and knees, feeling around under the bed once more for the chamber pot.

"Where the hell is the damn thing?" he said out loud.

Squinting, he grabbed the bed railing and stood, half pushed himself erect, and took a box of matches from his pants pocket as he moved to the small table upon which rested the oil lamp. Stutley opened the box, spilling most of the contents. He blinked and felt around the top of the furniture before finally snaring one of the pesky little matches. His fingers gripped the glass of the lamp and he lifted it to light the wick. As he struck the match and watched the flame ignite, he caught a glimpse of a large form off to his right, by the window.

Stutley froze.

A big man stood there silhouetted by the moonlight. The details were obscured by Stutley's myopia and the absence of light, but he could tell the man was dressed in a dark colored shirt and pants. He wore a black hat pulled low on his forehead, and the lower portion of his face was covered by a bandana. One of his gloved hands held a huge gun, which, thankfully, was pointed at the floor.

"Don't light the lamp," the masked man said, his voice somewhat muffled, but distinct.

Stutley didn't move until the match burned down, searing his fingers. He hastily shook it out and swallowed, suddenly feeling almost sober.

"Didn't want to disturb you if you had business to do," the masked man said. "You armed?"

"No."

The masked man moved forward, and Stutley felt a strong hand tracing over his body. He felt the pressing urge to void his bladder again but didn't dare speak, hoping he wouldn't pee his pants.

The masked man stepped back into the shadows and holstered his gun.

"What's your name, dude?" he asked.

Stutley swallowed, now feeling the twin urges to both vomit and urinate.

"My name's Lucien T. Stutley," he said in a voice fraught with a trembling weakness. "Who're you?"

"Never mind that. You don't look like no outlaw. What're you doing here?"

"I'm a writer. A novelist." He gestured

toward the chair by the bed, which held his traveling bag. "I have some in there I could show you."

The masked man ignored the offer. "Who are you to Donovan?"

"No one. I hardly know the man."

"You two looked pretty friendly."

Stutley felt like an iron hand was gripping his bowels now. Whoever this stranger was, he'd obviously been watching him.

"I'm not from around here," Stutley said, desperately searching for words. "I'm from back East. New York City, actually. I'm out here at the behest of my editor —"

"I ain't interested in your life's history. Got one of my own. What about Donovan?"

Stutley licked his lips and wondered how he should play this one. Who was this masked stranger, and what was he looking for? Finally, he found the courage to speak.

"He wants to be a legend, like Jesse James. The man's a self-absorbed maniac. Wants me to write about his exploits in one of my novels. He thinks he's got this magnificent plan to get rich."

The masked man was silent for a few moments, then asked, "What kind of plan?"

Stutley swallowed as a new thought danced through his alcohol-laden mind: What if Donovan had sent this big masked hooligan up to his room to scare him? Could this be some kind of a test of his loyalty?

"I don't know," he blurted out.

In the semi-darkness Stutley saw the masked man's hand reach for the butt of the pistol holstered around his waist.

"Mister." His voice was low and even. "I ain't got the time or the inclination to play. What's Donovan got planned?"

Stutley was on the verge of pissing his pants. He thought about asking if he could please use the chamber pot but couldn't find the words to speak.

"I ain't got all night," the masked man said.

His voice held power and authority.

"He's going to rob the train," Stutley blurted out. He watched to see if the masked man was going to draw his gun and shoot.

He didn't, and Stutley relaxed a bit.

"The train? When?"

"In the morning. Around first light." Stutley swallowed, recalling the plan Donovan had so meticulously laid out for him. "The train's already on its way from Denver with a load of freshly minted gold coins."

"How's he know when it's coming through here?"

Stutley let out a small laugh. "One of the

soldiers told him. The fort's been monitoring the train's progress so they can provide a guard, if anything untoward begins to happen."

"Un-what?"

"Untoward. It means not favorable. Inauspicious."

The masked man was silent, taking it all in.

"How do they know when the train's gonna get here?"

"Donovan's got look-outs posted at the fort. One of them heard about a wire they sent earlier about when the train's expected. He's also got men stationed by the water stop."

"How's he figuring on stopping a train? He gonna block the tracks?"

Stutley felt a flood of excitement now, the urge to void his bladder suddenly subsiding as quickly as it had arisen. He shook his head. "He's got it all worked out. There's a set of dead-end tracks that were supposed to lead to the town here, but they were never finished. There's a switching lever on the regular tracks that'll transfer the train onto the dead-end. Once the engineer realizes it and hits the brakes, it'll be too late. Donovan has got three wagons and a bunch of horses ready to take the gold."

"There ain't no guards?"

"There's a contingent of soldiers on board guarding it. Supposed to be twenty of them."

"Twenty soldiers? And Donovan thinks he can take all of them?"

"He's got —" Stutley stopped. Dare he say more? If Donovan found out he'd been spilling the beans, especially about the Bulldog, it would mean a certain and very unpleasant death.

The masked man rested his hand on his pistol again. "He's got what?"

Stutley breathed in and out several times in rapid succession. Certain death might be a possibility from Donovan, if he found out, but he wasn't here now, and Stutley could sense that this masked man was also someone to be obeyed.

"He's got a Bulldog."

"A Bulldog? You mean a Gatling gun?"

"Yes," Stutley said. "He's going to use it to kill the guards, and then he and the rest of his men will drive the wagons in and take the gold."

"The Gatling gun — where'd he get it?"

"I don't know. He said he took it from some soldiers."

"When's all this supposed to happen?"

"The train's supposed to be passing by

the old Temptation station around sunup."

The masked man said nothing for several seconds and then moved to the open window. Thrusting one leg through the opening, he paused and turned.

"Best for you if you forget I was ever here," he said.

With that, the rest of his body went through the opening, and he disappeared into the night.

Stutley barely managed to find the chamber pot in time.

CHAPTER 9

Cherokee Village
The Indian Territories

Reeves and Bear rode into the Cherokee village, which was lighted only by the same campfire that had been burning the night before. The old man, whose name they'd subsequently learned was Running Wolf, sat in virtually the same place in front of the fire, smoking a long pipe. They had Cooper tied up and belly-down across the saddle of a third horse. The Indian agent bellowed with each step the animal took. He had already vomited numerous times.

"At least let me sit in the damn saddle," he said.

Reeves ignored the request and told him to be quiet. They came up to the far side of the fire, and both Reeves and Bear dismounted.

Bear started speaking in Cherokee dialect, but Running Wolf raised his hand.

"We will use the white man's tongue, out of respect for the great warrior." He waved the stem of the pipe in Reeves's direction.

"There you go with that white man stuff again," Reeves said with a grin as he raised his hand in greeting.

The old Indian's face creased with mirth. "I see you have bagged some game. A not-so-wild pig, from the looks of him."

Cooper, who was still belly-down over the horse, swore.

"Chief," Reeves said, "this man's under arrest, and I'm taking him back to Fort Smith. But we need to go collect a few more. All right if we leave him here for a time?"

"A time?" Running Wolf asked.

"You can't leave me here," Cooper said. "Not with these people." His voice had a labored, sluggish sound to it, most likely due to his semi-inversion.

Reeves again told him to be quiet, then added with a sly smile, "You're supposed to be representing these folks, ain't you? I'm figuring it'll be a good chance for you and them to relate."

"You son of a bitching nigger!" Cooper yelled.

Reeves ignored the insult and turned back to the old man. "How about it? You agreeable to watching him for a spell?" He reached into his pocket, took out another silver dollar, and held it up.

The old Indian's eyes gleamed in the flickering firelight. "Another of those pretty silver ladies?"

Reeves flipped the coin to him.

The old Indian caught it. "It'll take more than this."

Bear appeared and tossed him a bag of jerky. Running Wolf opened the bag and smiled. "I will watch him." He bit off a piece of the jerky and began chewing loudly. "Now it is his turn to be hungry and watch me eat."

"You old son of a bitch," the Indian agent said. "I'll cut your damn guts out and feed 'em to the damn dogs."

Reeves strode over to the horses and grabbed the Indian agent's ear. Twisting, he pulled the man's head, forcing him to look up at him.

"You best be watching your mouth. You're going back to Fort Smith to stand trial 'fore Judge Parker, and he ain't gonna take kindly to what you've been doing to these people you supposed to be helping, much less leading them rangers into that ambush."

"Go to hell, nigger," Copper said.

Reeves chuckled. "I'm gonna take particular pleasure in watching you hang, mister."

He released the ear and pulled Cooper from the saddle, letting the man land hard on the ground. The corpulent Indian agent groaned in pain. Reeves reached down and pulled him to his feet. Cooper attempted to spit at Reeves, but the lawman was too quick and grabbed the fat jowls of Cooper's face in a gloved hand.

"I'm only gonna say this one time," Reeves said. "You're under arrest and going back to Fort Smith to stand trial. How you act, what you say, gonna make the difference if you hang, or just spend the rest of your life in a cage. But make no mistake, you cause any more trouble, and you ain't gonna make it back. Understand?"

Cooper didn't say anything, but after a few moments he nodded slightly.

Reeves shoved him toward Bear. "Let him relieve himself in the field there, and then put him in the wagon."

Bear nodded and slipped his Winchester 1873 rifle from its scabbard and shoved Cooper. "Move, lard-ass."

"At least untie my hands." Cooper's rough tone had diminished to a whine.

"Just keep movin'," Bear said, giving him a shove. "You stink bad enough already."

Cooper bit his lip, glanced back at the

Lighthorse, and then lowered his eyes to the ground. His next words were barely a whisper, but Reeves could hear them.

"Listen, Indian, I got some money stashed. Over two thousand dollars. You let me go, I'll tell you where it's hid."

"I bet you will," Bear said. "Get moving."

Reeves watched the two depart and turned back to the old Indian. "He ain't gonna cause you no more problems, Chief. And I'm gonna tell Judge Parker what's been goin' on 'round these parts."

"Judge Parker." Running Wolf chuckled silently in the darkness. "Many moons have come and gone, and, with them, more and more of the white men come. Soon, they will take this land from us as they took our lands before, and as they took the buffalo."

Reeves stood silently, figuring the old Indian was right.

Bear came trotting back to them, shaking his head.

"He'd already shit his drawers," he said. "Pissed in 'em, too. So I just locked him up in the wagon. Left his hands tied and put the irons on his legs."

"We gonna probably be needing more of them irons," Reeves said. "We ain't going back till I got all the men that killed them rangers."

Bear raised his eyebrows. "We probably gonna need another wagon then. I seen a couple of 'em in the stable in town."

"Maybe we'll grab one then." Reeves looked at him. "What was he saying to you?"

Bear grinned. "He was telling me how he was gonna make me a rich man. Give me the two thousand dollars he's got stashed. All I had to do was let him go."

"Probably the money he's been getting from stealing and reselling them government cattle."

"Yeah," Bear said slowly. "And since it was meant for my people, maybe I should take charge of it. Be a fine bit of money to bring back to the Lighthorse. Do a lot of good."

"Do a lot of good for these people here, too," Reeves said.

"People?" Bear snorted, holding his hands up in a questioning gesture. "What people? I don't see no people."

Reeves smirked and cocked his head toward the horses. "We best be getting some extra guns and ammo. We got us a train robbery to stop."

"How many men you think he's gonna have with him?"

Reeves shook his head. "Does it matter?"

Bear heaved a sigh. "Like I said, we're gonna need a couple more wagons."

Donovan's Room
Temptation

Donovan set the bag containing the money from the hollowed-out books on the feather-bed and looked around his hotel room for a suitable hiding place. He wasn't certain if anyone had noticed his trek from Cooper's office but felt certain he couldn't take the chance that someone might have suspected something. He'd left Boswell's body there. No sense wasting any more time disposing of that idiot. Cooper would be next.

Maybe I'll leave him in the privy with a bullet up his arse, Donovan thought. That would be appropriate.

His gaze went back to the bag as he tried to figure out where he could hide the money. He debated whether to take the time to pry up the floorboard and put it with the money from Hobb's metal box. But that would be putting all his eggs in one basket. Most of his men would be leaving in a few hours for the rendezvous with the train, and that would leave his room wide open for the scavengers like Henry, Polly, and, of course, Pocahontas to come poking around. None of them could be trusted. And if he couldn't

305

find Cooper, that snake would certainly come looking as well, especially once he discovered the dead man in his office and the missing money.

The sounds of drinking, yelling, and fighting carried up the stairs from the bar.

Donovan sighed. He'd have to be closing things down relatively soon, lest the lot of them be so stinking drunk that they'd be tripping over their own feet. He'd need them sober enough to hitch up the wagons and then make quick work of unloading and loading the gold coins. Once the train failed to make the next stop east, the army would be alerted, and they'd come looking. The wagons would slow travel down. Of course, he could take the Bulldog with him. That would effectively end any concerns about a meddling cavalry.

Perhaps the simplest solution is the best, he thought. *Put all my eggs in one basket, and watch that basket.*

Grinning at the felicitousness of his own wit, he removed his knife and worked the blade into the small gap between the floorboards.

More noise drifted up from downstairs.

Donovan paused to check his pocket watch. Three forty-five. He'd give it another hour or so, then move all of these louts out to the country.

The early bird catches the worm, he thought.

Additionally, with Boswell shooting the two guards, it meant that Donovan would have to place at least one man at the water stop to assure the engineer that everything was fine. He could use Boswell's uniform. They'd have to wash the blood out.

The soldiers on the train most likely would be getting off to relieve themselves and stretch their legs while more water was being taken in up by the engine, so it would be prudent to make sure those dead bodies were out of sight. He'd have to send someone dependable to get that done and then give the signaling shots that the train had departed the water stop. And he'd decided to let Texas-Mex do the shooting with the Bulldog this time. Donovan had noticed the envy in the Mexican's eyes as he'd watched the Gatling gun spit death at its incredible rate during the Ranger ambush. Donovan knew this one required too much planning, too much synchronization, for him to operate the gun. He needed to stay in over-all command, like a general directing his troops. Besides, how hard would it be to point the Bulldog in the right direction and turn the bloody crank?

It was so simple, an idiot or a fool could do it with ease.

He smiled, thinking it might be time for him to compose another limerick.

Then the board loosened, and he used the point of the blade to pry it up. The limerick would have to wait.

He looked down. The stack of money lay neatly in the space. Donovan removed Cooper's stash from the bag and packed it into the opening. He was barely able to cram it all in there and fit the board back in place.

Donovan smiled. It was a nice bit of sweet sauce to cover the cake. Tucking the pocket watch back into his vest and standing, he could almost envision the illustrated cover of Stutley's book:

A larger than life depiction of himself, standing over a Gatling gun, under which would read the title: *Marion Michael Donovan, the Rob Roy of the West.*

The Railroad Line
The Indian Territories
Reeves scanned the area where the railroad tracks came to an end and tried to figure out where Donovan might set up the Bulldog for the ambush. He and Bear had taken the long way around the town to avoid be-

ing seen, and now it was getting close to sunrise. The moon was full, so it provided some light, and Reeves felt grateful they'd been able to find the dead-end tracks, which were overgrown with weeds. He thought again about what the dude had told him and pondered if the man was to be believed. But what other choice did he have? Riding into town to confront the outlaws before they left seemed like a foolhardy proposition. He and Bear would be both outnumbered and facing the enemy on its home ground. Then again, the odds wouldn't change much being out here, but at least he and Bear would have the element of surprise. They'd be able to move about more to choose their own places to fight. Their main objective would be simple: locate that Gatling gun and get control of it before Donovan gunned down the soldiers. They'd still face long odds, but there was nothing Reeves could do about that now. Not with another massacre about to occur. He wasn't sure if they could stop it, but one thing he did know: they had to try.

He thought back to the ambush of the rangers. In that one Donovan had shown some battlefield savvy. Maybe the man had a military background. He'd set up on the high ground, led the rangers into a trap.

Not very honorable, but smart, nonetheless. In the saloon he'd been the obvious leader. Reeves knew it would be dangerous to underestimate this man and regard him as just another outlaw. And he had a substantial force with him. Reeves hoped they'd all continued their drinking long after he'd left Temptation with Cooper.

He looked at the dead-end tracks again. They branched off from the main set here with a lazy fork-like separation and continued to nowhere for about five hundred yards or so. It was still dark, and chances would be good that the engineer most likely wouldn't even notice they'd been misdirected until it was too late. Reeves tried to make the calculation as to how much distance the iron horse would travel before stopping, but he had no frame of reference. He'd never been on a train, and comparing something like that to a horse-drawn wagon was practically impossible. A heavily laden wagon going at top speed was difficult to stop, but with that you'd be dealing with live animals. If they saw danger or an obstruction ahead, they could be redirected and slowed down. The train had no way to do that other than applying the brakes.

Once the train got on those dead end tracks, it wouldn't stop until the rails ran out. He'd briefly toyed with the idea of trying to shoot the man at the switch lever, but there was no place to hide and wait. It would be tantamount to Bear and him facing down the gang without any cover at all. They'd be cut down, and the track switch would be thrown. No, they had to let this one play out and try to get control of that Bulldog.

Bear rode up next to him and leaned over in his saddle.

"You thinking the same thing I'm thinking?" Reeves asked him.

The Lighthorse nodded. "They're probably gonna set up the Gatling gun over there on that high ground. The range they used to shoot them rangers is about the same, provided the train gets stopped over there."

Reeves followed Bear's pointing finger.

"So," Bear continued, "I'm guessing the best place for us to hide is over in that gully there."

"Looks like. We can tie up our horses there and stay outta sight."

"And sneak up on them, Indian-style," Bear said with a smile. Then his expression changed. He dismounted and knelt on the ground, placing his ear to the dirt. After several seconds, he looked up at Reeves. "Riders coming. A lot of them."

"Let's go. It's getting close to sun up."

As he was turning his horse around, Bear straightened up and jumped on his horse's back. "Hey."

Reeves stopped.

"I don't suppose it would do any good for me to suggest we hightail it back to the Indian village and just let this thing be, huh?"

Reeves said nothing.

"I mean," Bear continued, "we got what we came for . . . the Cherokeo chief. And we could come back with a posse and clean out that town."

"What about that train? No time for us to come back with a posse."

Bear smirked. "Whatever you say, *Gimoozabie.*"

"Be sun-up soon," Reeves said, taking out his gun and checking to make sure he had a full load. "We better get ready."

Chapter 10

On the Outskirts of Temptation City
Stutley slid off the back of the wagon as it
came to a halt. It was early morning but
still dark, although the sky to the east was
suffused with a tincture of pink. They were
about half a mile from the town now, by the
area where the set of dead-end tracks ran
out. The place where the train ambush was
going to unfold, and a lot of men were going to die. The air smelled sweet somehow.
Did that portend death?

He swallowed and took out his notebook
and pencil. Was he ready? Should he stay?

But what choice did he have now?

He couldn't ride a horse very well, and, if
Donovan found him missing, there'd be hell
to pay.

He had no other choice. He had to remain.
But the thoughts of those soldiers being cut
down by the Gatling gun started to weigh
on his conscience. Up until this time, it had

merely been a fancy, a vague image, but soon he would be witnessing the carnage firsthand. What would it be like seeing death on such a massive and merciless scale? Could he handle it?

He tried to push the doubt from his mind. After all, this was what he'd come West to see, to experience. This was going to give him the knowledge to take his writing to the next level.

He thought again about what was about to come and felt a sudden twitching in his gut.

"Keep the horses and the wagons out of sight over there," Donovan yelled. "And make damn certain they're tethered to something solid. Any man whose horse runs off after the gunfire starts will be shot." He affected a stern look and gazed around at the near-frozen group, then he started laughing. A spattering of laughter emanated from a few of the members of his gang as they began dismounting in a disheveled manner and tying up their horses.

Stutley had no doubt that many of them were as terrified of Donovan as he was at that moment. He thought back to the mysterious masked stranger who'd been in his room a few hours ago. Had that been real, or had it only been an alcohol induced dream?

"Finn and Texas-Mex," Donovan said, "move the Bulldog into position. A couple of you others go over to the other side of the tracks in case any of the blue bellies jump out the other side of the car."

"Want us to shoot 'em if'n they do?" one bedraggled cowpoke asked.

Donovan glared at the man. "No, you bugger. I want you to kiss them on their bloody arses."

The cowpoke, who was obviously still under the influence of the rot gut, blinked with an incredulous expression.

"Of course you'll shoot them," Donovan said. "We have them in a cross-fire. And go throw that track switch on your way over there. Make sure it's tight."

Stutley watched as the outlaws spread out in the darkness, each man armed with a rifle and at least one handgun apiece. It was going to be bloody, and, with that Gatling gun, it would be a damn turkey shoot. Those soldiers wouldn't have a chance, unless that masked man had managed to warn them somehow. But how could he? It had been only a couple of hours since their late-night conversation. Hardly time enough for the stranger to ride all the way to the fort to try to intercept the train. And, even if he got there, how could they get word to the engineer? Still, Stutley somehow hoped the man had tried, and perhaps the train wouldn't come after all. At least that way there was a chance that the carnage might not unfold.

He had another thought: what if the masked man had warned the army, and they sent a contingent of soldiers to apprehend Donovan?

Stutley suddenly worried about getting caught in a full-fledged gun battle.

That might be even worse.

He heard the distant crack of three gun shots, the signal from the lookout at the water stop that the train was on its way.

It wouldn't be long now.

Stutley looked at the sky again. The pink had given way to a yellowish glow, the great circular edge of the rising sun silhouetting the scarce trees and bushes against the incipient brightness, lighting the way toward impending death.

He caught a glimpse of Donovan's face as he watched the big half-breed lift the Bulldog out of the wagon as if he were picking up a sack of grain. The brute was powerful. He set the Gatling gun on the ground, and he and the unctuous Mexican began to roll it up the embankment, where its barrel would be aimed toward the tracks.

Stutley heard a distant chugging sound and could imagine the wispy trail of blackish smoke filtering upward from the engine's smoke stack as the train approached. The sound grew louder, and he began to feel a slight vibration under his feet as the train veered suddenly to the right, coming in their direction.

Donovan laughed and turned to Stutley.

"Better get over by the horses, laddie," he said. "It's time to dance with the Devil as the sun comes up."

Reeves and Bear crept through the fading darkness as the yellowish light began to fill the sky behind them. It was nearly dawn, and, once again, Reeves knew somebody was about to die. Most likely a lot of somebodies. He and Bear had tied their horses in the small gully and traversed the rest of the way on foot. There was no way to stop the approaching train, so Reeves figured they had to let part of Donovan's plan play out. He saw men moving about fifty yards ahead and dropped to a prone position, motioning for Bear to do the same. The ground vibrated with the weighted momentum of the approaching locomotive.

Reeves could barely discern it in the nascent light. Down by the tracks, three of Donovan's men scampered across to the other side and crouched down.

"You see 'em?" Reeves asked.

Bear grunted. "I'm more worried about the ones on this side of the tracks. They got the Bulldog."

Reeves continued scanning the area. A cluster of perhaps ten to fifteen men were huddled by three wagons and a buckboard. About twenty yards away from them, two men were pushing what appeared to be the Gatling gun up a slight incline. The one doing most of the work was the enormous half-breed Reeves had seen in the saloon. The other, he guessed, was the Mexican, judging from the sombrero.

Donovan was out of sight, but Reeves could hear the familiar Irish brogue shouting out orders. The Irishman was close enough to direct his plan of cutting the soldiers down with the Bulldog and then sending in the rest of his men to mop up and unload the gold into the wagons.

Reeves slapped Bear's shoulder and pointed to the two men with the Bulldog.

"We gonna have to take them first," Reeves said.

"Then what, *Gimoozabie*?"

Reeves frowned and said, "Then we'll see."

The noise and ground vibrations grew stronger. Reeves pointed as the black, chugging iron machine emerged in the early morning light, barreling along, not slowing at all, toward the dead end of the tracks and its inevitable crash. They watched as the train continued forward, like an immense, unstoppable monster, then suddenly bucked and jumped as the front end ran out of rails. The momentum carried the huge metal beast forward, spraying fountains of earth from each side of its pointed, spear-like front end, accompanied by the groaning of metal and the ripping sound of the soil being pierced. It veered left along a slight declivity in the ground, the rest of the cars jumping and twisting like a gigantic sidewinder slithering through a field of grass. Twisting metal screamed in the darkness, along with the sound of artificial thunder.

"We gotta move now," Reeves said, getting to his feet.

He looked and saw the two men readying the Gatling gun, the half-breed and the Mexican. Donovan had moved farther away, standing by a group of wagons and a cluster of cheering men.

"After we take out the Bulldog, you move

to the other side of the train and get those three over there."

"I hope them soldiers know I'm a friendly Indian. Eh, *Gimoozabie*?"

Reeves said nothing.

Bear laughed. "I had to get it in one more time. Might not get another chance. What you gonna be doin'?"

"Takin' care of the rest of 'em," Reeves said as they began a quick trot toward the outlaws.

The train finally jerked to a trembling halt after traveling about twenty or thirty feet. The cars shook with a residual tremble and finally ceased to move.

Several of the outlaws began a series of hooting cat calls. The side door of the boxcar opened, and three soldiers jumped out, obviously shaken and unsteady, but trying to hold their rifles at the ready. More soldiers continued to pour out the open door, but many staggered and fell. The first burst of the Bulldog tore through the hazy morning air, illuminating each round with a bright flash from the rotating barrels in the still dusky morning light. The first rounds hit the side of the boxcar, missing the soldiers.

"Turn that damn thing a little to the left, Finn!" someone shouted from the cluster of men. Reeves recognized the voice: Donovan.

Reeves was almost there now. He saw the big half-breed lifting the end of the Gatling gun, rotating it to aim the barrel toward the emerging troops. The Mexican held the crank.

"That one's mine," Bear said.

Reeves covered the final yards in ten steps and slammed into the big half-breed. The big man grunted and fell to the side, his derby hat flying off his head. The Mexican whirled and pulled out his gun, but Bear kicked it out of the man's hand.

The half-breed pushed himself off the wheel of the Bulldog. Reeves slammed his fist into the big man's face. The breed grunted and spit out blood. Another punch flattened the his nose. The two men stood opposite each other. Moving with an unexpected quickness, the half-breed lurched forward, encircling Reeves in a bear hug. Reeves felt the enormity of the breed's strength and wondered if it was greater than his own. He exhaled and tried to take another breath but could barely fill his lungs. The giant exerted more pressure, and Reeves thought his ribs would break. He managed to pull his right arm from the encircling grip and swung his elbow into the breed's jaw. But the bigger man seemed unaffected and kept applying the pressure.

"I'm gonna break you," he said.

Reeves repeated the elbow blow to the half-breed's temple, and the pressure eased, allowing Reeves to get his left arm free as well. He jammed both of his hands under the breed's chin and pushed with all his strength. The pressure lessened a bit more. As Reeves bent the giant's head back he could feel the big arms weakening. Reeves chopped a blow into the other man's throat, and the crushing grip was totally broken.

The giant staggered back, and Reeves smashed a hard, overhand right on the breed's flattened nose. A gusher of blood poured from the damaged nasal cavities. The big man lumbered forward, his arms outstretched, but Reeves sidestepped and delivered a hooking left punch to the giant's side. He fell to one knee, a savage expression on his face.

The half-breed reached downward, his hand coming up with a gun, but Reeves already had his out, the hammer cocked back. He squeezed the trigger, and the flash from the barrel burst over the breed's face. The gun tumbled from the giant's hand, and he pawed for an instant at the round hole in the center of his expansive forehead before dropping like a felled buffalo.

Reeves turned and saw Bear and the Mexican, about twenty feet away, engaged in a knife fight. The two men circled each other, not allowing Reeves to have a clear shot. The Mexican lunged forward, his knife flashing. Bear deftly swatted the blade hand away and danced to the side, his mouth set in a taut line. They circled again, each man feinting and slashing.

A gunshot sounded as a round bounced off the wheel of the Bulldog. Reeves pointed his revolver at the shooter, one of three of Donovan's crew now running toward the Gatling gun. Reeves shot the man in the chest. He fell and rolled down the embankment.

Next, Reeves aimed at the other two men and shot them as well.

More bullets kicked up little clouds of dust near Reeves's feet. He crouched and glanced back at Bear. The Mexican leaped forward with a powerful thrust, but Bear parried it and shoved his own knife deep into the Mexican's gut. The man emitted a howling gasp.

"Who's a *tonto mierda* now?" Bear asked in a guttural voice.

Reeves holstered his gun, ran to the Gatling gun, and strained to lift it so he could swivel the barrel toward the group of outlaws. He grabbed the handle and began rotating the crank. The circle of barrels began their deadly spinning cycle, spitting out death and sending out flames half a foot long. The screaming outlaws began to fall in twisted heaps. Bear moved off to the side with his Winchester and said, "I'll get them other three."

Another bullet whizzed by Reeves, and he rotated the crank again. Three more of the bad men jerked and fell. Their ranks looked devastated.

Reeves saw two running figures about forty feet away, one pulling the other. He took what cover he could behind the gun and drew his Peacemaker, but, before he could fire, he saw the two of them scrambling onto a buckboard. In the increasing daylight, Reeves saw they were Donovan, and that dude, Stutley. Donovan held the other man in front of him and fired his gun over the dude's shoulder.

The bullet pinged off the Bulldog's barrel. Reeves ducked and came up, aiming at the departing buckboard, but he couldn't get a clear shot. Not with the writer still in the way.

Reeves turned and glanced back at the scene. There was little movement among the remaining outlaws, all of whom lay scattered in twisted, unnatural positions.

Bear was suddenly beside him, breathing hard.

"Got all three of them, *Gimoozabie.*"

"Get our damn horses," Reeves said. He holstered his weapon and looked toward the soldiers, who were positioned in a haphazard manner outside the boxcar. Most of them still staggered drunkenly in circles.

That crash must've knocked the hell out of them, Reeves thought.

"I'm Deputy Marshal Bass Reeves," he called out in a strong, clear voice. "Who's in charge of you men?"

He pulled back his vest so his badge was clearly visible and began walking down toward the still-disoriented soldiers, hoping none of them would take a shot at him.

Reeves repeated himself.

A couple of the young troopers looked around.

Nobody answered.

"Who's in charge here?" Reeves yelled again.

Finally, a young looking man in a uniform waved his arm. Reeves was close enough now to see a pair of yellow bars on the young man's shoulders as he stood up.

"I am," he said. "I'm Lieutenant Cates."

The lieutenant looked like he had a set of whiskers a cat could lick off.

"Indian!" one of the young soldiers yelled and pointed his rifle at Bear, who was walking up with two horses in tow.

Reeves jumped forward and grabbed the barrel, lifting it upward so that it fired harmlessly into the sky. The horses began jumping around at the gunshot. Bear turned and held the reins of the frightened animals, keeping them from rearing up.

"Hey, I'm a friendly Indian," Bear yelled.

"Hold your fire, you damn fool," Reeves said. "Him and me just got through savin' your sorry asses."

The young trooper sheepishly looked at the ground. "Sorry."

"You best be, boy," Reeves said, glaring at the man as he released the rifle barrel.

"Aw, don't be too hard on the kid, Bass," Bear said with a smirk and a wink. "He's probably heard tell that the only good Injun's a dead Injun."

"Nobody fire unless I give the order," the young lieutenant shouted. He turned to Reeves. "Marshal, thank you for saving us. We'd have been goners for sure if you hadn't come along."

"Best get control over your troops, Lieutenant," Reeves said. "We still got a ways to

326

go 'fore this is settled."

"I suppose you may have a point." He spoke slowly, pursed his lips, and then turned to another man wearing sergeant's chevrons who had walked up to them.

"Sergeant, check the status of the men and report back to me."

The sergeant nodded and waddled away with a somewhat uneven gait. The young lieutenant turned back to Reeves.

"What do you need us to do?"

Reeves glanced around. "Take custody of those outlaws, or what's left of them. Best have some of your men roll that Bulldog down here just in case there's more trouble."

The lieutenant's head bobbled up and down, and he began repeating each of Reeves's suggestions.

"And commandeer them horses up there," Reeves said. "Send a couple of your men back to the fort to tell 'em what happened. Get some reinforcements out here."

The lieutenant barked out more commands.

"Tell them riders to be on guard," Reeves added. "Might be some bushwhackers between here and the water stop."

Bear had the two horses calmed down. Reeves stepped over to his mount, grabbed the saddle, and swung up onto the horse's back. Bear did the same.

"You're gonna need another engine out here to right this mess," Reeves said, gesturing toward the tangle of derailed cars.

"Wait," the lieutenant said. "Where are you going, Marshal?"

Reeves reined his horse in the direction of the town.

"The man that set this ambush up ran off in a buckboard," he said. "He killed seven Texas Rangers. I got to settle up with him."

"But they've got a head start. How will you catch them?"

"It's what I do," Reeves said. "Besides, I know where they're heading." His boots dug into the horse's flanks, and the animal shot forward. "If any of them outlaws is still alive," he yelled over his shoulder, "keep 'em for me. I'll be back to collect 'em later."

Temptation

Donovan reined in the horses, bringing the buckboard to a stop as they arrived in front of the saloon. Stutley had fallen into the back section and remained there, clinging to the seat with an expression of sheer terror stretched across his face. His spectacles were askew.

If Donovan hadn't been so angry, he would have laughed.

But there was nothing to laugh about, he told himself, recalling that line from Robert Burns: *The best laid schemes of mice and men go often askew.*

His certainly had.

How in the hell had such a grand plan gone to hell so quickly?

And where had those two strangers come from to thwart things with such effectiveness?

Donovan had recognized one, the Negro who'd come into town the day before. Had he been scouting for another gang, or working for the law? Donovan guessed the latter, since he'd turned the Bulldog on the men instead of waiting until the soldiers had first been eliminated.

He sighed as he tied the reins around the brake and jumped down from the seat. Luckily, he'd left a saddled horse tied to the hitching rail that he'd planned to use to ride alongside of the wagons filled with all those recently minted gold coins. He imagined the sight in his mind's eye while surveying the deserted street. At least there was no sign of Cooper lurking about. Tracking down and shooting the Indian agent before leaving Temptation would be a small, parting consolation, but Donovan didn't have the time. He had another consolation in mind now, a larger one, and didn't know how long it might be before the army or the law arrived. But, given the confusion back at the railroad, he expected he'd have enough time.

"What are we going to do now?" Stutley asked, sitting up in the rear of the buckboard.

Donovan went to the saddled horse, removed a pair of leather saddlebags from across the animal's rump, and slung them over his shoulder.

"I'm going to collect my pay for this misadventure and be on my way, laddie." He looked wistfully at the poetaster and raised his eyebrows, thinking of the less-than-satisfactory ending to the novel Donovan had once envisioned. "It seems you'll have to use a bit more of that poetic license to tell the tale of the Rob Roy of the West."

Stutley flashed what appeared to be a very nervous smile, his head bobbling up and down in trepidation. "Sure, Mister Donovan. Whatever you want."

Donovan laughed. " 'Tis the luck of the Irish," he said as he turned and headed for the batwing doors of the saloon and the hidden cache in his room.

Henry, the barkeep, was behind the bar watching as Donovan entered. His two

330

afternoon delights, Polly and Pocahontas, stood in the hallway leading to the rooms of the hog ranch.

Donovan made a clucking sound. He was going to miss this place. Ever the gentleman, he tipped his hat to the ladies. Polly squealed and jiggled her more than ample breasts. The Indian girl remained motionless.

"Henry," Donovan said. "Have you seen that bugger Cooper around?"

"No, sir."

"Well, if he does show his ugly face while I'm up in my room, do call out. Understand?"

Henry nodded.

"I'm clearing out," Donovan said, starting to ascend the stairs. "And I'm giving you my full interest in ownership of this establishment."

The barkeep's eyes widened. "Thanks, boss. I mean, Mister Donovan."

"So keep an eye out for anyone on the street, as well. I'll be right back."

He ran up the stairs and dug the key for the door to his room out of his pocket. After slipping it in the lock, he turned it and gave the door a push, taking his gun out as he did so. A quick survey of all the nooks and corners proved the room empty of any threatening figures.

Empty, just like my coffers, he thought. Then he looked down at the floorboards.

Well, perhaps not completely empty. At least he had this one last consolation prize.

Donovan holstered his gun and shoved the bed to one side. Removing his knife, he knelt by the loose floorboard. He fitted the edge of the blade between the juncture of the adjoining boards and began to pry it up. After a few seconds it popped loose, and he gazed down at the money he'd stuffed into the space. Official Union greenbacks. Enough to give him a new start. Perhaps even enough to launch him into respectability. Setting the saddlebags on the bed, he opened each pouch and then began removing the money from the hiding place.

The shadows shifted subtly, and he was suddenly cognizant that he'd left the door ajar. A vision of Cooper sneaking up behind him flashed through his mind. Whirling, he turned and extended his gun toward the figure.

Pocahontas was standing there watching him. She was wearing her torn buckskin dress, and her face looked clean and fresh, like she'd just finished washing after a good night's sleep. He felt a brief stirring in his loins at the sight of her ripe body.

Donovan relaxed and stuck the gun back in its holster.

"Unfortunately, I don't have the time to spend with you now, my darling." He resumed his task.

She stared at the stacks of greenbacks.

He shrugged. "Just a little something I put away to tide me over while I beat a somewhat hasty retreat."

"Is that Hobb's money or Cooper's?"

"Actually, both." He turned and began packing the stacks of currency into one of the saddlebags. "But it's mine now."

She kept watching him stuff the money into the leather container.

Donovan grinned at her. "And how did your interlude go with Cooper last night? I hope you showed him a good time. I paid for it, you know."

"He's a pig."

"Ah, I'd be agreeing with that assessment." Donovan tied the first saddlebag shut and started packing the second one. "Speaking of our mutual acquaintance, I haven't seen him around today. Would you happen to know where he went after he finished last night?"

"He left."

Donovan didn't relish the thought of leaving Cooper behind alive and able to spill his guts if and when the law or the cavalry or both soon arrived.

"Did you want to take him with you?" she asked.

"Hardly." Donovan laughed. "I just have a bit of unfinished business to conduct with him."

"Want me to guard your saddlebags while you go look for him?"

Donovan frowned. The thought that it might be prudent to kill her for what she'd seen entered his mind, but he decided against it. After all, he did have a bit of a soft spot for this dark-skinned beauty. Even with that scar on her nose, she was a fine figure of a woman, and she had spirit. And, as for Cooper, the bloody lout was more than likely still sleeping off a night of drinking and debauchery, and there wasn't enough time to track the bastard down. Perhaps he'd get what was coming to him once the authorities arrived.

Better him than me, Donovan thought as he stood.

It appeared he was going to have to watch his back on the way out of town, which would best be done post haste.

Pocahontas was still staring at the heavily laden saddlebags.

"Cooper stole that money from my people," she said.

The lassie's avarice was showing.

"Your people? Come now, lass. Don't you think that's stretching things a bit too far?"

She said nothing.

He smiled. "Well, I am in a bit of a rush, otherwise I'd take you for one more ride."

"Mister Donovan," Henry called out from downstairs. "Somebody's coming."

"Is it Cooper?"

"No, sir. Looks like two riders."

Donovan's smile faded. "Just two?"

"Yeah, looks like . . . And, hey, I think one of them's that nigger from yesterday."

Donovan's smile returne,d and he looked at the girl. "Well, what do you know? The good lord's still holding me in the hollow of his hand."

Donovan had been shocked to see the darkie manning the Bulldog with such alacrity at the ambush site. How had he figured things out? Why had he interceded? He'd managed to ruin the best laid schemes.

Perhaps his return to Temptation was an act of providence. A last chance to set things right.

Donovan winked at the girl, grabbed the saddlebags, and strode out the door.

Reeves saw the abandoned buckboard in

front of the saloon. A horse was saddled and tied to the hitching rail. He'd figured as much. The tracks into town from the railroad had been easy to follow. Donovan most likely wanted to stop and grab whatever stash he had before hightailing it. Reeves swung his leg over the saddle and signaled for Bear to dismount as well. He took out one of his Peacemakers and said, "He's most likely in the saloon. Watch out for the bartender. Got a scattergun behind the bar."

"He's mine," Bear said, patting his Winchester.

They approached the batwing doors in rapid fashion, stopping on either side of the opening. "Donovan," Reeves called out, "this is Deputy Marshal Bass Reeves. I'm placing you under arrest for the murder of them Texas Rangers."

A loud laugh sounded from within, and Donovan yelled, "Come on in and have a drink, darkie."

Reeves and Bear exchanged glances and burst through the doors, spreading out to each side as they entered.

Donovan leaned against the bar, a bottle of whiskey and a glass in front of him, a wry smile on his face. A pair of densely packed saddlebags were next to him. Two women, Walking Deer and another, a blonde girl, stood off to the side and watched the scene intently. The writer dude sat off in the corner, his face puckered like a sour prune.

"I was just getting ready to depart for greener pastures, gentlemen," Donovan said. He raised an eyebrow. "But I sensed there might be a bit of unfinished business between us to attend to first."

Reeves stared into the other man's eyes, which displayed a strange merriment.

Donovan canted his head. "A Negro deputy marshal?"

"That's right."

"Ah, yes," Donovan said. "A freeman and a lawman. I had a funny feeling about you the other day." He brought the glass of amber liquid to his lips, drank, and then exhaled with seeming satisfaction before slamming the glass onto the bar. "I even thought about composing a limerick about it."

Reeves watched the man's hands. "I ain't in the mood to play. Give up now, and I'll see you get a fair trial back at Fort Smith."

"A fair trial?" Donovan refilled his glass. "You mean before I'm hanged?"

"That'd be up to Judge Parker."

The bartender's eyes shifted back and forth between the two men.

Reeves glanced at him. "Keep your hands

on top of the bar, mister barkeep."

The bartender scowled, then spat, but complied, resting his hands on the inside edge.

"You womenfolk best be leaving," Reeves said.

The blonde woman turned and scurried out of the room. Walking Deer stood defiantly in the juncture by the hallway.

Reeves brought his gaze back to the Irishman.

"Into Temptation there once came a darkie," Donovan said, reciting the words with a limerick's poetic cadence. "Everyone thought he was full of malarkey —"

"Like I told you," Reeves said. "I ain't got time for games. I'm taking you in for the murder of the rangers, and the attempted robbery of that train."

"Are you now?" Donovan picked up the glass with his left hand, his right still resting on the top of the bar. "How did you find out about the rangers?"

"You and your boys made the mistake of leaving one alive," Reeves said. "He told me who bushwhacked 'em before he died."

Donovan snorted a laugh. "Careless of the dastardly villain who perpetrated the act. And, just to satisfy my curiosity, what happened to Crowe and Franker?"

"I gave them the same chance I'm giving you. They didn't take it."

"Ah, that Crowe was a bit of a recalcitrant, wasn't he?" Donovan set the glass down without tasting the whiskey. "But I need to finish my limerick. And under his vest, the darkie wore a star with a crest, and Donovan left him under a tree."

"We're through talking," Reeves said. He was holding his Colt down by his leg. His thumb cocked back the hammer, already knowing how this one was going to play out. "You gonna come in peaceably?"

Donovan licked his lips, and he shook his head. "Not likely." The Irishman whirled, drawing his pistol and firing it.

Reeves dodged to his left, figuring the bullet would veer to his right. He brought up the Colt Peacemaker and squeezed the trigger. Donovan's body jerked, and he collapsed, his arms folding over the top of the bar, holding him erect. Reeves switched his aim toward the bartender, who was now bringing up the shotgun. Bear's Winchester roared, and the bartender's head exploded like a ripe melon. He twisted as he fell, grabbing at the rows of bottles next to him, causing an accompanying cascade of shattering glass as he dropped.

Donovan straightened up and struggled to

raise his gun again. Reeves shot the man between the eyes. The Irishman's head jerked back, then forward, and he fell forward onto the wooden floor, a crimson puddle widening around his slack, handsome face.

Reeves moved forward and checked Donovan, then stooped and snatched the gun from the dead man's limp fingers. He tucked it into the side of his gun belt and kicked the outlaw's arm away, then leaned down and ripped the sheriff's star from Donovan's shirt.

"You ain't deservin' to wear this," Reeves said. He pocketed the star and went to check the bartender.

Bear's bullet had gone in the man's cheek and out the other side. He was supine in the narrow expanse behind the bar, his eyes glazed over, a puddle of crimson framing his head.

"I told you I had him," Bear said. "Even though I ain't supposed to be dealin' with no white men here in the territories."

Reeves retrieved the metal rod with the five Texas Ranger stars strung on it. "I came for these, too."

Walking Deer walked over and stared down at the two dead men. Then she looked at the saddlebags still resting on the bar.

"It's Cooper's and Hobb's money," she said, pushing the bags toward Reeves. "What the Cherokeos stole."

Reeves looked at Bear, who nodded.

"Guess they belongs to you then," Reeves said.

Her dark eyes grew large, and she glanced toward Bear, who winked. The girl's lips trembled as they transformed into a smile. Reeves watched her grab the bags, turn, and walk out of the room.

He still held the ring of stars as he strode over to the dude. The writer's eyes behind his spectacles were as wide open as a pair of white dinner plates.

"Marshal," the dime novelist said. "That was you in my room last night, wasn't it? With the mask."

Reeves said nothing as he stood in front of him for several seconds, then asked, "What's your name again?"

"Stutley, Lucien T. Stutley."

"All right, Mister Stutley. You got something to write with?"

The dude took out his pencil and notebook.

"Need you to put something down for me," Reeves said. "Nice and neat." He recited the mailing address that the dying Ranger had given him.

Stutley printed it clearly on the paper and handed it over.

Reeves stared at the written words, admiring the clean, angular lines but not able to decipher them. He carefully folded the paper, put it in his pocket, then took out his last silver dollar.

"Here you go, Mister Stutley," Reeves said, flipping the dollar to the writer.

The dude caught the coin and looked at it. "Marshal, you don't have to —"

Reeves held up his hand. "I give them to folks that help me. And help the law."

He reached into his pocket and removed the star the dying Ranger had given him. His strong hands gripped the iron bar and he pulled the ends apart, opening the circle, and then slipped the seventh star onto the bar with the others.

"Got to mail these back to the rangers," Reeves said. "Much obliged for writin' out that mailin' address for me."

He turned toward the door.

"Ready, *Gimoozabie*?" Bear asked.

Reeves regarded him with a wry glance, then said, "Yeah. Let's go."

He strode toward the doors and went out, noticing that the horse Donovan had saddled was missing. He glanced down the street and saw the Indian girl hightailing it out of town in the buckboard, the horse tied to the rear bracket, galloping beside it.

Looks like she's off to a new start, Reeves thought. He silently wished her luck.

"Wait," Stutley said, pushing through the batwing doors. He looked at Bear. "What was that name you just called him?"

Bear grinned. "*Gimoozabie.* It means —"

"It means you best be keeping your mouth shut from here on out," Reeves said, already in the saddle. "Now let's get a move on. It's a long way back to Fort Smith, and we got some prisoners to collect first."

"But, wait," the dude said, pushing through the doors and onto the street. "What about Donovan? And the bartender? You aren't going to just leave them there, are you?"

"Be obliged if you'd see about burying 'em," Reeves said. "I expect there's still some decent folks in this town that'll help you with that."

"Best get that done before they start stinkin' too much," Bear added.

Stutley's head swiveled back and forth between the two men. "But I didn't even get a chance to talk with you, to thank you, to —"

"No thanks necessary," Reeves said. "And I ain't got time for talking."

The dime novelist looked up at the big man on the horse. "What did you say your name was, again?"

Reeves turned in his saddle and glanced down at the dude. "Bass Reeves. Deputy Marshal."

He turned forward and urged his horse into a trot, and Bear did the same.

They never looked back.

EPILOGUE

Stutley sat at the table across from Polly, who looked at him with a wistful hopefulness as she eyed the silver dollar in his hand. He shuddered at the thought and fingered the coin, all the while considering his options for developing and enhancing the events he'd just witnessed.

This would make a marvelous novel, if he could just figure out a way to get it all down in a believable fashion. Artistic license, that was the key.

A Negro marshal and his Indian companion. He jotted down a possible title: *The Dark Marshal.*

Nobody back East would believe it. Better turn the lawman into a white man.

He tried another: *The Disguised Marshal.*

No, that didn't sound right, either.

Why would a marshal wear a mask? He assumed Reeves did it as a subterfuge, but would the readers like that?

The Masked Marshal, he wrote next. The alliteration was too problematic.

Along Came a Marshal?

The word *Marshal* ruined the cadence of the words. He needed something with more panache. *The Masked Rider?*

He scribbled down a few more ideas, fingered the silver dollar again, and then it hit him like a silver bullet.

Why not make the hero a Texas Ranger instead of a marshal? But the story would have more drama if it were a man alone against the sort of overwhelming odds Reeves had faced.

Should I keep the Indian? Stutley wondered what the savage's name was.

He glanced over and saw Polly staring at him.

"That's a real nice looking silver dollar you got there, sweetie," she said. "I can think of a nice way you can spend it, too."

Oh, Lord, he thought as he caught a whiff of body odor heavily laden with perfume. He stared at Donovan's body lying on the floor. Henry's was still behind the bar. It was time to get out of there. Pretty soon the townsfolk would be meandering in to check on things, and Stutley worried they might assume he was in league with the outlaws. Visions of a lynch mob flashed in his mind.

Perhaps he could hide out in the boarding house until he could make arrangements to get the hell out of Temptation.

"Actually," he said, pocketing the silver dollar, "I've got to send a wire."

He smiled nervously, stood up, and grabbed his traveling bag, shoving all of his notes into his pocket, figuring out the story could wait. Perhaps, once he got back to the safety of Ohio, he'd tell it to his nephew, Pearl, who liked to be called by his middle name, Zane. The boy was fascinated with tales of the West.

As Stutley moved to the door, another title hit him, and he wanted to stop and write it down. This one had a nicer ring to it.

The Masked Ranger?

Maybe that would do.

Yeah, he thought. I kind of like that one.

POSTSCRIPT

Although this book features Bass Reeves, a real life hero of the Old West, it is a work of fiction and primarily intended to entertain. All of the other characters in this novel are products of the author's imagination, with the occasional exception of the mention of an actual historical figure. I should also mention that the character of Indian Lighthorse deputy, David Walks-As-Bear, is loosely based on a late Native American friend of mine who used to counsel me and give me advice on American Indian languages and culture. He was one of the smartest men I've ever met, and I did my best to render a portrait that would exemplify his outstanding character. I also put in a quick and somewhat veiled reference to an actual famous western writer who was a distant relative of mine. I made a concerted effort to try and capture the essence of the time period, and this included using some outdated, and nowadays "politically incorrect" words, but I felt this was in keeping with the traditions of the western genre. I also did an immense amount of research in an effort to make the work as authentic as I could, but I make no claims to its total accuracy and also acknowledge that I used a dash of artistic license from time to time to enhance the story when I felt it was necessary.

Much has been made in recent times of the theory that Bass Reeves was the inspiration for the fictional character of the Lone Ranger. While I grew up watching Clayton Moore and Jay Silverheels, and they were the heroes of my youth, I have no evidence that this theory is anything more than a fancy encouraged by historical coincidences. Reeves was an actual person, and, while he did purportedly give out silver dollars (not silver bullets) and ride a whitish-grey stallion (not a purely white horse) and did use Indian assistants as guides on his missions (like the Lone Ranger's faithful Indian companion, Tonto), I want to state that there is no direct evidence to point to all this influencing the Lone Ranger's creator, Fran Striker. But one thing is for certain: Bass Reeves was an extraordinary man, and his achievements deserve to be recognized.

Although I have the utmost respect for the real Bass Reeves, and the amazing things that he accomplished, I hope this book also stands as an homage to the western genre itself, and to the legends and mythology that grew out of a relatively short period of our nation's history. To that end, I once again freely admit to using a bit of artistic license from time to time.

After all, as it has been said before, legend often reads better than fact.

ABOUT THE AUTHOR

Michael A. Black is the author of thirty-one books, the majority of which are in the mystery and thriller genres, although he has written in sci-fi, western, horror, and sports genres as well. A retired police officer with over thirty years' experience, he has done everything from patrol to investigating homicides to conducting numerous SWAT operations. Black was awarded the Cook County Medal of Merit in 2010. He is also the author of over one hundred short stories and articles and has written two novels with television star Richard Belzer (*Law & Order SVU*). Black is currently writing the Executioner series (*Fatal Prescription, Missile Intercept,* and *Dying Art*) under the name Don Pendleton. His latest novel under his own name is *Blood Trails.*

The employees of Thorndike Press hope you have enjoyed this Large Print book. All our Thorndike, Wheeler, and Kennebec Large Print titles are designed for easy reading, and all our books are made to last. Other Thorndike Press Large Print books are available at your library, through selected bookstores, or directly from us.

For information about titles, please call:
  (800) 223-1244

or visit our Web site at:
  http://gale.com/thorndike

To share your comments, please write:
  Publisher
  Thorndike Press
  10 Water St., Suite 310
  Waterville, ME 04901